ALSO BY ED CONE

The Counterfeiter

ADAM & YVES

ADAM & YVES

ED CONE

New York 2023

Library of Congress Control Number: 2023911170

Library of Congress Cataloging-in-publication Data available upon request

ISBN 978-1-7332430-2-5

ebook ISBN 978-1-7332430-3-2

Epigraph from C.P. Cavafy, "Pérasma," in C.P. Cavafy, *The Collected Poems*, ed. by Anthony Hirst, trans. by Evangelos Sachperoglou (New York: Oxford University Press, 2008), p. 100.

Manufactured in the United States of America

2 9 1 3 8 4 7 5 6

First Edition

For Mikey & Xander, Louis & Kim

and, of course, Michael

ADAM
& YVES

Κ' ετσι ενα παιδι απλο Παναγιωτης Μαλανδρης
γινεται αξιο να το δουμε, κι απ' τον Υψηλο
της Ποιησεως Κοσμο μια στιγμη περνα κι αυτο —

And thus a simple boy
becomes worthy of our attention, and for an instant,
he too passes through the Exalted Realm of Poetry —

— C.P. Cavafy

— PERASMA (PASSAGE)

PART I

The Goddess

CHAPTER 1

New York Allows Same-Sex Marriage, Becoming Largest
State to Pass Law, *New York Times, June 24, 2011*
"Four members of the Republican majority joined all but one Democrat in the
[New York State] Senate in supporting the measure after an intense and emo-
tional campaign aimed at the handful of lawmakers wrestling with a decision that
divided their friends, their constituents and sometimes their own homes."

When he emerged from the No. 1 train in Midtown and set out on the two
blocks to his office, Adam felt a spring in his step that hadn't been there
before, not for as long as he could remember. It must be what walking with
wings on your feet feels like. Is that what happiness, true happiness does to
you? He couldn't help but wonder as he crossed Avenue of the Americas
and proceeded along the crosstown block toward Fifth. Traffic was surging
past, yellow cabs dodged daringly among the more patient cars and trucks,
and sunlight glinting off a nearby office tower nearly blinded him as he
approached the building where his architectural firm resided. He was hoping to make partner within a few years, and had some noteworthy projects
to his credit. And now, to top off his professional accomplishments at age
thirty, he'd followed his heart and found the love of his life. No, he hadn't
mentioned this to anyone at the firm, though he'd made a few friends there,
one good one in particular. But he had no idea when or how he'd send out
the news that he finally had a partner, when that partner happened to be
a man.

There'd been no shortage of women in his life, all of them good
friends, they all found out, some sooner, some later. At office functions a

striking female often appeared on his arm, and if the same woman showed up with him more than twice, that was enough to start the gossip mill and also to serve as a smokescreen, not one he'd consciously erected, but that had been the effect.

Yet in time he became more concerned about the subterfuge, and there it was—his life a living lie, to use a corny cliché, and he hated himself for it. But what was he to do? He thoroughly enjoyed women, respected them, believed they were his equal or better, and loved their company. He'd even managed to pull off a few what you might call affairs. But he'd never had his heart in it or, more apropos, his nether organs.

As for men, his attraction to them had trailed him since his teens, when it shifted into high gear. That's when he began to fool around. He even had what you might call relationships, but never long-lasting and never ultimately satisfying. The end point of these various entanglements had been a growing dissatisfaction with all romantic forays and a certain malaise, a feeling that something was incurably wrong with him. He'd probably spend the rest of his life flitting (he detested the word) from women to men, men to women without ever finding someone he could love.

Then he met Yves.

It happened over a piano. Not a piano you'd find at the Carlyle, where the descendants of Bobby Short keep the ivories in motion. Nor a piano at a dive in Greenwich Village, though it was in the Village where they first met. Perhaps on Perry or Charles, one of those enchanting side streets where the trees overhang a canopy as far as you can see, a street lined by proud brownstones and federal townhouses. There it stood—the Baldwin console, its stature midway between a spinet and an upright—right on the sidewalk. One could almost believe it had rolled up and parked there on its own.

A man with his back to him was fingering the keys. As he walked closer, his ear picked up a melody he recognized but couldn't quite place.

It was classical, and it sounded more staccato than the familiar version, because the man wasn't peddling. Then it came to him, and he actually said it out loud: "Chopin, Étude in C-major, the first of Opus 10."

The pianist glanced sideways and nodded while continuing to play. It was half a minute till he finished the piece. He held his hands to the keys for several moments afterward, as if a force within the piano kept them there. Then he straightened up and stepped back.

"Do you perform here often?" he couldn't help asking. "That's impressive playing."

"I'm impressed you recognized the piece."

"My sister played it at recital. I heard it for weeks on end while she practiced, till I swear I could have played it myself."

"Do you play, then?"

"No, I don't." He added, "I wish I did. I wasn't allowed to take lessons."

"That's a shame," the pianist returned. He looked to be a couple of years younger than our architect, who is about to introduce himself as Adam Stover. "No one should be denied the right to play an instrument."

"Do you think it's a right?"

"It's a right if anything is."

Adam nodded in agreement, remembering the time his dad told him it was enough that his older sister played piano and his younger sister violin. "The orchestra's full here," dad had declared. "You should be out playing baseball." And he did play, on a Little League team, for a few years, badly, but with determination. Then he asked the pianist, "I don't mean to get personal, but why are you playing this beautiful instrument here in the street?"

"Because that's where I found it."

"I see," Adam returned, his tone more doubting than affirmative.

"It's been abandoned."

"This beautiful Baldwin?"

"That's what the super told me." He pointed to the service entrance of the brownstone to corroborate his statement. "Someone who just vacated an apartment didn't want to take it and didn't want to pay to dispose of it."

"So he left it in the street?"

"Moved in a hurry."

"That ought to be a crime—abandoning a piano!"

The pianist nodded in agreement.

"It would be awful it if were just carted away and chopped up for kindling. I hope someone comes to rescue it."

"Someone has come."

"Who?"

"You're looking at him."

Adam glanced from piano to pianist.

"I'm taking it home with me."

"How?"

"That is the question of the day."

The two surveyed each other long enough for a few brief thoughts to be exchanged, then Adam asked, "Do you live nearby?"

"A few blocks. The problem is, I don't want to roll it there under its own steam. It needs a dolly or two to be properly transported."

"Where do you propose to get one?"

"I could get a couple from the super of my building, but I can't leave the piano unattended." He added with a grimace, "It's been mistreated enough for one day."

The architect made a quick calculation. "How long do you think it'll take you to get the dollies?"

"Twenty minutes or so—if I'm lucky."

"Tell you what. I have a little time on my hands. Why don't I wait here till you get back?"

"I couldn't ask you to do that."

"You don't have to ask me—I volunteer." He added in French, he wasn't sure why, "J'y suis et j'y reste." He was there to stay.

"Alors, vous parlez français …?"

"Oui et non. Et vous?"

"C'est ma langue natale."

He was French-Canadian, this so-called pianist, and that accounted for the almost imperceptible accent.

For the first time since the start of their encounter, the musician's concentrated expression relaxed. "Do you have a cell phone on you?"

Adam removed the cell from his trouser pocket.

"Give me your number and I'll keep you posted. If there's an undue delay, I'll come back and relieve you."

"Then how will you get the piano home?"

"I'll solve that problem later."

The obliging architect gave his number, then added, "My name's Adam."

"Yves."

A half-hour wait, punctuated once by the dinging of his cell, then a txt msg—On the way—and the musician reappeared around the corner with two dollies trailing behind.

"Thanks for waiting."

"My pleasure. Ready to hoist?"

Yves positioned a dolly at one end of the piano and the two of them heaved the instrument onto it. Then they moved to the opposite end and lifted the piano once again, until it seemed secure on the dollies.

"You know, there's no way I can thank you …" Yves began.

"You can't lug this beauty by yourself. Start pushing."

They rolled the piano along the uneven sidewalk, stopping twice to anchor it more firmly on the dollies when they hit a deep crack, then proceeded to the corner, turned right, and rolled down the next two blocks until they came to the avenue. Straining to lower the piano off the curb, they moved onto the street, but when they were midway across the broad thoroughfare, the piano slipped off one of the dollies just as the light changed.

A symphony of honking began pianissimo, and several vehicles moved menacingly closer as the two struggled to right their piano on the dollies. The honking was crescendoing when a truck swerved across the avenue from a far lane and a burly driver hopped out, threw his head back, and bellowed to the crowd, "Aww, *shaaadduppppp—!*"

With no more ado he lumbered to the piano and embraced it in a bear hug, the ladies in the tattoos on his upper arms wiggling seductively as he repositioned the instrument on its dollies and pulled it to the back of his truck. He signaled the piano's guardians to follow, then climbed onto the fender, opened the back doors, and lowered a sturdy wooden plank onto the street, preparing to roll the piano inside.

"How far you fellas plannin' to cart this baby …?" His matter-of-fact tone suggested they'd formally engaged his services.

"Couple of blocks over, then turn to your left, and one block more," Yves directed.

"Climb up to the cab while I lock her in," he ordered.

"I don't want to leave the piano here by itself." Adam embraced the Baldwin.

"It's illegal for you to ride in the back of the truck," came the mordant reply.

"Is it legal to take on passengers and a *piano* in the middle of a busy avenue?" Adam countered.

Yves tensed and started to say something, but the driver ordered,

"Ride at your own risk."

Adam hopped into the back and tossed a blanket over the piano, then secured it with a rope he found on the floor, while Yves joined the driver in the cab to give directions. As their savior closed his door and put the truck in gear, a cheering arose from the crowd that had gathered to attend this Manhattan melodrama.

"Man, that was some ride," Yves declared once they were inside his apartment, the piano centered on a wall of his sparely furnished living room.

"Nice apartment," Adam said. "May I ask you something?"

"Shoot."

"Why did you pick Chopin's first étude to play?"

"Good question. Because it's all over the keyboard."

"Good answer."

"Now I have a question: How much do I owe you?"

"For what?" Adam leaned an arm across the piano as if it belonged to him.

"First of all, for tipping the driver. What did you give him, by the way?"

"Sorry, that's proprietary information."

"Then there's your charge for riding in the back of the truck."

"Waived."

"The carting fee—pushing the piano all those blocks?"

"Gratis."

"And waiting for me to collect the dollies—that must have amounted to half an hour or more. How much for your time?"

"You made it back within the grace period."

Yves stepped closer to the piano as their negotiation was unraveling. "All right—there's got to be something I can give you for your efforts. I could never have done this without you." He was grinning now, a bit shyly, and, like Adam, had put his arm across his new possession.

"Look, I'm not in it for the money."

"I refuse to be let off scot-free. You've got to let me give you something for your time and effort. I'm afraid I have to insist."

Adam reflected, his brow furrowing. "There *is* one thing I might be willing to accept, but I'm afraid it's too much to ask—"

"Ask."

"A kiss."

The kiss was delivered on the spot.

But that didn't end their negotiation. After reflecting several moments, the architect whispered, "I can't accept the kiss either. I'm going to return it."

And that's how Adam met Yves ... But a corrective is in order here: Yves is not a pianist.

"You're not pulling my leg? You're actually a cellist—? But—you were playing a piano—!"

"If I'd found an abandoned cello on the street, I'd have been playing a cello when you happened by." Yves lifted the cup of espresso to his full red lips, blew, and sipped. They were having Sunday brunch at an outdoor café in the Village, their first date after adopting the piano a few days ago.

"You let me believe you were a pianist all this time, when you're actually a professional cellist—?"

"I suppose I've let you believe all sorts of things—if you put it that way. I have no control over your thoughts."

"But—your profession, what you do for a living, your daily bread—isn't that important enough to have told me about? I mean, what if you were married or something?" Adam scratched the back of his head, signaling his disbelief. The sun beaming down streaked his ash blond hair.

"What if I were?"

"Then you'd be an adulterer." He added as an afterthought (or was it?), "Or you'd be about to become one."

"I used to believe that an 'adulterer' was a person who conducts his affairs like an adult."

"Very funny. But aren't we getting off the subject?"

"Tell me what the subject is."

"Well, what in the hell do you *think* it is—?"

"I'm not thinking. I'm listening to you."

Adam's guffaw caused several sips to stop and heads to turn in the café, but he was having too much fun to care.

"I started lessons on the cello when I was six years old," Yves resumed. "When I was twelve I began piano, but not to perform; my cello teacher believed it was a good idea for me to learn to play a keyboard instrument."

"Do you think it was a good idea?"

"We would never have met without those lessons."

"I was never good with facts, but that's one I will always remember."

Yves put his hand on Adam's. The hand was retracted only when the waiter asked whether they wanted a refill of the coffee. It was perhaps just a reflex. After more coffee was poured Yves said, "I'm flattered by all your questions, but you haven't told me much about yourself."

"Alors, mon brave," he began, starting to acquire a new habit: interjecting words and phrases of French into his conversation. "I've mentioned I'm an architect, several years with the same firm, and gunning for partner—me voilà." He emended, "Sort of successful, single, solitary ..."

"Sexy," Yves finished the alliterative chain. His hand returned to rest on Adam's. "Now, what is the story beneath the story?"

"Oh, *that* story—? It's about falling in love with you. Shall we go for a walk?"

Summer was well along. The leaves were ripely green and the air was heavy with humidity and presentiment. They entered Washington Square from the northwest corner, loping diagonally across the park toward the fountain in the center, where the usual assortment of entertainers and gamesters were holding sway before an audience of wide-eyed tourists and jaded locals. Yves was wearing dark gray khaki slacks and a matching T-shirt, showing that he cared little for style but something for presentability. Adam wore a bright red T-shirt over tan cargo pants, both well fitted to his trim physique.

As they took possession of a bench with the assorted buildings of New York University as backdrop, Yves observed, "We passed near here when we brought the piano home."

"Your place is just the other side of the park, if I remember correctly." He'd left Yves' apartment in such a happy haze that he couldn't have told you how he made his way home.

"Good memory. Where did you say you live?"

A Pekingese with the obligatory pink ribbon in her hair scampered across the path in pursuit of an audacious squirrel. The new friends exchanged glances and grinned before Adam replied, "It's too far from yours, I can tell you that."

When he added, "I live on East Tenth Street, near Fifth Avenue," Adam couldn't tell whether Yves looked surprised, happy, or both. But he'd always remember that look.

"You're right—it *is* too far away."

"Would you like to see it?"

"Why not?"

They wended their way north out of the park, then turned right on East Tenth, a quiet side street extending all the way across Manhattan, eventually stopping midblock before an eight-story residence that was an anomaly among the four- and five-story brownstones anchored by the high-rises at either corner.

"We're finally home," Adam announced. He started up the short flight of stairs to the entrance, but Yves lingered on the sidewalk.

"Aren't you coming …?"

"I was savoring what you just said."

They took the elevator to the fourth floor. "The apartment faces to the back. The front apartments give onto the street. They're somewhat noisier."

"How long have you been here?" Yves asked as Adam unlocked the door and led them into a rectangular foyer where a dining table rested against one wall. A coat closet was to the right and the kitchen to the left, then an archway to the living room.

"I bought it two years ago—with help from my folks."

"Generous parents."

"Would you like to take the tour?"

"Sure, why not?" Yves followed close behind Adam as if he risked getting lost. Or maybe he just wanted to be near him.

A fireplace was centered on one of the walls, and the room was painted eggshell, aka white with a shading of tan, a warm color when Adam switched on the floor lamp. A photograph of Midtown Manhattan taken from on high, an antique map of Paris, and several black-and-white prints came in view.

"Isn't it curious how many shades of white there are?" Yves ventured as he walked around the room.

"It was a dreadful color before I moved in. When I told my family about it, they refused to visit until I had it painted."

"What was the color?"

"Rent-control green."

"Quel horreur! Did they like it when they finally saw it?"

"Hard to say. You know parents—they usually mean well. But the first words out of my dad's mouth were 'Is this all you get for our money?' *Our* money—did you hear that?" He glanced at Yves, who nodded, a trace of amusement on his face. "At least, they don't live here with me, though my little sister sometimes crashes for a day or two at a time."

"You live alone?"

"Yes, but I'm thinking it won't be for much longer." He added, "Let me show you the rest of the place."

They proceeded to a hallway that gave access to a bathroom, large bedroom, and tiny study.

"This bedroom's at treetop level and the windows face in two directions. Good for cross-ventilation."

"A corner room—I've always wanted one," Yves returned, stepping to the window. "What a sea of leaves you have out there. It must look like green waves when the wind blows. And your understated décor is very easy on the eye."

"Let me show you the study." Adam led them down the hall to the little room, which contained a settee, a desk, and a waist-high bookcase. A profusion of family photos populated the wall above it. "Rogues gallery," he explained.

"You'll have to tell me who all these folks are." A portrait of a middle-aged woman whose features resembled those of his new friend caught Yves' eye. He lingered over it for some moments.

"First, would you have something to drink?"

"Maybe some ice water."

In the kitchen he poured them each a tumbler of water, then led them to the living room.

The light was growing dim. Adam asked, "Have you lived long at your place?"

"Couple of years. I've been planning to move for some time. I think I've found a new home."

"Really? Where is it?"

"Where do you think?"

CHAPTER 2

Support for Same-Sex Marriage Is Up, *New York Times, April 26, 2012*
"In 2001, Americans opposed same-sex marriage by a margin of 57 percent to 35 percent. [In April 2012], 47 percent are in favor and 43 percent opposed."

"Is everything ready ...?"

"What's to be ready?"

"You know."

"What do *I* know?"

Lenora stopped reading the article for *Fashionista* she was editing but hadn't glanced up to meet her husband's eye. She didn't want to encourage him. She hoped their exchange had ended. She relished the quiet time before the arrival of guests at their nine-room Park Avenue duplex. Of course, her son wasn't exactly a guest. But he was bringing someone with him. Someone indeed.

"Well, I mean the drinks and appetizers, and all that." She resumed, "Did you remember the dessert ...?"

"What dessert?"

Al had also not bothered to look up from his copy of the *Wall Street Journal*, which he'd been skimming for the past quarter hour as they sat in their Park Avenue pad waiting for the doorbell to sound the alarm. Alarm indeed.

They'd been married almost forty years, and their marriage had settled into a set of routines that ranged from monotonous to irritating to endearing. Al's mind was tangled in his article, about the economy needing less government intervention, the newspaper's mantra. But who doesn't enjoy reading about one's cherished beliefs over and over?

"You know," he said at length, "the dessert—I was supposed to pick it up."

"Well, did you …?" Lenora fastened her eyes on her fifty-something husband with the stylishly graying hair and black-framed reading glasses slipping down his straight, prominent nose, a cultivated owl, uh, Al.

"No—I thought you would … You've always been so good about things like that …"

Things like that—in other words, everything her husband couldn't be bothered to do. And now, in typical Albert Stover fashion, he was attempting to give her credit for something she hadn't done that he himself was supposed to do but didn't. But the point was moot; they'd already decided a meal at home was inappropriate for this first meeting. (What if nobody talked?) A friend at her office recommended a new restaurant in Tribeca. The four would have drinks at the apartment, then cab it downtown. Afterward they'd return to Park Avenue for a piece of the cake no one had bothered to buy. At least that was the plan.

After a moment Lenora put in, "Maybe we should just let them starve."

The *Journal* fluttered to Al's lap. "There's child-abuse laws on the books for that sort of thing."

"Adam is hardly a child."

"Child-shmild—won't you be embarrassed to expose your bare pantry to your son and this mysterious friend of his?"

"What's so *mysterious* about his friend?"

"You know what I mean." Al was staring at her now, as if just starting to take her seriously.

"Frankly, I have no idea."

"Then let's put it this way." He wedged the *Journal* between the over-stuffed armchair and his overstuffed middle. "Our boy … *man* is in his thirties now and he's taken up with some guy as his roommate."

"I don't know what you mean by 'taken up.'"

"Don't be perverse."

"Be precise."

"What I'm saying is, he owns this nice apartment we helped him buy—"

"—I've seen the mortgage—"

"—and, after living alone there for a spell, he's taken some guy in."

"Go on."

"Well, if I were in his shoes—"

"You're not—"

"I'd either want to have a woman there or have my freedom. I mean, why does he want to be saddled with this musician …" He added, "and all that racket?"

"To help pay the maintenance."

"But a musician, and a guy at that?"

"Would you feel better if he were renting out a room to a penniless female?"

"This is not about *renting*. Why doesn't he have a *woman* living with him? That's what I'd like to know—not to share the rent but his damn bed."

"You'll have to ask him that."

"Why are you so nonchalant about this helluva mess?"

"That's what mothers are for."

Lenora continued tweaking her article till a sharp *buzz-buzz* shattered the silence—their children's signal since time immemorial that they'd come home from school or wherever they'd been.

"Keep calm," Al advised, his trembling hand rattling his *WSJ*.

He buried his nose in the paper just as his younger daughter wandered into the living room.

At the same moment, Adam materialized in the broad archway to the living room with "the friend" at his side. "Hello, Ali. What a surprise to find you here." He gave his sister a peck on the cheek.

Alison Stover stood tall and slender, her ash-blond hair the color of Adam's. Her broad, open face could look plain and even mannish, but when she did her hair and put on makeup, the discriminating called her beautiful. She'd piled that thick, full hair on her head tonight and held it in place with a mother-of-pearl clip. Her smile revealed straight, even teeth.

"This is my baby sister, Alison," said Adam to Yves, while his gaze alighted on his folks. "Ali, my friend Yves Montjour."

Yves took her fingertips and shook her hand in the taut European manner. "I could swear we'd met in Florence once," he declared, "though perhaps I'm remembering a Botticelli or a Raphael."

She started, just started, to smile, perhaps imitating her Florentine counterpart, her composure as undisturbed as paint on canvas.

Al approached the new arrivals, his hand extended so far in front of him that he could be seeking alms.

"Dad," gulped Adam, "I'd like you to meet my friend Yves, "Yves Montjour."

Alison darted an admonitory gaze at her father.

"Why are you staring at me like that?" Al attempted a whisper but exceeded it by decibels.

"Just remember, you're about to meet a cultivated gentleman."

Before Al could reply, Lenora and her black-and-white harlequin print joined her husband. "Welcome to our home, Yves. I'm Lenora Stover."

"How do you do, Mrs. Stover."

"Call her Lenny," Al directed.

"Dad!" wailed Adam.

"That's what she'd've told him herself," Al retorted. "She tells every-one to call her Lenny."

"Yves Montjour isn't *everyone*," interjected Alison. "And Mom's used to speaking for herself, Dad."

"Would you like to say something, Lenny?" Dad asked.

"Let's take orders for drinks. What can we get you, Yves?"

Yves hesitated, as if he meant to call her by name but wasn't sure which one. "A glass of wine, thank you."

"Vin rouge ou blanc?" she inquired.

"Rouge, s'il vous plaît," he returned. "You didn't tell me your mother speaks admirable French, Adam."

"I hope he's told you nothing about me." Lenora gestured for them to be seated. "I'd rather create my own first impression."

"I'm willing to wipe the slate clean." Yves took a seat beside her on one of the matching settees at either side of the malachite fireplace. "But then, I'd be erasing a catalogue of favorable commentary."

Lenora reddened a tad, a rare occurrence for her. "Perhaps you'll start a new slate, now that we've met."

Al sank onto the opposite settee while Adam stood at the fireplace, wondering how the evening would unfold. Yves and his mom were off to a good start. Dad would take charge of the conversation. Perhaps he should have met with them without Yves, to test the waters. He'd adopted a casual stance in breaking the news, and what safer way than a phone call? It didn't help that dad answered the phone. After the obligatory chitchat, he asked to speak with mom. "I'll give her a message—she's tied up at the moment," dad said. "Hmm, I can call back." "Whatsisabout?" The query was not in the script. "Really, Dad, I don't mean to bother—" "Bothershmother." No getting off the hook, new script needed. "I plan to bring a friend over for you guys to meet." He heard dad's voice at the other end of the line, addressing the recently unavailable Lenora. "Hey, Lenny, Ady wants to bring someone special over ..." Dad then asked the receiver: "Who is this Miss Right?" "It's ... it's ...—" "Goonimlisning," dad prompted. "Good evening, dear, how are you ...?" Mom's voice came through from another phone. "Adysgotsomethingtotelllyouuuuuuuu." "Dad makes it sound like a big deal or something." "Of course it's a big deal." "Yes, dear?" "I just want you to meet a friend, that's all."

"We'd be delighted," said mom. "Drinks and dinner?"

"No need to go to any trouble."

"Who said anything about trouble? Your mother'll know how to carry this out." As if a bomb squad were needed. Dad resumed, "Whaturwesupposedtocallthisyoungladyyyyy?" "Yves," said his son. "Eve?" said dad. "Adam and Eve? You hear that, Lenny?"

Now he was in for it, but he decided to leave it that way. They could thrash out the orthography later. Later came soon enough. In another phone call. This time his mom answered. "I need to explain, mom, that Yves is a guy ..." "A *guy* ...?" "I'll spell it for you, mom—" "I know how to spell 'guy,' dear." "Y-V-E-S; he's Canadian, French-Canadian." Mom went on automatic pilot; it was impossible to read her. All she said was, "It'll just be the four of us, then. Ali might drop by."

He'd meant to say more, to explain that he couldn't explain—should he try to explain that...? Mom got it. (But what would she make of it?) The subject had never come up. (Why did there have to be a *subject*? And why did anything have to *come up*?)

Mom's voice interrupted his uneasy ruminations.

"Weren't you going to get drinks, Albert ...?"

"I'll bring the drinks," offered Alison. She'd been viewing the proceedings with detached amusement.

"Red wine for me," said Lenora. Adam seconded it. "I'll have my usual," said Al.

"Well, here we are," Al began after Ali left the room. Turning to Yves, "What kind of living can one make playing the cello?"

Yves shot a quick glance at Adam. "As opposed to the violin or the viola ...?"

"Don't ask me," returned Al. "I'm no musician."

"He doesn't expect you to be a musician," Lenora returned. "He's asking you to clarify your question."

"I mean," Al began, his hands running up and down the imaginary strings of a bass viol, "Can you earn good money in that line of work?"

"I like to think of it as a profession," Yves replied.

"Yves is perfectly self-supporting, if that's what you're getting at, Dad." Adam hoped his frown would silence his father. He might have told him to mind his own business, but he didn't want the visit to get off to a bad start before it had hardly begun. Maybe Yves would view their exchange as a comedy routine. In truth, he'd often thought dad missed his calling.

"Don't musicians have unions these days, like actors and singers?" put in Lenora.

"We do indeed," Yves replied. "Those fights at the barricades paid off."

Adam flashed him an approving grin.

"Where do you perform?" Alison inquired. She'd returned with their drinks. She handed a squat glass of Scotch on the rocks to her father, the "rocks" clickering against the glass.

"Thank you, daughter." Al raised his drink. "Cheers, everybody— time for a toast."

"Remember, you can't take back your words," Alison cautioned. Her trademark deadpan served her well most of the time in family affairs. She was seldom hard on her dad; she loved it when he called her "daughter." He'd never called her older sister that.

"My words? I don't intend to recall them," Al declared as if he'd just given them a treasure. He took the measure of his audience, a director on stage. By the fireplace stood his wastrel son, keeping some distance from his new whachucallhim. Maybe the veil would fall from Ady's eyes, he'd see the folly of his ways. He could hardly help noticing how out of place this so-called friend looked since he'd inveigled his way into the family. At least the guy didn't lisp or flip his wrists. He seemed to be winning over Lenny. She rarely showed her hand to strangers. Lenny was more inclined to let matters take their course, unless she was forced to take a stand, as in a fire or flood. But she was sitting right next to the child abductor (okay, Ady wasn't a child, even if he was acting like one), and she seemed quite comfortable—she was practically encouraging the whattocallhim! But why was everyone staring at him now? The toast! He drew in his breath.

"I don't mean to, ahem, *string* this out, but here's to equal pay for violinists, violists, and cellists."

His audience groaned and he could sit down now and pretend to behave.

Alison, standing next to Yves, exchanged glances with him after serving the drinks. "You haven't told us where you perform."

"I play all over the place."

"She's talking about your professional life," prompted Al.

Adam winced. "How much longer must we endure him, folks?"

Yves gave him a wink. "I don't work at just a single venue. I'm free-lance, so I play wherever I'm invited."

"Any places we might know?" asked Lenora.

"Carnegie Hall, Avery Fisher, City Center …"

"The man gets around," chirruped Al, with a show of bonhomie.

◙　　◙　　◙

No sooner had our quartet departed, with several drinks under their belts, than Alison's cell purred. She reached into her purse, viewed the caller's number (no image for him yet), then replied, "It's too late for you to come over. They've all gone."

She'd told him they'd have flown the coop by eight. Why was he calling at nine, if he wanted to meet them? No, she didn't ask the question. He was not the sort of guy to pin down, or hold to anything he'd ever said—"Everything I say is meant to be forgotten," he'd told her. "My words have a short shelf life." All right, she got the point already. He was sui generis, though not without a certain charm she wouldn't attempt to define, if she had to describe him to someone. To her parents, for example, if he'd shown up at the apartment this evening, as planned and promised. That might have been a good time to introduce him. Her folks had plenty on their plate concerning Adam and his acquisition du jour.

That was beneath you, Ali—*du jour* indeed. What in the hell do you know about your brother's sex life? The only thing that's given you pause is the forever missing girlfriend for a man who, everyone agrees, is a catch. So maybe he hasn't met her, or doesn't want to settle. Or maybe he's just plain gay, if gay can be plain. Keep an open mind—remember, you didn't graduate from Sarah Lawrence for nothing. The poor guy has enough on his hands with mom and pop—not to mention Big Sister.

The voice in her cell whisked her back to the present. "Something came up—sorry I couldn't make it."

"There'll be another chance."

"You spend much time over there?"

"My darkroom's here."

"Maybe I can come see your pics sometime."

"Maybe I can come see your etchings." This reversal of the male's shtick got a chuckle from him.

"You don't want to come to my place, believe me."

"I don't?"

"It's a DMZ, a minefield of good intentions gone amok."

"What a poet you are."

"Call me Baudylaire. Seriously, it's a mess over here. When can I see you?"

"When do you want to?"

"Duh—now, of course."

"I'll have to ask my mom—but she's not here, unfortunately."

"You're a piece of work, you know that—?"

No, she didn't know it, but she knew her own mind.

But this one was different. Most guys she met seemed like little boys. But her ardent Italian (she'd met him in a figure-modeling class—he was the model), this Pietro, was different, an accomplishment in itself these days: he was a quixotic mess. No, she wasn't being too hard on him—that's what he'd called himself the last time they'd tallied his pro's and con's. But he was also talented, capable of self-reflection, understanding. In short, he was original. And that counted for a lot. But she wasn't going to hop-to when he snapped his fingers.

"So you get to have a good night's shuteye," he lamented, "while I cry myself to fucking sleep—is that our deal?"

"There might be better deals on the horizon."

"I hope they're a helluva lot better than this one."

"Cut the scream of consciousness. You'll survive, and I predict you'll wake up dry-eyed by tomorrow morning, or afternoon, or whenever."

CHAPTER 3

Biden Expresses Support for Same-Sex Marriages,
New York Times, May 6, 2012
Vice President Joseph R. Biden Jr. said on Sunday that he was "absolutely comfortable" with same-sex marriages and was heartened by their growing acceptance across the country, a position that moves well beyond the "evolving" views that President Obama has said he holds on the issue.

Obama Says Same-Sex Marriage Should Be
Legal, *New York Times, May 9, 2012*
[T]hat quick decision [was] … thrust on the White House by 48 hours of frenzied will-he-or-won't-he speculation after Vice President … Biden … all but forced the president's hand by embracing the idea of same-sex unions in a Sunday talk show interview.
President Obama's decision to endorse same-sex marriage undoubtedly entails some political risk, but recent polls suggest that public opinion is increasingly on his side.

Exiting the building, Adam wondered what Yves thought of the Stovers' fancy Park Avenue address, where residents had only themselves to look at—Fifth Avenue had Central Park—but still saw their status reflected back to them from across the divided avenue. Karolos the doorman, resplendent in maroon livery with gold braid, had already snagged them a yellow cab from the line of traffic inching past. After a brief to-do about seating arrangements, Adam nudged his dad onto the backseat, then motioned mom to follow. He whispered to Yves, "You're on your own, baby." Yves flashed him a grin and sank onto the seat beside, who knows, his future mother-in-law?

Adam hopped into the front seat as the driver asked, "Where would you like to go, sir?"

"Downtown," said Adam. His mother had not told him the name and location of the restaurant, and he was straining to overhear the conversation in the backseat, where his dad's voice was sucking up the oxygen.

"Exactly *where* downtown, sir?" prompted the cabbie.

"Anywhere," said Adam vaguely. So he'd finally introduced the man of the hour—of his life!—to his reasonably ordinary, ordinarily reasonable folks. And now the four of them were jammed in a cab as close as sardines.

"Just head toward Tribeca," suggested Adam. "You know where that is ...?"

"Tribeca? I believe I can find it," mused the cabbie, reaching up to adjust his turban.

"Sorry if I seem a bit jumpy," Adam advised under his breath, adding recklessly, "I...I think I'm in love," glancing to the backseat.

"Ah, the lady ...?"

"No, the man—one of them. Turn left here."

The cabbie glanced in the rearview mirror, then frowned.

They'd advanced only two blocks down Park. The divided avenue was clogged from curbs to curbs with vehicles whose occupants had counted on beating the rush-hour crush by setting out somewhat later—and got themselves in a traffic jam.

"Sir," ventured the cabbie, "I believe it is good policy to have a specific destination in mind."

"Of course." Adam tried to interrupt the conversation in the backset to find out where they were going, but it was difficult to make himself heard with his father's voice overriding the sound of the traffic. "If you have to ask the price of a yacht," intoned Al Stover, sounding as if he'd just priced such a vessel, "... you can't afford one."

"Should I make a right here, sir?" their cabbie peered hopefully at Adam, who agreed that they should get across town to take the West Side Highway. The cabbie pulled a quick right and headed onto the transverse road through the park.

"You can step on it now," encouraged Adam.

"Step on *what*, sir?"

"Just an expression—you're doing fine."

"… So I said to him, 'If you expect me to make a bid on your yacht'…"

The cab rumbled through a Central Park of black trees standing out against an indigo sky lit by myriad lights from the surrounding buildings. Papa Stover continued with his favorite stories, providing enough patter to prevent awkward silence or serious conversation. But his spouting wasn't bothering Yves. Adam's mom had clearly grown a mental carapace to tune out the verbiage. She was composed, fit, and fashionable. Her close-cropped hair betrayed only hints of gray, and if she had any wrinkles, expensive makeup concealed them. A likable woman, Yves decided, if a little distant, disappearing at intervals like the Cheshire Cat. Not distant in a snobbish way, but a woman who'd had her brush with life and was content to sit out the rest of the fray, reengaging only when it suited her. To Yves' mind, she seemed too circumspect to upset the applecart of her marriage, though the axel was sagging. How weirdly exhilarating to be sitting by someone who was about to become a big part of his life but who only a couple of hours ago was a complete stranger.

The cab rolled down the West Side Highway, the moonlit Hudson a luminescent strip separating New York and New Jersey. Then it zoomed past Fourteenth Street, that Berlin Wall between Downtown cool and Uptown glamour, swerved onto the exit at the Holland Tunnel, and began making several twists and turns through Tribeca's narrow streets.

"Mom?" cried Adam in a last-ditch effort to figure out where they were going. "Oh, yes, dear" said Lenny placidly, "It's the street just up ahead." The taxi clattered over ancient cobblestones to pull up in front of an unprepossessing façade on a street where fire escapes clung like exoskel-etons to the fronts of lofts and warehouses.

"Are you sure this is right, Lenny?" asked Al dubiously as the cab discharged its passengers. "It looks kind of rundown to me." Adam paid the cabbie, who departed their company with an entirely rearranged concep-tion of his new homeland. Surely the gentleman in the front seat was joking about having a man for a ??? in the back? But the lady was old enough to be his mother!

◘   ◘   ◘

The difference between the inside and the outside of a chic New York restau-rant can be the difference between blight and splendor. New eateries sprout daily on litter-strewn streets amid abandoned shops and decaying tene-ments with graffiti-scarred walls. Yet the glitterati find their way through, with reviewers close on their heels, or sometimes leading the charge.

When our four diners entered the restaurant, there was confusion about the reservation—no record of it. Mr. Stover launched a tirade that ended, "Do you know who I am—?" The befuddled maître d' signaled to a nearby waiter, and a table was promptly located for their party. Once seated Al confessed, "I never make reservations."

"Why not?" wondered Lenora, as if reading a script aloud for the first time.

"I just walk in and say 'I'm Mr. Stover.' Works every time."

After an uncomfortable silence, Yves said diplomatically, "You put on a good show. I might have caved, too."

"And probably lived to regret it," said Adam, sounding relieved. He was proud of Yves for keeping his composure under fire. No doubt mom and dad were devouring his every move and word. "Shall we give a glance at the menu?"

Their eyes scanned the single sheet that listed in a **PROMINENT TYPEFACE** the daily specials, without $$$. Waiters in white tie and black slacks and busboys in charcoal drab sailed past, their fleeting images reflected in the smoked-mirror walls. Suddenly a jovial voice broke in on them.

"Everybody keep your seats—I insist!"

A gentleman of middle years and middle girth beamed down at them as if he'd just said something clever.

"Uncle Max—!" Adam stood and offered his hand to the new arrival, who waved him away. "Don't disturb yourselves on my account, folks."

"What do you expect us to do?" asked Al with poorly concealed impatience.

"Please, please, keep your seats," Max continued to insist. His eye alighted on Yves, who finally declared, "Just following your command."

"I can see we'll get along splendidly, this worthy young gentleman and I," Max said. "And who might you be?"

"I'm always myself."

"Quick on his feet as well—though he's still seated."

"Do sit down, Max, you're creating a scene." As soon as she spoke, Lenora fished for something in her purse, dismissing the intruder from her attention.

"I can't possibly stay—if only for a few moments." Uncle Max drew up a chair, insinuating himself between Yves and Adam.

The waiter approached with a look of trepidation. Diners were supposed to sit evenly spaced in this no-price venue. The gentleman squeezing between the two young men was destroying the $ymmetry.

"Drinks are on me," Max proclaimed, with a wink at the waiter. Though no one replied, he tacked on, "No arguments, please," then added to Yves, "After that, you're on your own."

"I've been on my own all my life, sir," Yves retorted.

The irrepressible intruder drew back to get a better look at the outspoken fellow. "Is that a fact?" He continued to babble merrily while waiting for the drinks and at some point declared,

"Before I leave this family circle," his eyes once more centering on Yves after a furtive dart at Lenora, "you don't mind if I include *you* as 'family' here, do you?"

Yves nodded slightly.

"Just who *are* you, anyway? I've been wondering ever since you invited me to your table."

"Ady's boyfriend, that's who he is."

Max's head swiveled from Yves to Albert.

"For now," Al resumed, as eyebrows rose around the table.

Lenora announced, "I'm taking a powder, gentlemen."

"I'm going with you," declared Max, all but tipping his chair over as he rose to join her. "Nice to meet you, young man. I say, hang in there, won't you? This is some family, as I'm sure you're discovering." He turned and followed Lenora toward the ladies & gents.

◙　　◙　　◙

"That was really amazing."

"You liked …?"

"How could I not …?"

"You're just being kind—"

"Not at all—it was totally terrific, memorable even—je t'assure."

"I *do* believe you. It's just that, well …," Adam propped his chin in both hands as Yves lay on his back beside him. "I was so worried; I wasn't sure how it would work out."

"What's not to 'work out'?"

"You know, meeting my folks for the first time …"

"Is *that* what you're talking about—?" Yves flipped onto his side, "dinner with your folks—?"

Adam counterflipped to face him. "What did you *think* we were talking about?"

"The fabulous sex we just had—!"

"Oh, *that*." Adam exhaled, the breath rushing audibly past his lips.

"Qu'est-ce que tu veux dire, '*oh that*,' you little schmuck! It's the best sex I've had in ages—of course, I can't speak for you." Yves made as if to let his crest fall.

"*Schmuck*? Where did you pick *that* up? You're sounding like a New York Jew."

Yves ran his hand through Adam's hair. "Speaking of New York Jews, you never mentioned whether you're Jewish on your mother's side or your father's."

"I suppose I haven't."

"Which is it?"

"I don't give out such info."

"Why not?"

"Because it would allow you to pigeonhole me."

"In what way?"

"According to Jews, if my mom is Jewish, that makes me a Jew. If it's my dad, then I'm a Gentile. The point is, I don't leave that determination to others. If I say I'm a half-Jew—or Jew-half—c'est exactement ce que je suis."

"Makes no difference to me—I love both halves of you, you half-wit."

So why don't you tell me what you thought of my Jewish-Gentile Gentile-Jewish parents?"

"I thought your folks were great, no complaints here." Yves rolled onto his back, his eyes peering upside down into Adam's. "Friendly, outgoing, generous—especially your dad."

"Mind if we dwell on this a bit?" Adam drew the sheet to his chest. The soft ambient light from neighboring apartments was filtering into the room, an involuntary sharing of electricity and a reason to love your neighbors.

"Dwell away."

"Obviously, I'd hoped it would go well tonight."

"Obviously."

"So, you liked them both?"

"I liked your sister. She's cool."

"And my folks?"

"Your dad's a good guy. He goes off half-cocked, and loves the sound of his own voice, but he seems a reliable sort of bloke."

"You mean, the kind of dad who gives you your allowance on time?"

"Don't be defensive. I think he's someone you could count on."

"You mean, when the chips are down?"

Yves slid next to Adam as a breeze fanned the room and murmured innuendos while rustling through the trees in the courtyard below.

"My dad's a regular windbag. But if you get his attention, he's a sympathetic listener."

"I was intrigued by your mom. She was along for the ride but didn't ask me a single thing about myself."

"She was assembling the evidence. If any blanks remain, she'll start her interrogation. But you won't be aware of it."

"So I should keep my guard up for a while—?"

"I wouldn't worry about it. Mom doesn't approach things directly. She comes and goes without making a stir. She'll slip into the apartment with two or three shopping bags and stow them away before you notice she's entered."

"I don't think I've ever seen my mom with a shopping bag," Yves confessed. "We were poor—simply put. Mom's clothes came from a widowed sister who passed them on—once they went out of style."

"And your dad?"

"We've never talked about him, toi et moi."

"That's why I'm asking now." Adam reached for Yves' hand.

"He left us when I was a kid. I rarely saw him after that. Mom had her hands full, raising me and my little brother. She took in laundry, sewing—a cliché, I know, like something out of *La Bohême* …"

"I was thinking Zola…"

"*L'Assommoir*, right on. Then I got a scholarship to college, and after that my education was pretty much assured. So I'm not exactly your Park Avenue type. You may have noticed."

"Do you think that makes a difference to me?"

"Does it?"

"Are you trying to start our first fight after two months in paradise—?"

"Me? Fight? What's gotten into you?" He cuffed Adam's cheek, his clenched fist barely grazing the skin.

"I love you, you know." He cupped Yves' chin with his free hand, then kissed him. "That's what matters."

"You don't care what your parents think of me?"

"I mean, I want them to like you, but if they don't, that's their problem." Adam released his hand. "But I'm sure they liked you. I got no bad vibes, as you'd put it."

"Not even when your dad asked me whether I planned to be in New York for any length of time?"

"He was probably referring to your touring schedule."

"No one said a thing about touring schedules. As I mentioned, I thought he was a good guy, but I had the distinct impression he considers me a supernumerary—just a walk-on in your life, till you come to your senses."

"I think you're being thin-skinned."

"I wouldn't be so sure." Yves' voice lacked its usual self-confidence.

"Maybe it's just as well if he doesn't put much store by you—by *us*—for the time being."

"In other words, we should disappear off his radar like we don't exist? Now, there's the voice of commitment!"

"Silly ass—! You know that's not what I mean." Adam threw both arms around Yves' neck. "Make love to me again, you blithering idiot—!"

Later, as they lay in each other's arms, Yves whispered, "There's one more thing about tonight—at the restaurant—that seemed a little—how should I put it?—*remarquable* ..."

Adam was drifting off while still clinging to Yves.

"This Uncle Max of yours ..."

"Maximilian Bombek, what a character. Uncle Bombast—he's not a real uncle; he's mom's cousin several times removed, I've never understood the connection. Ali says he's not removed enough."

"He said something that stuck in my mind. I thought I'd run it past you."

Adam twisted a lock of Yves' hair with his thumb and forefinger.

"We were speaking together, just the two of us; I think you and your dad were arguing about the New York Public Library's plans for a facelift."

"Sounds like something dad and I would squabble about," Adam returned dreamily. His eyelids had closed, fluttered open, closed once more.

"… when he asked what made me decide to play the cello."

"What's so odd about that? You're a musician, aren't you?"

"I never told him I was a musician. The subject never came up."

"You must have said something about it?"

"Nothing at all. That's something I'd distinctly remember."

CHAPTER 4

Gay Marriage Withstands Legal Threat, *New York Times*, October 23, 2012
New York's highest court declined on Tuesday to hear a challenge to the state's gay-marriage law, ending the only significant legal threat to same-sex weddings in the state.

Her key turned in the lock for that satisfying *clickkk* and her hand slipped off the lion's head of a brass doorknob. Before leaving the elegant little shop, which nestled in the East Sixties off Lex, she glanced through the sheath of plate glass handsomely lettered in gold:

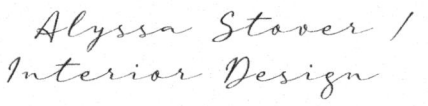

It'd hardly been two years since she signed the lease, and she had enough business to float her brainstorm of an enterprise. In fact, she had more customers than she could deal with comfortably, but she turned no one away—and worked long hours. By every measure, her venture was a success, though her own father had bet against her. Dad had wagered she'd close her doors within six months. "I can hear it now," he'd pontificated, "the client will want to recover the sofa in chintz and you'll insist on satin. You're too hifalutin to run a business, Aly." But she'd won their bet hands down—she was covering the Upper East Side in that glossy fabric.

As she headed for home, she remembered the letter. She'd left it on her desk so she wouldn't forget it. Then the call from Josiah broke her concentration. Pesky Josiah! Whose sleeveless undershirts were a cause for reproach, despite her sartorial directive to wear V-necks. "What difference does it make if my undershirt shows in twenty-first-century America?" he'd reply whenever she raised the subject. "Men go around in flip-flops and cargo pants these days, and you're worried about my undershirt? If it's any consolation, my U-shirts are from Barney's and my U-pants are from Brooks."

"U-pants—? Sounds like a submarine fleet," she'd snapped, "not something you'd wear next to your skin! If you hope to make a slam dunk while getting to first base with me, please remember—I'm a decorator—details matter!"

"I loff you, I loff you, I loff you!" he vociferated on that day not so long ago. He was pursuing her down Second Avenue amid the jumble from the much-overdue subway line now snaking for three measly stops beneath the East Side thoroughfare.

"And please stop saying 'Loff' for 'Love'—" she chided over her shoulder. "You sound like a Lon G-island Jew!"

"But, I *am* a Lon G-Island Jew—!"

Why did that episode come to mind whenever she thought of Josiah Grynszpan, her unencouraged paramour?

She wasn't sure what she'd done to attract him—she certainly hadn't tried. He'd peeked into her shop several times, he'd explained later, whenever he passed by on the way to his, a few doors down. Then one day he stepped inside hers disguised as a customer, fussing over a display of fabrics, running a finger across several to check them out. Later, as she began to see through his disguise, she realized he was a sheep in wolf's clothing. That's what she called him to her friends; she called him other things as well.

After weeks of resistance, she accepted an invitation to lunch. But over a BLT sandwich (his) and egg salad (hers), his confession of love propelled her out of the café. In hot pursuit he chased her down Second Ave, until she ran out of steam.

Was it the oxygen deficit that cast him in an altered light? She gasped for breath, leaning against a storefront, his hands plumped down on either side of her as if he were doing vertical push-ups against the wall. And her. Was there, in fact, something to be said, she was starting to wonder, for a man who'd chase you down Second Avenue, broadcasting his love to the world? No one else had ever chased her down Second Avenue, or any other street. She'd heard it said that you can't resist someone who loves you. But was Josiah Grynszpan to be her fate? The will to resist urged her to ask herself, Why wasn't someone named Theophilus Witherspoon IV tailing her down Second Avenue—or, for that matter, the Champs-Elysées of Paris, France?

Of course, Josiah Grynszpan had time to pursue her. How busy could his old curiosity shop keep him—books and bed linens. Whoever heard of such a combination? It's a wonder he had any customers at all.

"I sell the bedding along with the books, Aly—"

"The name is Alyssa."

"... *Alyssa*, because folks often mistake my bookstore for a linen shop."

"Is it any wonder, considering the name you gave it?

"Between the Covers?"

"It sounds like a porn shop—"

"... so instead of disappointing all the walk-ins, I stock sheets and pillowcases as well."

It was pointless trying to win arguments with Josiah; he always managed to outtalk or outargue her. So she gave in. And accepted dates with him. They were getting somewhere—he was checking out Jockey-brand T-shirts.

She pulled back the accordion gate that guarded her shop and unlocked the door to retrieve the letter. It lay exactly where she'd left it. She'd been so excited that she'd put off opening it till she had a quiet moment. Her emerald eyes focused momentarily on the square envelope, its stamp bearing the inscription Ελληνική Δημοκρατία, Greek Republic. Then she stashed the letter in her purse, closed the shop, and walked to her apartment a few blocks beyond in the East Seventies.

◙　◙　◙

"Look who's finally come up for air! Nice to see you're back again, Adam."

Adam didn't have to raise his eyes from the drawing board to know who was speaking. The bantering, confidential tone was typical of Trent.

He glanced up from his plans for a new entrance to an elite private school on the Upper West Side. Trent Duncan, his best friend at the firm of Appleby, Bartleby & Drumm, stood more than six feet. Though approaching middle age, he held himself like a man ten years younger—straight back, erect shoulders, flat abdomen. His plush silk tie picked up the muted browns and golds of his Tattersall shirt and brown calf belt. The tie was purposely askew, to make you think its wearer paid little attention to his appearance?

"Glad to see you, Trent," Adam rose to extend his hand, but Trent grasped him by his upper arm. "I expect you to tell me everything."

"What are you talking about?"

"Fess up—coyness doesn't suit you."

"Who's being coy?" Adam glanced around to be sure no one was outside his office. "Are you free for lunch any time soon?"

"How about drinks instead, after work?"

"You've got yourself a date."

They met at a Midtown bar that reeked of expense accounts. A hostess ushered them to a table by a window that gave onto the multitude of New Yorkers scurrying past and muffled the snarl of passing traffic, which was moving hardly any faster than the pedestrians.

After the waitress took their order, Trent asked, "Out with it—are we celebrating?"

Adam shrugged. Grasping the table as if fearful it might rise from the floor, he managed to say, "We can celebrate anything you wish."

When the waitress returned with their drinks. Trent lifted his glass but caught himself. "I don't toast when I don't know what I'm toasting."

"You and your toasts," Adam muttered, not without an edge. "Here's to your health and happiness."

"Trent raised glass and eyebrows. "And here's to your … your …?"

"What are you trying to say—?"

"I'm waiting for you to fill in the blank."

"All right, goddammit, there *is* someone—now drink your fuckin' Scotch!"

Trent took a sip of Dewar's and squelched a smile. "All I'm asking you to cough up is—everything."

"There's not much to tell." He tacked on, "I've been coasting along alone, and suddenly I'm not alone anymore. End of story."

"Then congratulations are in order?"

"Do you congratulate someone for being happy?"

"You're happy?"

"For the first time in my life. Or it feels that way. Don't ask me to explain. I can't."

He'd not known Trent to betray a confidence. And Trent had opened up to him on several occasions. Their friendship was launched about the time that Trent's marriage was dissolving. He'd asked Adam's help with a project that had gone off track, and his failing marriage was disclosed as the reason. Trent had told no one else at the office about his domestic turmoil, and the confidence that the older man placed in him cemented their friendship. Thus began their bromance.

"Where did you meet, if I may stick my nose in here?" Trent eyed him intently.

"On the street."

"Soliciting?"

"Don't blow this out of the water."

What a relief it would be to unburden himself and talk about his cellist. What if he tossed caution to the wind and recounted the tale of Chopin's étude and the abandoned Baldwin?

But Elias Fothergill, senior partner, Appleby, Bartleby & Drumm, was gazing down at them.

"Talking about me behind my back, are you?" The older man slid onto the seat beside Adam, as if they'd been expecting him.

"We were discussing Adam's new project," Trent burbled. Adam felt the nudge of Trent's brogan against his tasseled loafer.

"Always glad when an employee of Appleby puts the interests of the firm ahead of personal concerns."

A buttoned-up gentleman with an unerring instinct for business, Mr. Fothergill was not a founding partner, but he didn't differentiate himself from the architectural firm that he'd guided to preeminence.

"I take it I'm not intruding," he proclaimed, all evidence to the contrary.

"Not at all," came Trent's breezy reply, "but I must leave you gentlemen to attend an event I've been dreading all week." He took a couple of bills from his wallet and placed them on the table. "This should cover our drinks, Ad."

Before Trent was out of earshot, Fothergill said, "Wouldn't you know, this obviously involves some tedious female."

"One can only sympathize," said Adam, wondering how he'd survive this unexpected session with the boss.

"The only thing worse than a tedious female—waiter, Chivas on the rocks," Elias Fothergill continued, "is a tedious male."

◘　　◘　　◘

It was a day when summer unleashed its assault on the city after a cool, damp spring. A day when office workers overstayed their lunch break. A day when men rolled up their sleeves and women raised their skirts to catch a welcome breeze. A day when lovers lay in grassy parks while pledging undying love and other foolishness. A day for losing your head if it came to that, or keeping your wits if you could still think straight.

Alison Stover's head lay in an unreliable lap that kept threatening to disappear, owing to the restlessness of its owner. He was sitting in Washington Square Park. He hadn't expected her head to land there. He'd never kissed her, though he'd certainly tried, always rebuffed, not without humorous consequences. On his first attempt, she'd pushed him away so hard that he landed in a trashcan. The second time, he tried to pull a fast one—a kiss behind the ear, they were standing in front of Carnegie Hall before the doors opened—and she gave him a shove, whereupon he fell flat on his ass. An usher appeared to assist the unfortunate suitor back to his feet (the venerable hall was leery of lawsuits).

So imagine the shock of her suitor when his beloved's head plopped into his lap without warning. And then the surprise of the century: "Aren't you going to kiss me …?"

He tried to kiss her but couldn't because she was lying down. So she rolled from his lap, and he gazed into her eyes while searching for something to say.

"Will you ever be ready?" she complained, as if she'd been urging him to kiss her for weeks.

"You're such a tease."

"Opportunity is knocking."

"Have I ever told you—you're a goddess?"

"You're thinking of someone else."

"Why do you always credit me with the worst intentions?"

"At least I credit you."

"So there's not a single romantic bone in that stunning bod of yours?"

"You're welcome to check my medical records."

This time the young man's lips met no resistance. A stopwatch would've timed the kiss at forty seconds or so. When their lips parted, she ran her fingers through the copper curls that fell across his forehead. When he drew breath, he sighed, "We must try that again."

"You'll need an appointment. Don't you need to be somewhere now?"

"Are you banishing me after all I've been through—?"

"Was the kiss such a slog?"

"Why are you sending me away when I'm prepared to spend the rest of my life with you—?"

"Maybe that's why. Do you smell rain?"

Clouds were churning on high, their sudden onset in defiance of the cheerily optimistic weather report.

"So you're a meteorologist?"

"We'll get to that later. Meanwhile, my brother doesn't live far from here. We could drop by his pad, to miss the downpour."

"What if he's not home."

"I have a key."

"What kind of brother would entrust his keys to a girl like you?"

"We share a business relationship."

He was following her across the square. "I cat-sit for him when he's away."

"What's this brother like, if I may inquire?"

"You may, since you have." At the intersection, she thrust out her arm to stop him from stepping into a line of automobiles. "He's reasonable, responsible, reliable."

"And no doubt rarefied. Would I like him?"

"You'll have to decide for yourself."

"Is he married?"

"Not yet."

"He has a fiancée?"

"Maybe."

"What does that mean?"

"It hasn't been announced. Nothing's been announced."

"Would I like her?"

"Whom?"

He spelled it for her: "His presumed f-i-a-n-c-é-e." (He even said the *acute* over the first *e*.)

"That's one *e* too many."

"What are you talking about? Do you deign to correct my French?"

"His fiancé—one *e*. What are *you* talking about?"

"A guy?"

"As I said, one *e*."

◙   ◙   ◙

They reached a shady street of brownstones and gentrified tenements arched by overhanging elms, and Alison led her charge to a building midblock that was taller than its neighbors. Its limestone façade sported traces of Art Deco with stylized thunderbolts crossed by streaks of turquoise and jade, a modest knockoff of Rockefeller Center. A panel of buzzers mounted in the outer lobby stood in for a doorman to announce guests and deliverymen.

Alison pushed a button, and before long they were buzzed in. En route to the elevator through a lobby faced with polished marble, she told her companion, "You'll be on your best behavior, you hear?"

"Scout's honor."

"Were you ever a scout?"

"What do you think?"

Adam answered the door in cut-off sweats and a sweatshirt whose sleeves had been shortened to the shoulder. "I'll tell Dido and Aeneas you've come to visit," he announced.

"Tell them we're avoiding the rain. They'll get it—they're cats," she replied. Then in mock-formal mode: "Ady, may I present my friend Pietro Tresceri."

Her companion extended his hand. As Adam clasped it and was on the point of saying something, Alison said, "You may call him Treachery if you wish."

"Well, then, Treachery, I'll be en garde but do come in."

He led them into the living room and had just invited them to take a seat when Yves appeared. He ran his eye over the newcomers, and before Adam could introduce him, said, "Nice to see you again, Alison."

"Likewise, Monsieur Yves." She lowered herself onto the sofa next to a blue-gray Persian cat, then patted the seat beside her, as if Pietro were also a domestic animal. "I see you've survived that dinner on the town with my folks. Pretty ghastly, I imagine?"

The start of a grin morphed onto Yves' lips.

"I expect the truth—" she encouraged.

"On the contrary, I think we all had a fine time, don't you, Ad?"

"Yes," agreed Adam, "Dad behaved."

"You must have worked a spell on them."

"That he did," said Adam. He elbowed Yves gently. "Mind getting these folks something to drink, mon ami? Fruit juice, mineral water, and we also have beer.

"Nothing for me," piped Treachery, who'd remained standing. "Gotta go."

All eyes turned on him. "Something I hafta do—I almost forgot."

"What in the world could that be?" asked Alison.

"I've forgotten again already."

Glances were exchanged by all present but for Aeneas, who twitched his tale as Dido, a fat white Angora, jumped up beside him, then rolled onto her back.

"I'll see myself out," said Pietro-Treachery.

CHAPTER 5

Supporters of Same-Sex Marriage See Room for
Victories, *New York Times, October 30, 2012*
Six states and the nation's capital have legalized marriage for gay and lesbian couples. But in 30 states, voters have limited marriage to a man and a woman through
constitutional amendments; in addition, same-sex marriage has been blocked in
referendums like those in California in 2008 and Maine in 2009.

"Step into my office, son—"

Elias Fothergill addressed junior male members of Appleby, Bartleby
& Drumm as if they were errand boys, standing in their office doorway and
attempting a casual pose that made him seem even more stiff and intimi-
dating than usual.

Worse, he'd caught Adam off-guard as he stood on the threshold of
his office. The associate partner, under most circumstances alert and atten-
tive to his work, had been lost in thought. He'd been running through his
mind the surprise visit from Alison and her friend with the odd name.
Treachery? It was cool that his baby sister felt free to bop into his pad with
friend in tow. Ali hobnobbed with all kinds of characters. This one seemed
not a bad sort. Yet, his sudden exit—what was that all about? Everyone has
appointments and dates that can't be broken. But the guy vamoosed as if
he'd heard a shotgun. And Yves' take on the matter? Not till later that evening did the subject come up. They were in bed catching an episode of *Law
& Order*, when a character appeared who reminded Adam of the fugitive.

"That guy looks remarkably like Ali's friend this afternoon, don't
you think?" He reached for a handful of popcorn from the bowl in Yves'

lap. He stirred up the popped kernels to vibrate the bowl, hoping to snag Yves' attention.

"Hmm—?"

"That fellow who was here with Alison today …?"

Yves didn't reply, but when the character reappeared on the screen, Adam remarked, "That guy we just saw today—I'll swear there's a resemblance."

"To whom?"

"To whom do you think—?" Yves had seemed particularly distracted that afternoon, but could he have forgotten someone they'd just met?

Adam muted the remote. "Hey, what's up with you?"

"Don't be lewd," came the mock-disapproving reply.

"I was asking you about the guy we met this afternoon, Ali's friend. Don't you see the resemblance to the actor on the TV?"

"My mind was somewhere else."

Mr. Fothergill looked up from Adam's plans, which he'd brought to his desk. "I've been examining your project for the school's new entrance," he began tentatively, not a good sign.

"Yes, sir?"

"You've done some good work here, Stover. You've clearly put some thought into it, no argument there."

"As you can see in this sketch …," Adam stepped behind Mr. Fothergill's desk for a better view of the plan, "the building wasn't much to begin with. The school has been around for a while, but it lacks architecture, sir. It's a pastiche of different styles. In working with it—rather, *around* it—I chose the glass façade, which doesn't clash with the stone, brick, stucco, and wood that's already there. It's hardly the Louvre, as you can see."

"I see, I see, … a worthy first attempt."

"*First*, sir …?"

"I'm not suggesting you *entirely* rework it." Fothergill clasped his hands as if to warm them.

Adam flexed his forehead to suppress a frown. He'd spent days juggling materials and a variety of approaches to confront the jumble of styles the school presented. He'd run several tentative sketches by Trent Duncan, and they'd both agreed on the solution that now lay on Fothergill's desk. If the boss expected another attempt, he'd hardly know where to begin.

"The truth is," Fothergill said, "the school is going all out to punch up its image." He dropped his voice. "I have it from the headmaster, a long-time acquaintance—and client. Appleby, Bartleby & Drumm redesigned his co-op a few years ago after their latest tuition hike. I can tell you their overall concern, my boy, in three words: image, image, image."

"They want a new look?"

"It's a neighborhood school snuggled away on the Upper West Side. They're trying their best to lure a stream of limousines from Park and Fifth for the kiddie drop-offs each morning. And when those sleek Cadillacs and Chryslers slither up in front of the school, the school desires to put on its best façade, if you will."

"Of course. What do you suggest."

"It's not for me to tell you how to draw your plans. I'm sure when you go back to your desk, you'll come up with a serviceable solution."

"Serviceable, sir?"

He left Fothergill's office and meandered back to his desk, his shoulders drooping as if heavy stones were weighing them down.

◉   ◉   ◉

She tossed her jacket over a chair and sank onto the sofa. Then removing the envelope from her purse, she took the rhinestone-studded letter opener from the table beside her, a gift from Josiah. When she ran it across the faintly pink envelope, it made a soft, scratching sound, as if the tinted missive were whispering to her.

The room around her vanished into the dimness as she held the letter before her, its stamp depicting the Acropolis.

"Αγαπητή μου φίλη Άλυσα," it began in Greek, To my very dear friend Alyssa.

The letter resumed in English, salted with Greek expressions: "I have huge έκπληξη [surprise] for you—έρχομαι στη Νέα Υόρκη [coming to New York]. Business and pleasure—you know how I love to mix them. Soon we be together again. You have room—soon you have guest! In ten days I be on your doorstep." The letter was signed

Για Πάντα, Αφροδίτη

Always, Aphrodite

Aphrodite of Athens—the most beautiful woman in the world! The letter's few short lines brought back a scene that seemed as vivid as when she left Greece two years ago: the Aegean's wavelets erasing her footsteps as she stepped across the sand, Aphrodite in the skimpiest bikini, Venus on the Half-Shell with her fair skin bronzed by the August sun, and close behind, his thick dark hair standing straight up as he emerged from the water, his brilliant sapphire eyes staring into her soul, or so Alyssa imagined—Manolis, the one man she'd ever loved (besides Theophilus Witherspoon IV, of course).

Had she been rash to abandon her life in Greece and return to the States to start her decorating business? The decision tore her in two, partly because of the effort it had taken to get there, partly because of the life she found when she'd arrived in the Hellenic Republic. She'd completed graduate school and worked for a couple of years in various East Side galleries where her mom had pull through a distant cousin, then applied for a scholarship from her university for a fine arts program in Greece. After finding an apartment in the fashionable Kolonaki neighborhood of Athens and immersing herself in the program, she'd met Aphrodite, and was quickly absorbed into her circle of friends.

Greece was a new world to her, and so were the Greeks. They stood much closer to you than her fellow Americans and were quick to argue, quick to anger, and quick to forgive. Passion reigned; she might have fallen for one ardent pursuer after another, if the multiplicity of offers hadn't canceled one another out. Aphrodite was helpful in this area; she considered few potential suitors good enough for her American friend, until Manolis.

Alyssa had met him by chance at a beach south of Athens. She was lounging under a large umbrella with Aphrodite and companions when the oversized beachball landed smack in her lap as she lay soaking up the sun, her mind drifting nowhere in particular, hardly expecting to meet the man of her dreams. *Plop.*

"Would you mind returning the ball?" He stood before her, his weight shifting from foot to foot, impish and impudent.

The ridiculously large yellow sphere, a miniature sun dropped from the heavens, now half covered her. It could have kept two afloat at sea. "What makes you think I speak English?"

"Your newspaper." He glanced toward a copy of the *Herald-Tribune* lying beside her.

"It's not mine."

"The ball isn't mine either," he grinned. "I have no claim to it whatsoever."

"Then you have some serious explaining to do—"

◙   ◙   ◙

"Who's sitting in that empty chair?"

"What do you mean?"

"Think about it."

"I'm thinking. But nothing comes to mind."

"Then can you honestly say you're thinking ...?"

Yves pressed his back against the back of the chair and stretched his legs. His sneakers made a wheezy sound as his heels slid over the rough wooden floor. "What does 'honesty' have to do with it?"

Dr. Norman Nuddelmann, LCSW-R, CBT, MSW, LMHC, adjusted his horn rims to peer across the tiny room in which he received patients. Montjour, Yves had been in his care now for a little over a month, in that stage that Dr. Nuddelmann liked to call, unclinically speaking, "feeling our way." "The point I am trying to make is that such a question as you just asked cannot be answered, anymore than one could report who is sitting in an empty chair."

His patient blinked once, twice, bit his lower lip. "It was just a question."

Dr. Nuddelmann, whose name had hijacked so many letters of the alphabet that he often abbreviated it even in formal writing, blinked then said, "Tell me more about this latest development in your life."

"I'm not sure there's much more to tell." Yves' thumbs and fingertips conjoined in a miniature church steeple, which he pressed to his lips. "As I said earlier, I have a partner, a partner for life. I have never loved anyone this way before. I love him completely, with no reservations," he hesitated then resumed, "and I couldn't possibly be happier."

Dr. N smiled and nodded, as if he himself had wrought this beatific state in his patient.

"But there has to be an explanation for why I felt—quite recently— such a strong pull toward someone else."

"Someone you know?"

"Yes, but someone who hasn't been in my life for a while." He glanced about the little room, which had a single window of the type found in ancient castles. It was so narrow you could barely shoot an arrow through it, if you were trying to kill your therapist. "So, what do you make of this?"

"What do *you* make of it?"

Yves shrugged. "It makes me feel shallow and superficial."

Dr. N's eyebrows arched.

"Like a fickle schoolboy who can't see a good thing when it's staring him in the face. Or—more appropriately, in my case—lying next to him in bed."

Dr. Nuddelmann's head bobbed, perhaps a touch of Parkinsonism. Then his patient declared, "I probably don't deserve someone like Adam. Adam would never cheat on me, or stand me up for someone else. He's honest and serious and hardworking. Whatever he devotes himself to, he's faithful to it."

"*It?*"

"It. *Me.* You know what I mean."

"Hmmm."

"So what should I do?"

"What do you *think* you should do?"

"I don't want to lose him, I can tell you that."

"Are you afraid of losing him?"

Yves slapped his cheek with his opened palm as if he were trying to knock sense into himself. "I think what I'm trying to say … you may need to help me out with this …"

Dr. Nuddelmann was not one to launch rescue missions for patients needing verbal filler. But he nodded encouragement.

"… is that I'm afraid of making a misstep."

"Such as …?"

"*That* is the question."

Neither spoke for half a minute or so. A truck rumbled past on the quiet Village street a flight below. A door slammed. A pipe clanked. Dr. N remained sphinxlike.

"What if I do something rash or foolish? Not intentionally, mind you, but on impulse?"

"Impulse?"

"Like agreeing to meet this guy, or even dropping in on him, just to see what he's up to."

"What he's up to ..." came the psychological echo.

"I mean, what if it happened?"

"Are you afraid it will happen?"

"I'm concerned about this pressure in my groin that hasn't let up since I last laid eyes on him."

"What have you done about it?"

"The pressure?"

"Hmm."

"Made love like crazy—to Adam."

Dr. Nuddelmann reflected. "Seems like a constructive response."

"Yes, but—it feels like I'm cheating on my partner."

"Do you think of the other person when you're making love to Adam?"

"Of course not! I only think of Adam."

"Then why is it cheating?"

"Because if I hadn't run into the guy—through no fault of my own, I assure you—I wouldn't be so sexed up, and I wouldn't be taking it out on poor Adam."

"Does he mind?"

"He loves it." Yves' brow furrowed. "Or he says he does."

"Does he?"

"He hasn't asked me to stop."

"Well, then …?"

"But I can't escape the feeling that I would be … that *Adam* and I would be acting differently if it weren't for this other guy."

"How is that?"

"Ordinarily, each of us is pretty self-sufficient. Adam comes home from work and goes straight to his drawing board after fixing a snack. That's when I take out my cello and practice, sometimes just to keep my fingers nimble—and off of him. I usually do my practicing in the morning when he's at work. But my playing doesn't seem to bother him. He's never complained. He has a sister who played classical piano, so he's used to hearing the stuff. I haven't met her yet; he says she's a handful, that she can be prim and proper and all that—"

"All what?"

"Well, that she might give us some trouble when she finds out."

"Finds out what?"

"About us."

"What about us. I mean—*you* …?"

"Well, that we're together now."

"I see."

"Then what should we do?

"What do you *think* you should do …?"

"I don't know. We're all adults here. We should be able to figure it out."

"Not so fast." Dr. Nuddelmann sat straight in his chair for the first time since the session began. He was leery of patients figuring things out before he could help with the figuring. "This sister, where does she stand in the family hierarchy?"

"Alyssa? She's Adam's older sister."

"Is she domineering?"

"He seems to have a healthy respect for her."

"What do you make of her?"

"As I said, we haven't met yet, though I think we shall, soon."

Norman N. looked up. His eyes grew smaller as his glasses slipped down his nose.

"His folks have invited us to a meet-and-greet, so to speak. At least, that's how Adam billed it. In fact, I could use your advice about how to approach this formidable woman."

"I'm sorry—our time is up," came the time-worn mantra. A toilet flushed in a nearby john. Another patient was on the runway.

So Fate, with the kindly midwifing of Dr. Nuddelmann, terminated their session, because if there was anything Dr. N was averse to, it was giving advice. But such unspoken counsel was about to be superseded by events. It turned out that Yves would not have to face the Gorgon after all: he was not invited to the family powwow.

"I'm sorry if I wasn't clear, dear," Lenora apologized in a phone call to her son the night before the "family" dinner. Her voice rose on the word *family*. As the family diplomat, she'd been deputed to break the news.

"I just don't get it," said Adam. His breathing rasped through the receiver in short gasps. "Yves is my family, too."

"Yves is a lovely young man."

"Then why isn't he invited anymore?"

"I quite understand your feelings, darling. Your father thinks it would make for a smoother ride if just we old-timers assembled this time around—"

"What 'old-timers' are you talking about?"

"The very immediate family."

"Yves is immediate to me, Mom, we're a couple. You can't get more immediate than that."

"I quite understand, dear. Next time he'll be included, you have my word."

"For someone who doesn't cook, you have more pots and pans than Macy's Housewares." Alyssa surveyed her parents' immense-for-New-York kitchen. Her father inherited the apartment from a relative. She was a child then, in the days before new owners were infected with the mania for gutting baths and kitchens upon taking possession to install zero-degree fridges large enough to store two corpses at a time. "What can I do to help?"

Alyssa surveyed the platters of roasted vegetables, chips, dips, sliced cheeses, and pastas. "I can't remember the last time I ate a home-cooked meal in this house."

"I can say the same thing." Albert stepped into the kitchen. "Who eats this stuff, anyway?"

Lenora failed to reply to their comments, her feathers folded flat against her sides, refusing to be ruffled, as she refused to cook.

"Looks pretty tasty to me." Alison appeared in their midst, a clutch of photos in hand. She had a way of materializing out of nowhere, in this case out of the servants hall. That spacious room behind the kitchen contained a circular stairway for the use of the long-departed servants who once populated the apartment's many maids rooms, four in the Stover apartment, two upstairs, two down. Alison had converted one of the maid's rooms to her photography darkroom. And she sometimes crashed in the maid's room beside it, instead of returning to her pad in Chelsea.

The doorbell drew their attention from the culinary discussion. "That's Ady," said Lenora.

"Doesn't he have a key?" asked Alyssa.

"He hasn't been using it lately."

"Why on earth not?"

"Separation-individuation," ventured Alison in the tone of a disinterested psychotherapist.

"What are you talking about?" asked her dad. "And why are we standing around in the kitchen?"

"Would someone get the door?" prompted Lenora, as if she were needed in the kitchen to tend to the cold cuts and takeout.

"I'll get it." Alyssa marched to the foyer, with Albert and Alison in her wake. The opened doorway framed her brother in linen slacks and white button-down oxford, with bouquet in one hand and bottle of Sauvignon Blanc in the other.

"The prodigal son," announced Alyssa."

"The preppie incarnate," emended Alison.

◳   ◳   ◳

He was feeling like a fifth wheel. Was he such an egotist to expect the conversation to revolve around him? Why was no one addressing him directly? What was the reason for this confab, he wondered, alone and ignored in the middle of the room?

Until Alison remarked as they were finishing their sorbets at the dining table, "How is Yves, Ady? You haven't mentioned him all evening."

Adam migrated from the rock to the hard place. Just the day before, he'd had to explain to Yves how he'd been disinvited to the family dinner, and now he knew he was in for a grilling from the Park Avenue set. He'd concocted an off-white lie for Yves, that he, Adam, had been mistaken about the invite, that his mom said it was meant to be such a blah blah affair that they'd be embarrassed to allow an outsider into the family circle. The elephant, no longer in the room but an "outsider," saw right through it, though he pretended to go along with the deception. "Your mom misses her boy. She seldom gets to see you," Yves had murmured. But he'd reflected nonetheless for some time before responding after Adam broke the news. In truth, Adam couldn't imagine his mother admitting to missing anyone; she was as self-contained as the *Winged Victory*. All he'd replied was, "Yeah, something like that." Valiant under fire, the elephant-outsider offered, "Anyway, I have that Bach cello suite to get under my fingers. Better for me to stay home." They'd exchanged glances—sad little looks with fake smiles—as Adam reached for his partner's hand, but Yves had already turned to leave the room.

Before he could reply to Alison's question, Alyssa, who'd hardly turned her head his way since his arrival, declared, "Big news, folks—my friend Aphrodite is arriving from Athens this weekend." She glanced in triumph around the table, as if they'd awaited the tidings for weeks.

"Love that name," said Albert. "I hope she lives up to it."

"You have nothing to fear in that department," Alyssa boasted. "She's drop-dead gorgeous."

"In that case, you can fix her up with me!" Al winked at his son.

"Steady, Dad," said Alison.

"I expect we'll have a fine time while she's here." Alyssa's eyes swept the table then came to rest on Adam, "if all goes well."

"What's not to go well?" Adam hoped he didn't sound defensive.

"Greeks are a conservative people. The entire nation is Orthodox Christian, as you know," she exclaimed as if stating the obvious. Then to make sure in case it wasn't obvious, she tacked on, "Every last one of them."

"Greeks also have the highest rate of sexual activity in Europe," interposed Alison, "perhaps in the entire world. I can check that out for you."

"Where in god's name did you hear something like that?" asked Albert.

"In the *Economist*. You said I should learn more about business, Dad, so I took out a subscription. Greeks also smoke the most."

"I could use some help in the entertainment department," Alyssa said. "Not that any guy worth his salt wouldn't jump at the chance to be with her. But there's always that shortage of eligible men in New York," she claimed, conveniently overlooking the hundreds of thousands waiting in the wings at any one time. She directed the full force of her gaze at her brother. "Of course, I'm not looking for help here."

Though the rest of the family may not have felt the temblor, the tectonic plates were shifting under Adam.

"What kind of help were you looking for?"

"Since you asked, someone to squire her around after she arrives. But I wouldn't want to put you out or anything."

He was at a disadvantage, not knowing what she knew about his "domestic situation," as his father had referred to it obliquely a couple of times this evening. If she were in on it, she'd certainly disapprove—she'd be the first in line. Had appearances ever mattered more to anyone than to Alyssa Stover?

"I could help out in a pinch."

"That's kind of you, dear," said Lenora, a neutral referee awarding points.

Al inserted, "If this chick's all she's cracked up to be—"

"She's not a chick, Daddy—"

"What is she?"

"A goddess!"

"I can meet the goddess's plane when she arrives." Adam eyed his sister across the table, emotion drained from his voice.

"Thanks, I've got her arrival covered."

"Then sometime after that—lunch? dinner?"

"Very good of you." Alyssa lowered her praetorian guard. As her battlements slipped away, a thought flew over the parapet that she might kill two birds with a single stone, or not *kill* them but something more constructive. Her brother could be perverse and obtuse at times. Whatever dreadful situation he'd gotten himself into—her folks were hopelessly vague about it, but she could put 2 + 2 together and come up at least with a 3—there had to be a way around it, and she'd find that way.

Had appearances ever mattered more to anyone than to Alyssa Stover? How did she get to be so conservative? She sounded at times like a Southern Baptist. And it was 2012!

CHAPTER 6

The Black Vote for Gay Marriage, *New York Times, November 1, 2012*
[N]o matter which side you are on, the gay marriage question in the black community has forced a conversation, which is taking place in the pulpits and the pews, the hair salons and barbershops—and ultimately at the ballot box.

He was wondering why he bothered to have sex. Self-service was the way to go. No arguments, no misunderstandings, no come-ons without payoff. The tip of his knob had tinged from puce to pink to purple he'd been stroking it so long. As he lay in bed, serving himself, he'd been gazing out the window at the couple in the apartment across the court. Were they watching *him*? After several moments of this seeming double voyeurism, the pressure in his loins surged and he realized he'd not been thinking of Alison—he was fixating on someone else.

He'd been chasing after Ali for weeks. She'd have nothing to do with him at first. He'd exposed himself to her on several occasions—in drawing class, where he modeled three times a week, a freelance nudist. Had he lost his appeal? Her sovereign indifference might have discouraged a less frantically persistent ego. But he'd held to the course: was anything more desirable than a woman who resisted? No, he didn't think he was god's gift to women, or to men. Yet he'd attracted one, a man of intellect and talent.

He'd met Yves Montjour at an audition for aspiring violinists, accompanied by other instrumentalists as needed. Yves was on cello, he was on piano. As pianist, he set tone and tempi for each tryout. But it turned out that the cellist had a musical mind of his own, and there were movements in Beethoven's *Archduke Trio* where they ended a note apart. At times he actually "felt" a tug and pull of resistance from the cellist, who was inclined to take the tempi more slowly. It was the oddest sensation, as if the cellist were physically gripping his chest and restraining him.

At the end of the day, as he was passing through the lobby of the recital hall, he encountered the ornery cellist. The cellist glanced up from a black notebook he had his nose in, and their eyes locked. He was on the point of walking out to the street but instead turned and declared,

"You have decided views about a musical score."

The cellist returned the notebook to his pocket. "They don't pay me for the number of notes I bow per minute."

"I thought this was supposed to be a cooperative enterprise."

"You didn't cooperate."

"We should've had this conversation before we started playing."

"It's too late now."

"It's never too late."

His words started tumbling out of their own accord. Was he making an ass of himself? Apparently the cellist didn't think so, for he said when he could get a word in,

"Your playing blew me away."

Then the ineluctable ice-breaker. "Shall we go for a drink?"

He remembered Yves' smile as he resumed stroking himself while stealing another look at the couple across the way. They were standing at the window, but he couldn't tell whether they'd noticed him yet.

They'd wandered down brightly lit Bleeker, the Main Street of Greenwich Village, with its hopeful storefronts of leather goods, jewelry shops, lingerie emporia—consumer society on enticing display. Every so often they'd stop before a bar, exchange glances, then continue on, till the cellist ventured, "I know a quiet place with a piano bar a couple of blocks away."

"Not a cello bar?"

The hostess seated them by the window, where they might have watched passersby, but they were too intent on each other to look away from their conversation. After they finished their second beer, the pianist confessed,

"If you asked me to go home with you tonight, I wouldn't even know your name."

"If I didn't ask you, you still wouldn't know it."

"Do I think you're going to ask me?"

"I'm not a mind reader. But I can tell you with absolute certainty—I don't live far from here."

They forged their way into Yves' darkened living room and groped through the intimate obscurity toward the back.

"I wonder where this leads," asked Pietro.

"Are you having second thoughts?"

"Third."

They undressed each other in the hall and Yves eased them into the bathroom, where he lit a candle and turned on the shower. He led his companion under the showerhead and scrubbed him down with a bar of soap that smelled of wax and desire. The warm water teased his skin but not as much as the cellist's tongue discovering the creases and folds of his body.

Afterward the cellist rubbed their bodies dry.

"Why just one towel—?"

"Just one shower."

Yves led them to the bedroom, the one towel yoking their shoulders.

Pietro crawled into bed, his damp curls sinking into the pillow. A shaft of light cast an irregular halo around the curls as Yves slid in beside him.

At dawn next morning, his eyes still closed, he reached for the cellist but came up with a pillow instead. Had Yves left for work? He imagined

Yves' arms around him. Those arms had "pulled" him away from the music at the tryouts; now he imagined Yves' arms pulling them together.

◨　　◨　　◨

"Better—much better indeed …"

Elias Fothergill retreated a step from Adam's desk and patted his young colleague's shoulder. It was a lifeless pat, as if the wrist that produced it were too limp to spring back.

"Thank you, sir."

"They'll be ready to start construction before you know it," he beamed. "How does it feel, my boy, to give a school a facelift?"

He hated the plan. It violated every principle of aesthetics. When executed by the school, the unimposing premises would resemble a glitzy brothel. That's what he'd told Yves as he was working out the remaining details.

"When they complete the renovation, I'll be known in architecture circles as a second-rate whore."

"I love whores."

"That's not the point."

"The point is, I love *you*, even if you're not a whore." They were sitting on the sofa together. Yves rested his hand on Adam's thigh.

"Don't."

"Why not?"

"Because you'll arouse me."

"Now, I find *that* offensive."

Yves' eyes, a deep violet blue, could flash with fire that intimidated him. He was new to this live-in-lover setup. More than once he'd provoked Yves' ire without meaning to.

"What's offensive?" he asked, his apprehension at the fore.

"What do you mean, it *will* arouse you? You're not aroused *already*—?"

"Fuck these plans!" yelped Adam. He slipped to the floor, yanked Yves' trousers down, and went to work.

Afterward, as Yves lay on top of him, Adam's plans crushed between them (no panic—photocopies!), the associate architect murmured, "Now you probably *do* think I'm a whore."

"Actually, I think you're the best lay in town. But didn't you want my opinion on something …?"

His cheeks reddened at the recollection of that amorous escapade. "I guess it feels like a relief, sir."

"Relief?" queried Mr. Fothergill.

"To have it over with."

"Nonsense, you should be proud of your work. In fact, I plan to send you up there to present the plans in person."

"Me, sir—?"

"After all, you're bound to be the best advocate for your own project. Toodledo."

Later that afternoon, as he was about to leave for a meeting, his phone rang.

"Ady, are you free to talk ?"

"Could it wait?"

"It's quite urgent," urged Alyssa.

"Can we touch base a bit later—?"

"She's on the way! Isn't that fantastic—!"

"I have this meeting coming up—"

"She arrives this weekend—she'll be here for a whole month!"

"That's really swell, Aly."

"I thought you'd be glad to hear! And I wanted to tell you that …"

She wanted to tell him about so many things that he had to scribble a message for his secretary to postpone his meeting. Later that day, as he passed Mr. Fothergill in the hall, his boss asked him to step into his office, the spider to the fly.

"Close the door, would you?"

Trapped in the web.

Adam took a seat across from Mr. Fothergill's crocodile smile.

"I've been intending to bring this up for a while, Stover."

Fothergill's eyes sought the ceiling, as if he'd spotted an insect there, and Adam began to panic. This was no time to get the ax. A mortgage. A family to impress. A lover to care for, though Yves paid him rent.

"Yes, sir?"

"It's about my wife."

"I hope she's well, sir?"

"Very well, very well indeed."

"I'm glad to hear it."

"I think she's never been better."

"Thankfully."

"You're a sensitive man, Stover." Fothergill smiled broadly. "You've never been to our place in the country, have you?"

"I've not had the pleasure, sir."

"Don't you think it's time we put an end to that?"

"To the pleasure—?"

Fothergill shrugged like the humble soul he wasn't. "We'd like to extend an invitation to spend a weekend with us at our house upstate."

"How kind of you, sir. May I ask when?"

"Why, as soon as you can come. We were thinking within the next couple of weeks. Could you scan your calendar and fit us in?" Before his underling could reply, Fothergill resumed, "It's just our little plot of land," the "plot" in question, in fact, a Valhalla-on-Hudson. But who ever said modesty is unbecoming?

"I'm honored by the invitation, sir."

"You must bring someone along—I leave the choice to you, of course."

"Of course, sir."

It sounded like a dare.

◉　　◉　　◉

"How do you know she'll fall for your brother?"

"Why wouldn't she? He's tall, tanned, tony."

"A variation on the tall-dark-handsome theme—it just might work."

Josiah stroked his whiskers. He hadn't shaved this morning. He often went without shaving. His customers didn't seem to mind. Several mentioned that his Bogart beard (some called it "shadow") went with the film-noir interior of his bookstore, gray-stuccoed walls spattered in violet and charcoal. Between the Covers specialized in gothic horror, mystery, and adventure, plus those sheets and pillowcases. And a smart reason for the bedware: what indie bookstore can survive in the brave new world of Amazon and B&N if it fails to entice online shoppers away from their next click?

Alyssa had taken the day off to help him shelve new inventory. All she could talk about was her latest project, a match between her brother and the goddess arriving from Greece.

"On the half-shell?" he'd inquired.

"She's not an oyster, Josiah. You wait and see!"

He'd learned an essential skill for getting along with his lady unfair: to hear out her schemes while keeping his counsel. He reached down from his perch on the ladder and grasped a handful of paperbacks she was handing him.

"Are you okay up there?" she inquired after listening to him heave and sigh.

"Having trouble finding room on this shelf—no big deal."

She recalled the first time she'd helped him shelve books. Though Between the Covers was lined ceiling to floor with bookshelves, it had run out of space in several key genres and he'd sent her to three nearby bookstores to borrow their "shelf-stretcher." Only after she'd traipsed to the third shop and the manager, with the most controlled demeanor she'd ever beheld, informed her that his shelf-stretcher was on loan to another store did the lightbulb light up. After delivering the dressing-down of his life to poor Josiah, she stormed out of the store. Her boyfriend stuck a BACK IN 1 HOUR sign on the door and chased her down the street. He made matters worse when he exclaimed, "I was sure you'd catch on after the first store, my darling …!"

"Get the hell out–I never want to see you again—!"

Alyssa stormed into her shop and then to its back room, Josiah trailing and pleading behind her. Having never brawled in his thirty-seven years, he lacked the skills and strategies for confrontation and had no idea what to do. She slapped him twice, then pushed him so hard he fell onto the couch.

"You don't make a fool of me, Josiah!" she shrieked, almost in tears. "Don't you dare!"

"How the hell else am I supposed to get your attention," he shot back, starting to get the hang of how couples battle. "I was *trying* to entertain you."

"Entertain me? *Entertain me?*" I don't want to be entertained!"

"I wanted to make you laugh!"

"I don't want to laugh!"

"Maybe we could laugh together."

"I don't think so."

"Maybe you should learn to laugh a little at yourself."

"No, not that, not ever!" She was crying now.

"Well, then, what *do* you want?" he asked desperately. Then, more gently, "What do you really want, Alyssa?"

Alyssa, in the process of pushing him back as he struggled to sit up, stopped. No one—certainly no *man*—had ever asked her that before. Suddenly, she leapt on him foursquare, tugging at his T-shirt with a wicked smile. "Cut out the games, here's what I want."

After it was over, as they lay in each other arms, softly giggling, Alyssa sat up and declared, "Josiah Grynszpan, you are good in bed!"

"At least, on a couch," he replied in the comfort of satiety, but, noticing a photograph on a nearby table, asked,

"Who's the man in that picture frame …?"

A handsome fellow with WASPish features—straight nose, high forehead, thin lips, chiseled chin—stared out at Josiah from across the little room.

"Theophilus Witherspoon IV."

"Why is it that such names are always followed by roman numerals?"

"Old family."

"My family's old, but there's not a roman numeral among us."

"That's because …" Alyssa glanced from Josiah to the photo. She didn't finish her remark.

They drifted off to sleep, and when they awoke the moon was keeping watch outside the window, while the sign he'd posted at the entry to Between the Covers had become as outdated as an old calendar.

CHAPTER 7

States' Votes for Gay Marriage Are Timely, With Justices Ready
to Weigh Cases, *New York Times, November 7, 2012*
The justices tend to say they are not influenced by public opinion. But they do
sometimes take account of state-by-state trends, and the latest developments will
not escape their notice.
On Tuesday, Maine and Maryland became the first states to embrace same-sex
marriage through direct democracy, and Washington State seems poised to follow
once all of the votes there are counted.

He set his bow across the music stand. He'd hardly drawn it over the strings
since he'd opened the cello case this morning, when Adam left for work.
Visions of another man kept crowding into his brain and other parts
of his anatomy, distracting him from the suite he was trying to master.
Treachery—it stuck against his front teeth when he tried to say it. The *T-r*
combination at the beginning of a word was hard to pronounce in English.
Those sounds were better apportioned in his native French, a softer language in which the *r* tended to glide down the throat and disappear by the
time the next letter had to be articulated. And the real name? It was coming
to him now, a corruption of an Italian family name—Tresceri.

"It's what my friends call me, that's the origin of it," the cocky Italian
American explained on their second date, which unspooled two days after
their first encounter, starting with a phone call. "It's me—when can we
hook up?"

"Ready when you are."

What was he saying? He who was always circumspect, now tossing
caution to the cyclone. It felt like a cyclone when Pietro entered his bed.

He'd never had sex like that, as if a force of nature had seized him by the tail and turned him inside out as night faded to day. Then to awake late with the young man sprawled beside him, dead to the world. But he had an appointment and couldn't linger, couldn't ask *When do we meet again*. He just pulled the door quietly behind him so it wouldn't click or shudder when he left the apartment, then set off to put the sleeping beauty out of his mind, a failed attempt.

They met in Washington Square Park at five that afternoon. He found him sprawled on a bench, a baseball cap covering those curls.

When he caught Pietro's eye, he asked, "What have you been up to?"

"Stripping naked."

He slid onto the bench beside him.

"I do it now and then—for money."

"That's probably the best reason."

"It's not what you think."

"What *do* I think?"

"That I'm a two-bit whore." Pietro pulled off his hat and tossed it at his benchmate; it struck his chest then fell to his lap.

"Hiding something under there?" His mischievous companion pointed his toe to ground zero.

"You have a wicked mind, you know that?"

"I was posing for a drawing class."

"Would you like to grab a bite, my treat? You can pose for me afterward."

◉   ◉   ◉

"I'm not a whore. I only act like one."

"But you get paid for it?"

Their eatery was hidden on a lane of the Village whose two- and three-story dwellings resembled more a small town than Gotham.

"I'm a model."

"Touché."

"You may touché away at will."

"You'll be my whore?"

"No, cuz I won't charge you nothin'."

He learned that second night they spent entwisted like pretzels that Pietro not only played classical and jazz piano but also posed for drawing students to make ends meet. He'd come to the city from a town buried in the wilds of Pennsylvania, escaping from a past he'd already forgotten to a place where he could "expand," as he put it. His dad was a baker, his mom a seamstress. His goal: never again to set eyes on a bag of flour or a pincushion, that St. Sebastian of the sewing box. "I'm breaking *freeeeeeeeeeeeee!*" he foretold. He—not his folks, not friends, not even Jesus Christ Incarnate— would determine who he was.

"Who are you, by the way?"

"I'm figuring that out, as I go."

They used condoms the second time around. The first time he'd lost his head, until it was too late. It was the most foolish thing he'd ever done.

"Don't worry," said Pietro. "I haven't had sex in a while. And I never take chances."

"You just took one."

"I live by exceptions."

"You know what I think? You're quite the chatterbox, but I suspect that hidden depths lurk deep within you."

"Then dig deep."

As thoughts of that episode from his past receded, he picked up his bow and drew it across the strings. The piece was flowing into his fingers now. He could feel them coming alive in response to Bach's steady rhythm, a commanding force that drew him in and made him forget his boisterous lover, but only as long as he continued to play.

◘   ◘   ◘

It lay smack in the center of his desk, the discreet envelope with its faint blue tint and deep blue border. A careful hand had placed it at right angles to his blotter pad. He knew what it contained and opened it with a sense of foreboding. What if he tossed it into the wastepaper basket and claimed he'd never received it? Nah, Fothergill would appear with a "replacement" next day.

"Did you receive the wife's invitation?" Mr. Fothergill poked his predictable head inside his office that afternoon.

"Thank you, sir. How very kind."

"Splendid," beamed Mr. F, as if he'd granted an extravagant request. "When may we expect you?"

"May I get back to you—" He caught himself, "… to Mrs. Fothergill, about the date?"

"No hurry. Tomorrow morning will do, I'm sure."

When his boss left, he picked up a bejeweled letter opener, a gift from Alyssa, and made an incision in the envelope, wishing the innards would say YOUR FATHER HAS A MOUSTACHE. But the note read:

ERZSÉBET KAROLINA AND ELIAS FOTHERGILL REQUEST

THE PLEASURE OF YOUR COMPANY, ETC.

His heart and head sank in unison. Of course his reply would be in the affirmative. There was no escape.

He'd invite Yves to join him. The trip would be idyllic—the two of them away together for the first time from the hurly-burly of the city—a honeymoon. He pictured them hiking through a woodland of hidden trails or swimming nude in a pristine pond, this excursion into paradise. But reality insisted on having its way. Appearing in public with his one and only, and actually acknowledging him as that special one of a lifetime? What would happen next? He tried to picture the faces of his hosts when he'd introduce Yves. *Mr. & Mrs. Fothergill, may I present my boyfriend lover partner fuck buddy,* Yves.

A mellifluous voice interrupted his anguished musing. "Would you be up for a bike ride after work?" asked Trent, sticking his head in the door.

"You bet!" He was thankful for a distraction.

Each kept shorts and T-shirt at the office for trips to the gym. After work they changed clothes and walked to a nearby bike shop with rentals. They entered Central Park at Sixth Avenue and followed the Park Drive North till it paralleled Fifth Avenue, its limestone façades gleaming di$creetly in the brilliant sunlight of late afternoon. They climbed the hill behind the Met museum, past a half-hidden bronze cat whose menacing presence goaded cyclists to peddle harder, then veered onto the Great Lawn, where they reclined their bikes on their sides as they reclined themselves at the edge of Turtle Pond.

"Trent, I have a problem," he blurted out as soon as they were settled in the grass.

"Join the club." His companion raised his Ray-Bans over his head and peered into the distance, as if summoning reserves of wisdom to impart to his younger friend.

"I'm already a member. Can we be serious?"

The lids closed slightly over Trent's soft brown eyes, which were zeroing in on him.

"Fothergill's invited me to spend the weekend at his country place."

"Welcome to another club," said Trent. "We've all made the trek up there. Guess it's your turn now."

"But I—"

"Take it as a sign of confidence. You've made your mark. You've been accepted into the inner sanctum. That ghastly school entrance you designed—"

"Not my fault—!"

"It's probably what did it."

"That's not what I'm worried about."

Was Trent scrutinizing him more closely now? Or was he projecting? It was time to come clean. So this is what it feels like, the churning in the gut, telling the first of his friends that he was living with another man, that he might possibly even be …

The word caught in his throat—G - A - Y—three insignificant little letters, but in such a combination, like those chemicals that are harmless when isolated from each other but lethal or corrosive or explosive when combined? But he had to say something.

"I have something strange to tell you, Trent."

"I think I can take it, as long as it's not *too* strange."

"Too strange?"

"As long as you're not violating all sorts of social taboos."

To Adam's raised eyebrows, Trent emended, "Frankly, you don't seem like the kind of guy who'd do such a thing."

"There's this guy I'm living with."

Trent nodded.

"He's my partner."

Another nod.

"I love him."

Trent reached over to shake his hand. "Congratulations!"

Adam blinked to stanch a tear. His relief was so palpable it was overwhelming. He barely murmured, "Like, … it's okay …?"

The sun's rays peeped out from behind a row of sheltering trees and Trent pulled his shades back over his eyes. "I've never understood why sexual orientation is such a *thing* with people, this mania for classifying one another. We spend most of our lives doing our jobs, waiting in line, going to war. We spend so little time in bed—it seems all out of proportion to fixate on who's in the sack with you."

"Sounds pretty enlightened to me."

"As for labels," Trent continued, "I wonder why we don't just simply label the *act* of sex. 'I had a heterosexual event last night—tomorrow I may have a homosexual event,' et cetera. Stick the label on the activity, not the person."

A pair of frisky dachshunds galloped past, playing the canine version of Cops 'n' Robbers. "But without labels, how would you tell who was straight and who was gay?"

"Ask, if you have to. Don't you usually know?"

"Do you mean, do I have gaydar?"

"Yup."

"I'm not sure there is such a thing. Are you?"

"I dunno, but I think it works the way that judge explained when he said he couldn't define pornography but knows it when he sees it. Back to you—of course it's okay! I hope you'll be very happy together. I look forward to meeting the lucky guy."

"That's generous of you." Tempted to ask Trent to keep his confession to himself, he ventured instead, "Maybe the three of us could have lunch sometime."

"Sounds good to me. I promise not to be jealous."

"Why would you be jealous?"

"Don't put it past me, which is to say, don't take anything for granted."

To Adam's quizzical expression he said, "Hey, man, that's a life lesson."

He wished Trent's shades weren't covering his eyes, the better to tell whether he was pulling his leg. "Trent, you're such a good friend, it makes me want to hug you."

A patchwork of clouds had gathered above them. Trent pushed his glasses onto his head again and said, "You may give me a hug at your wedding."

"But that could be some time into the future."

"No surprise there, my friend. Isn't the future always a few steps ahead of us?"

Not until hours later, as he was dozing off beside Yves, did Trent's remark rise to consciousness—*at your wedding.*

Yves' rump was rubbing against his, the heat now transferring between them. He rolled over and slung an arm around his bedmate, who was emitting those *shussshing* murmurings that come with the onset of sleep. As he lay there, his mind kaleidoscoping the events of the day, he started to wonder about Trent's remarks. Clearly, Trent was secure in his masculinity; he could afford to joke about a subject that most males shy away from instinctively, or reflexively, or defensively. But then, why had he never fallen for Trent? His officemate had every attribute that would appeal to a gay man. Maybe he, Adam, wasn't gay after all? But then, what was he doing in bed with Yves? He quickly resolved that self-interrogation at this time of night could lead to madness. He flipped onto his other side, taking the bedcovers with him, then reached over and pulled the covers up to Yves' chin.

As Yves' warmth permeated his body, he felt as if they were blending into a single person. The image of two men atop a wedding cake appeared to his mind's eye. But then, how was he going to marry the love of his life when he hadn't the faintest idea how to present him in public? It was a while before he fell asleep.

◎   ◎   ◎

During that restless night, a Boeing 747 was arcing across the European continent from southeast to northwest on its approach to North America. When it reached the forks of Long Island, it had begun its descent, heading for JFK International Airport. Its passengers had fastened their seatbelts and brought their seats forward for their imminent arrival in the New World. After a smooth landing, pilot and copilot stationed themselves at the exit door, flashing their assembly-line smiles as passengers deplaned. Suddenly, the pilot's ersatz expression froze and he nudged the copilot with his elbow, the time-dishonored gesture of one guy to another when a knockout catches his eye.

That same expression was mirrored on the face of his companion, who let out a low whistle and exclaimed under his breath, "36 24 36."

PART II

The Rook

CHAPTER 8

Push Expands for Legalizing Same-Sex Marriage,
New York Times, November 12, 2012
Nine states and Washington, D.C., have now legalized same-sex marriage. Though it remains unpopular in the South, rights campaigners see the potential for legislative gains in Delaware; Hawaii; Illinois; Rhode Island; Minnesota, where they beat back a restrictive amendment last Tuesday [November 6]; and New Jersey, where Gov. Chris Christie vetoed a bill to legalize same-sex marriage in February.

A rapid shift in public opinion is bolstering their cause as more people grow used to the idea of same-sex marriage and become acquainted with openly gay people and couples.

"Is that her …?"

"You mean *she.*"

"The one in the bright orange dress, with the faux leopard jacket …?"

"What is this, Twenty Questions?"

"Just trying to be helpful." Josiah scratched the back of his head. They'd waited an hour in the International Arrivals building at JFK for a flight that had already landed. Three times Josiah thought he'd seen their passenger. He'd struck out.

"I've told you, she's the most beautiful woman in the world," Alyssa scolded. "Your three guesses don't come close." She craned her neck as another gaggle of passengers straggled toward them.

"Wait a minute," exclaimed Josiah, with increased authority. "I think I see her—that must be her, I mean, *she*, … coming toward us—!"

Alyssa inclined her head.

As the new arrival approached, Josiah exclaimed, "Oh my god—!"

Alyssa and the new arrival let out a *whoop*, then clenched. When they broke apart, the arriving passenger glanced at Josiah. "Who is this cute little man?"

"Little man—?"questioned Alyssa, as if she no longer recognized anyone from her present life. "That's my little Josiah—"

Josiah explained, "Είμαι το μωρό της."

Aphrodite's eyes popped. "Your boyfriend speaks—Greek—?"

Alyssa looked mildly shell-shocked.

"Do you understand what he said?" asked Aphrodite.

"He said 'I'm her baby.' When did you learn Greek, Josiah?"

"Last night."

"Then you'll be my μωρό, too," beamed Aphrodite. She slung her arm through his and they headed to the baggage claim.

The Lincoln town car crept along the perpetually clogged Van Wyck Expressway toward Manhattan. Josiah sat in front. From the back of the cab a patter of English mixed with Greek reached his ear. At length he felt a hand poking his shoulder and heard Aphrodite's lightly accented English. "What are we looking at over there?"

When he turned to face her, he saw that his fellow passenger's makeup had worn off and her hair was tousled by the wind. Yet he could hardly miss the underlying beauty—the regular features, proportion of height to width, perfectly spaced eyes with a trace of circles from sitting up all night, Garbo on an off-day.

"That's the skyline of Manhattan," he explained. "Note the Empire State Building standing out over there."

"Is that the tallest building in the world?"

"It's the tallest in Manhattan, not in the world."

"It's the symbol of America, isn't it?"

"At least the symbol of New York. Some would say the Statue of Liberty stands for America."

"The one with those crowds huddling at her base ... yearning to break free?"

"Very good," returned Josiah, "but I think she said to *breathe* free."

"Asthmatics, were they?"

Josiah couldn't decide whether Aphrodite was a wit or a scholar. Either way, her looks lived up to their rep.

◙   ◙   ◙

In a converted maid's room of her parents' Park Avenue pad, now her dark room, Alison removed her sketch from the bulletin board for a closer look. Not bad, she thought as she examined the lithe form of the male nude. She recalled the drawing session. The young model's intent stare had made her uneasy. He'd hardly taken his gaze off her, though she was sitting at the back of the room. At first, she thought it was happenstance. Didn't models, like ballet dancers, fix their eyes on a distant spot as part of their posing? His bod was much more attractive than the usual male specimens, with their rolls of overlapping flesh that appeared to be melting.

But her model was not just looking into the distance; he was pointedly staring—at her. She made several quick moves to test her hypothesis, and his eyes blinked each time she jerked or bobbed or swayed. Then let him fixate! It gave her all the more chance to capture his roguish expression.

After class, when she ran into him in the hall, she encountered that same look when their eyes locked and he declared,

"Please don't ask me whether we've met before."

"I was not about to ask you anything. But it appears you're the same off-stage as on."

"What is *that* supposed to mean?"

"Everyone else just poses, but you—"

"What about *me*?"

She was trying to decide whether she should be intimidated to be standing so close to a man she'd just seen in the buff, even if he was awfully cute. "You're equally impudent, whether you're posing or not."

"How do you know I'm not posing now?"

"I *don't* know—"

"Well, since you know so little, I don't suppose you know we're going for coffee?"

They settled into a miraculously unoccupied table at Starbuck's. "You must tell me why you do this posing thing," she began.

"Moola."

"Isn't it embarrassing to get up with no clothes on in front of a bunch of strangers?"

"Do you think it would be less embarrassing if I knew everyone in the audience?"

She started to reply but he interrupted. "I find it thrilling."

She winced as he moved his chair in so their knees could have touched, had he not held back.

"And this is how you support yourself, running around naked?"

"What would you think if I said yes?"

"I'd say you're an exhibitionist."

"Oh, I'm definitely that," he proclaimed. He didn't add that he was also a musician; he'd save that for later—he was sure there's be a later. "What do *you* do when you're not interviewing naked men?"

"Photographer."

"Cool, man. What do you photograph?"

She explained she worked for a city agency that hired her to shoot scenes around the metropolitan area that could be reprinted in promotional material for the tourist trade.

"Perhaps you'd like to include shots of me?" He rose and took the stance of the *Discobolus*. "The first shot is gratis, then half-off for the rest. I can give you a model release to cover all of them, save you some red tape."

"You may sit down now."

He slid onto the seat beside her. This time his knee was touching hers.

She reattached the drawing to the bulletin board and stepped back to view her work from a different angle. She'd posted charcoal sketches of an old woman, a man in a turban, a child gazing into the distance. But her eye kept returning to the young man, Pietro. He'd asked for her contact information that day they met, but she'd refused to give it. She did agree, after considerable cajoling, to take his cell number just in case ("Of what," he'd asked, "an atomic attack?"). At least it subdued him. She couldn't imagine calling him. He wasn't her type. To be sure, she had no idea what her type was, but it was definitely not a cheeky, naked male model.

But he was not to be put off. After drawing class next day, he waited for her outside the posing room, then pounced as she left the building.

"Where are you heading?" he demanded.

"Top secret."

"What are you up to?"

"Classified."

They'd entered Washington Square Park and were proceeding through it.

"I have to talk with you!" he asserted as they neared the fountain in the center.

"What about?"

"Classified. Would you mind slowing down—?"

She kept to her brisk pace, that ash blond hair fluttering off her shoulders.

"All right, slow down or else—"

She continued her headlong gait, and for a fleeting moment she thought he'd veer away. Instead, he yanked off his pullover and tossed it to the ground.

She was now facing him in his undershirt.

Hopping from one leg to another, he pulled off sneakers then socks in rapid succession.

Passersby were starting to accumulate on the pathway.

He scampered behind her and dropped his jeans to the pavement, exposing a pair of red-and-white striped boxer briefs.

The crowd was now jostling for a better view of the performance. The space around the performer shrank like a beam from a spotlight growing ever smaller as it zooms in on its target.

"Go, man, go—!"goaded raucous voices from the crowd.

He hopped onto a bench and, gripping his undershirt from the waist, yanked it over his head. Clutching the straps, he twirled it like a lasso, then let go, a diabolical leer where his mouth used to be. As the crowd grinned and guffawed, the shirt flew through the air. It landed on the face of a passing cop.

A roar went up from the crowd as the undaunted performer jammed his thumbs inside the waistband of his underpants and prepared to slide them down. But a commanding voice bellowed, *"Stop—!"*

The crowd fell silent as the police officer strode into their midst. He held out the undergarment as if presenting evidence at a trial.

"Exactly what do you think you're doing, sir?" His eyes swept the crowd then fastened on the striptease artist. The honorific "sir" addressed to the nearly naked young man provoked a chorus of laughter. This seemed to please the cop, who got a charge out of upstaging the stripper. Before the offender could respond, Alison stepped between them and declared with unassuming self-confidence,

"Beg pardon, officer—we didn't mean to cause a commotion. We're doing a skit for an advanced drama course at the university." She pointed randomly to one of the buildings at the perimeter of the park. "We were just adding the finishing touches."

"Drama course—?"

"We had to perform it before a live audience." She added, as if it would make a difference, "It's for extra credit."

The officer registered the good-natured reaction of the crowd, tossed the undershirt back to its owner, and shook his head to signify *boys will be boys*. He waved a magnanimous hand for the assembled to disassemble. His parting thought: *Time for the wife to change my tighty-whities for them colorful britches.*

She glanced again at the drawing and couldn't suppress a smile. She'd even let him walk her home, once he'd put his clothes back on, asked him up for coffee, and introduced him to her roommate, Jenny, who worked at the Art Students League in Midtown Manhattan.

Later the incredulous Jenn asked her, "How did you have the presence of mind to rescue him from the cop?"

"My brother calls me the 'cool head' of the family."

Later, Jenn requested an elaboration of the striptease in the park. Alison filled in the details, reeling them off as if reciting a recipe. Jenn remained silent for some time, then passed judgment: "He was trying to go out with you. That's not a crime. Maybe you should hop off that high horse you've been riding."

She started to protest, then recalled that she hadn't had a date in months. The last couple of admirers got the cold shoulder and never asked her out again. Perhaps it *was* time to hop off that horse …

◨　　◨　　◨

Was she hearing voices? Sometimes the pipes groaned like humans. She'd even responded once or twice while deep in concentration, startled by the sound of her own voice. But was it actually voices she was hearing this time? Her folks were supposed to be attending a fund-raiser. She cocked her ear. These were human, not pipe, sounds, and there was no mistaking her mother's silken alto.

She repinned her sketch of Pietro to the bulletin board and wandered through the kitchen to the dining room. Her mother was standing with her back to her.

"Mom …?"

Lenora Stover was the true cool head of the family, but right now she looked flustered. She ran a hand through her hair, as if to buy time.

"How are you, dear? I didn't expect to find you at home this evening."

"I'm not at home, Mom; I'm at your house."

"Touchée."

"Was someone here?"

Lenora glanced around the room. "Not that I know of."

"Didn't I hear you talking with someone?"

"I was on the phone. That must be what you heard."

"That's odd. I thought I heard two voices."

"I must have left the speakerphone on. Someone was calling my cell for your father."

"Where is daddy, anyway?"

"He's still at the foundation. I came home early. I can take only so much of those moneygrubbers. Would you join me in a glass of sherry, dear?"

"Sure, why not?"

Lenora poured them each a glass from the brass bar at one end of the room. "Why don't we take it upstairs?"

She led the way up the spiral staircase to a large sitting room. A blanket of deep sapphire had descended over Park Avenue, but countless lights from nearby buildings pierced the darkness. They imparted a cheery glow to the dimly lit room, where mother and daughter reclined in easy chairs on either side of a marble fireplace.

They sat quietly, each absorbed in her own thoughts, till Lenora asked, "Work is good?"

"Work is fine."

"I've noticed several new photos in your dark room. Very nice."

"Thanks."

"Social life okay?"

"I suppose."

"Are you seeing anyone in particular?"

If she said *yes*, she'd have to go into detail; if she said *no*, they'd have nothing to talk about.

"It's hard to tell."

More silence, which soon prompted the following: "I've been out with him a couple of times. I don't know if it's going anywhere."

Lenora raised an eyebrow.

"He's amusing, I'll say that much for him. It's a plus—men can be quite dull."

Her mother nodded.

"I'm not sure he's someone I'd want to bring home."

"He's *that* amusing?"

"He might hang by the chandelier, or do a handspring when I introduced him."

"I'm sure you could introduce him without running too grave a risk."

"He's already met Adam."

"Really? Where?"

"We stopped by Adam's place the other day. We were down in the Village and needed to get out of the rain."

"Did he behave?"

"Adam always behaves."

Lenora couldn't repress a smile. "Your friend."

"He didn't stay long enough to act up." It was in fact the first time she'd thought about Pietro's hasty departure. He'd been so hot to be with her, vowing eternal love and other forgettable nonsense, then out of the blue he scrams. Okay, he was not one for consistency. Yet it was a little odd that he left so suddenly. What was the cause, mood swing? She'd have to ask. Of course, that might make her seem too interested. But would that be so bad? What was Jenn's remark about a high horse? She'd laughed it off at the time. But was she, in truth, afraid to dismount?

"How was my son?"

Alison grinned in spite of herself.

"Did I say something funny?"

"I've never heard you call Ady your son."

"But that's what he is."

"It sounds possessive—out of character for you."

"Am I such a cold mother?"

"A cool mother."

"Is there a difference?"

"Probably, not a big one." She hesitated. "Perhaps you're feeling a bit insecure because you're about to lose him. I almost said 'to another man,' but you're not a man."

"That we can agree on."

"Do you like Yves?"

"He's an accomplished young man."

"You're damning with faint praise."

"What do *you* think of Yves—and Adam?"

"I think they're cool."

"Why?"

"They love each other. They're doing something about it. Happy ending."

"What do you think they're doing about it?"

Alison glanced out the window for several seconds. "I think the question is, would you accept him as a son-in-law?"

"Do you think it'll come to that?"

"The papers are full of articles these days about gay marriage. It's the wave of the present."

"Did you know your brother was—?"

"Never thought about it—till now."

"Now what do you think?"

"I guess you might call Ady cutting edge."

The sound of traffic heaving and honking along Park Avenue reminded them that the city was alive and well.

"Would you care for more sherry?"

"I probably should be going." She rose to leave but instead asked, "What does dad say about all this?"

"Your father? He hasn't said much on the subject."

"That's a first."

"I'm not sure he knows what to think."

"I'm surprised he hasn't blown his stack."

"I think you need to be more concerned about your sister."

"Alyssa? I'm sure this hasn't gone down well with her. If anyone in the family, the city, the entire world is concerned about appearances …"

"Her friend from Greece has arrived."

"Aphrodite? It's just like Alyssa to have a friend with a moniker like that."

"She wants to throw a party in Aphrodite's honor. She's hoping to have it here."

"Do you object?"

"She's kind of put me on the spot."

"How is that?"

"She's concerned about Adam bringing his friend along."

"He's not just a *friend*, Mom."

"And that's the problem. If he *were* just a friend, I could tell him we didn't have room for one more."

"You can't tell him that now."

"I don't intend to. He's already put out with me for uninviting his friend—or whomever—from our dinner the other night."

"Alyssa put you up to it?"

"I shouldn't have given in. I need to make it up to him now."

"He and Yves should come in drag. That would give her something to bitch about!"

"Life is complicated enough."

"You're doing the right thing, Mom. You don't suppose she expects Adam to squire Aphrodite around?"

"I'm not sure what she expects."

Alison glanced at her watch. "Gotta run. Thanks for the sherry. Don't get up—I'll let myself out."

After grazing her mother's cheek with a kiss, she stepped out of the building to a warmly glowing evening on Park, and Karolos hailed her a cab. It swerved to the curb and swallowed her, then headed down to Chelsea.

CHAPTER 9

Same-Sex Issue Pushes Justices Into Overdrive,
New York Times, December 9, 2012
[T]he court went big on Friday, also taking the case from California filed by Theodore B. Olson and David Boies. Their case seeks to establish a constitutional right to same-sex marriage in the remaining states, almost all of which have laws or constitutional provisions prohibiting it.

Like the men's clubs of old, Al's social club was an alternate reality where boys could definitely be boys. It was hidden amid the mélange and melee of Midtown Manhattan, its façade so undistinguished you could walk right past it if you weren't eyeballing the address on your way. The interior reeked of leather with hints of Brut cologne and air-freshener.

The club originated not around academic or civic but business interests, and Al often dropped in to catch up on the news or have a conversation with the likeminded, which required little thought or commitment. You never knew whether your conversation of today would be resumed tomorrow or forever forgotten.

Thus Al was nonplussed when his friend Bernie McGregor or McCallister—remembering names was not required here—caught him smoking a Cariños Robusto and brought up a subject they'd discussed only recently—Al's son.

"You tell me he's getting on at that construction firm of his?" Bernie asked.

"*Architecture*," corrected the proud dad. "His star is rising, from what I understand."

" 'Cause I might have a job for him. He's the one getting married, if I remember rightly …"

The Middle Western twang that Bernie brought with him to the city years ago rang uncomfortably inside Al's head, and the combination *son* + *marriage* put him on guard. Had he let something slip about Adam's new, what to call it, "arrangement"? Had Bernie made inquiries about Adam's marital status as a prelude to proposing a business deal?

Al seldom talked about Adam. Not because he didn't love him, though he never said he did. What was there to say? Of course he loved him—Ady hung the moon! Was he proud of him? What a question already! He was the perfect son, he couldn't imagine a better one. What was this Bernie-talk about marriage? Could he have heard about Adam's—(go ahead, spit it out)—partner?

The idea was inconceivable. No, that "idea" hadn't grown on him, despite Lenora's prophesy when they tête-a-tête-ed on the subject. "It could be worse," she'd said. "How?" "He could marry a gold digger." Such talk always sent them to square minus one. But how could his boy do such a thing with some guy he picked up off the street? It was unnatural, and you didn't have to be a biblical scholar to know that!

Yet the suspicion persisted that he was somehow responsible for Adam's new direction, though Lenora had pooh-poohed his concerns, which she called a combo of hubris + hutzpah. Still, hadn't he done *something* to make the boy turn out this way? That baseball team he forced the kid to join, when he wanted to play piano? Maybe Adam tried so hard to please him that it threw him off balance. Maybe if he'd let nature take its course, Adam would have gotten "music" out of his system and developed normally. Was that why his son hooked up with a musician? Was it rebellion, pure and simple, a misbegotten getting-even? He'd heard that this same-sex business was catching on, and same-sex marriage might soon be legal. Of course, it was the modern age, but when was it not the "modern age" for fathers facing off with sons? But why *his* boy? Why couldn't his boy be just plain fucking normal? Was that too much to ask …?

"Sorry, I didn't catch what you said," said Bernie McGregor or McClintock. Al took another puff on his Cariños Robusto and blew a squall of smoke into the air. He'd almost forgotten he was having a conversation with a clubmate who'd turned out to be a little too nosy for comfort. He'd have to wing it.

"You know how kids are these days, my friend. I can't tell if mine are coming or going."

"I get your drift," snorted Bernie, flicking the end of his cigar on the edge of the ashtray—and missing.

回   回   回

He wasn't sure how long he'd been awake. They forgot to shut the blinds before they turned in last night and the sun was shining between the slats, their elongated shadows falling across the ceiling like bamboo shoots. He was imagining he'd awakened in some exotic clime beside a handsome stranger. That stranger, aka Yves, was wearing the same style boxers and V-neck Tee as he wore. So much for exoticism.

Once upon a time they'd gone to bed clothesless. Lately, one or the other had begun to hit the sack clad in something or other: track pants, sweatshirt, even jeans one night when he fell asleep while reading. Of late, the bedclothes had morphed into boxers and Tees. Was their passion waning? And when (and why?) did they start wearing the same style underclothes?

But there were more pressing matters than sleepwear and their fanfuckingtastic love life to worry about. Like the invitation from the Fothergills. He still hadn't mentioned it to Yves, he couldn't say why. He kept waiting for an opportune occasion, but why did it have to be an occasion, and opportune? Why didn't he just come out and say "We're invited for a weekend?" Well, why not?

As the days passed and the pressure mounted, a disquieting thought began to dawn: he hadn't reconciled himself to introducing Yves as his lover to anyone but his family. How long did he think he could coast without letting the rest of the world in on the news? It was time to face the issue squarely, if he was serious about the relationship.

Of course he was serious! He couldn't imagine losing Yves after waiting all these years to find him. Yves was perfect. His only complaint, if it was even that, is that Yves could be touchy on issues of social class, for someone so otherwise self-assured. This touchiness could erupt unexpectedly. At breakfast recently, the subject came up of private vs. public schools in America. He'd declared that many state and public schools were as good as their private counterparts (he himself had attended Dalton and Amherst, then architecture school at Washington University), to which Yves replied, "Easy for you to say; you had the bucks for either." Once Yves had asked him about his parents' doorman Karolos, and he'd replied that doormen were handy for collecting your packages and laundry. Yves retorted, "Then you think we should move to Park Avenue?" He couldn't let that one pass. "Do you have a problem with Park Avenue?" When Yves dismissed the pointed query with a wave of the hand, he'd added, "Dark secret coming up: I was born on West End Avenue." To which Yves retorted, "That's just as bad, my friend—it's another Park Avenue, without the parkway." Maybe his Canadian lover had a point. The pundits were saying that the molasses of social mobility in America's much vaunted classless society were more viscous than Britain's. But why were they feuding about social class when they faced an infinitely larger issue?

He felt a tug on the sheet; Yves had rolled next to him but was still sleeping peacefully. He ran a hand over Yves' chest. His lover was a paragon. Yves' train was always on track, always on time, always advancing toward its next destination, while his own train was often stuck or sidelined in the station or waylaid in the railyards by confusing or conflicting signals. If Yves had received an invitation to visit his boss over a long weekend, he'd have come straight to him and told him to pack his bags. Yves was resolute; he was also self-accepting. Yves had known he was gay since he was a kid; he didn't question his sexuality, nor was he ashamed of it.

Was that the issue, then? Was he ashamed because he was gay? In fact, *was* he gay, or just ashamed? To reply *yes* meant sticking a label on himself, a mark of Cain? It meant announcing that he was off-limits to women. It meant exposing the most intimate details of his private life to whoever entered the room. It meant subjecting himself to possible scorn and ridicule, even in ultra-liberal New York. Was he prepared to take such a step? Was that why he hadn't told Yves about the invitation? Well, was it?

◙   ◙   ◙

"Hi, Mama, it's me—"

Lenora held the phone away from her ear and wondered, Aly or Ali? In the split second that complex thoughts can flash through the mind, the absurdity of her daughters' nicknames struck her full force and she almost laughed out loud. How many times had these pet names sown confusion in the household? "Ask Aly." "I gave it to Ali." "I think Aly has it."

It was Aly. Alyssa, to be exact.

"Yes, dear."

"Have you decided?"

"Decided what?"

"You know."

"If I knew, would I be asking?"

She knew, but she wasn't ready to throw in the towel, and the bathmat along with it. Alyssa had cornered her. She'd agreed to host a cocktail buffet in honor of Alyssa's friend from Greece. That in itself was no big deal. Al would order the liquor and she'd cater the eats. They had plenty of space: large living room connecting at one end to the library and at the other to the dining room, plus a spacious foyer. They could accommodate many guests, and it made sense for Alyssa to hold her affair at the Park Avenue apartment. But the terms and conditions were the sticking point.

"The party."

"I thought I said you were welcome to have it here."

"Yes, but, the details, Mama."

Details, otherwise known as sticking points. Of all her children, the eldest was the most difficult. Alyssa had the brashness of her father and the guile of her mother, a challenge at the best of times. But she was determined not to cave. Her own words reverberated in her head from her last conversation with Adam, before their recent family dinner: "Next time he'll be included, you have my word." She sucked in her breath. "I told you, you're welcome to invite as many friends as you wish, but I can't in fairness tell your brother whom he can bring, if he decides to bring anyone."

"What do you mean, *if*?" Alyssa interrogated. "All right, there's a slim chance he'll come alone, but a fat one he won't. What then?"

"You do the proper thing and introduce him and Yves to your guests."

"How am I supposed to introduce that creature?"

"That's entirely up to you, dear. As for the creature business, he's perfectly presentable."

"What do I tell Aphrodite?"

"Tell her nothing."

"What if she asks?"

"Tell her he's your brother's friend."

"You make it sound so easy."

"I wouldn't worry about it if I were you."

"What is she going to think?"

"We can't read her mind." Lenora paused then added as if to conciliate, "At least, not in advance."

"What if you told Adam he had to come alone?"

"I'm not going to tell my grown son whom he can bring to a party."

"You absolutely won't, then—?"

"My advice: don't be so concerned about appearances."

Sunday A.M., around ten or so. The *New York Times* strewn over the glass-top coffee table, at one end of which a box of fresh croissants from the local bakery, the pastries crowding their container like fat guinea pigs, the smell of almond paste and chocolate pervading nearby nostrils. Two pairs of feet visible beneath the table, one pair in sleek open sandals, the other shod in faux fur bunnies that could almost pass for real. A voice asking in nearly accent-free English with a British tinge: "When am I going to meet this brother of yours?"

Noting Alyssa's hesitation, she added, "Is that how you say it …, '*going* to meet'?"

"It's the present progressive, like the Greek simple subjunctive, kind of."

"Some grammarians are arguing now that there's no true subjunctive in my language. But let's talk about your brother."

"I was wondering when you were going to ask." Was she only wondering, or was she dreading the question? She'd been all set to show off her bro to the goddess from Ellas. Adam was certainly a catch for any woman. But now that he was in his silly metro phase, metro+ in fact, she'd been hard-pressed to decide what to do about him. Adam and Aphrodite were a natural pair, each other's dreamboat, a modern-day Antony & Cleopatra minus the asp. But then he'd thrown her this curve, imagining he was enamored of a homo, just because it was all the rage these days? A wacky fixation that couldn't last, but inconvenient timing nonetheless!

"You can't image what a busy fellow he is—I told you he's an architect with a prestigious firm in Midtown. I mean, they're not building Parthenons, but they do pretty impressive stuff. He's just completed an award-winning remake of one of the most exclusive private schools in the city. But don't fret, my dear—he knows you're here and he's chomping at the bit to meet you."

"*Chomping?*"

"He's as excited as a horse at the gate, so to speak."

"Your brother is horsey?"

"Δηλαδι—so to speak—"

So what if truth gets stretched for the sake of tact? Didn't her own father say she could use some improvement in the Tact Department? Ady would come around; he just needed a push, a bit of priming, once he understood the stakes. And met the goddess.

"Is he coming to your party?"

"You mean *your* party? Of course, darling! He wouldn't miss it for anything."

Nuff said, you'd think. But to be on the safe side, she dropped the following: "I even told him to bring a friend along, in case he didn't live up to your expectations, okeydokey?"

Aphrodite took a croissant from the box and pinched off the end, popping it into her mouth and savoring the flavor. "It's okeydokey if he brings a whole gang of friends. By the way, what does *okeydokey* mean?"

He awoke with a start, threw his legs over the edge of the top bunk, and slipped to the floor. He made sure his feet didn't hit Zambo, who was still snoozing in the lower bunk. At least there were only two of them now in the "dorm"—the bedroom of the apartment that he shared with three very unrelated others in Alphabet City, that domain east of First Avenue where streets are named for letters of the alphabet, owing to a lack of imagination on the part of the City Fathers. Roommates Karla (for Karl Marx) and Morri (for Jim Morrison) were already up and out, she to a dance class, he to heaven knows where.

Gotta get outta this hellhole, Pietro thought as he lurched from bedroom to living room to kitchen, where every inch of countertop was covered by dirty crockery, greasy pots and pans, books, magazines, newspapers, a Kiss lunchbox, and a pair of ballet slippers—for a start. He rinsed a mug nestled behind the Pisa tower of unwashed plates and located the one saucepan that the inhabitants of apartment 4-A had solemnly agreed to keep clean at all times; they'd also agreed to maintain a roll of toilet paper but hadn't worked out the details. He filled the pan with water and set it on the stove to boil.

Once the java was steaming, he took the newspaper from a stool and sat down to sip but didn't read it, surveying the compact chaos of the spacious kitchen. It was a cozy arrangement, this living with his "menagerie," as he described them to friends. He'd spotted the ad for the apartment on a bulletin board in the building where he posed naked. That was a couple of months ago, after he'd broken up with a girlfriend who'd thrown him out when she'd caught him ... he couldn't quite recall the reason—alcohol was involved. He had to move fast, and the menagerie took him in without checking references (there were none). So it was a place to hang his nonexistent hat, until he'd met Alison Stover. That raised the possibility, if their romance went according to plan (which didn't exist) that he might soon have a decent place in which to settle down. He was certainly sweet-talking her in that direction, not that she'd offered to add his name to her lease yet, or even laid out the welcome mat. But there was always the possibility ...

... and then he'd encountered Yves Montjour once again. But Yves was involved with another man—incredibly, Alison's brother! This was entering a new realm, in fact, outer space. Had Pennsylvania been so dull that he had to throw himself now into every tangle that Gotham offered—one contretemps after another? He'd brought down the house at a chamber music concert in which he was performing, when a cell phone interrupted the sublime third movement of Brahms's Piano Quartet in G-minor and it turned out to be *his* cell—and he'd taken the call! He'd even left the stage for a minute, at which point the audience decided it was a comedy routine and went wild. At another event, he went to great lengths to introduce two guests at a party, breathlessly providing the salient details of one to the other, only to find out they were married. And other such brouhahas.

Was he about to enter yet another with the Alison-Yves-Treachery triangle? ("Treachery," his nom de guerre now. "Pietro" was becoming passé, with its associations of recycled clothes from county fairs and S&M the daily fare, spaghetti & meatballs.) If he continued to pursue Alison, there'd be no way to avoid Yves; sooner or later their paths would cross again. He'd see to it.

How had they left it? *He'd* left it. He'd walked out on Yves, in such a way that Zambo subsequently called "unpropitious" when he was regaled with the latest version of his roommate's "life story." They'd been drinking vodka out of the same bottle one night at the apartment, when Zambo put the question, "Explain to me why a dude as cool as you isn't hooked up with someone?"

"I was."

"Who with?"

"A guy."

"So you're gay?"

"I'm all over the map of late."

"What happened?"

What happened indeed. The actual event was shrouded in the mists of an alcoholic haze. He'd moved in with Yves on impulse, accepting a spur-of-the-moment invitation that might have been more a rhetorical question, as Yves had put it—"Had you thought about moving to a new pad?" He'd brought along little more than a suitcase and a stack of musical scores, figuring he could always collect the rest of his stuff from wherever he'd been living. During that first week, he was starting to think he'd finally arrived—a tidy little apartment with one of the nicest guys he'd ever met, who seemed to see the best in him. But he wasn't very good at leaving well enough alone.

One night, he'd met a woman at a bar, and she'd invited him to crash a party at the apartment of a "friend." They'd dropped in long enough for him to ascertain that the lady in question had no "permanent abode," as she put it, so he invited her back to his, uh, Yves' place for what was meant to be just the evening.

Zambo then asked, "You brought her back to your boyfriend's apartment? What were you thinking?"

"It's the sort of thing I do on automatic pilot."

"I see," said Zambo. All too clearly.

Treachery added, "Every time I'm on automatic pilot, I crash."

"Tell me about it."

"Anyway, who should come waltzing in on us but Yves. He found us making out in the living room. And more than just making out, I should clarify, in fact…"

"Hmmm. What'd he do?"

"Who?"

"Yves."

"Yves? What about Yves? Oh, *Yves*? Turned and fled. So I grabbed my stuff and swooshed outta there."

"Did you leave the chick behind?"

"Probably." He paused for several seconds. "Never thought about her again—till this moment—come to think of it."

Zambo took another swig from the bottle. He was a sympathetic listener, a regular kind of guy in his late twenties, the kind of fellow you'd take home to mama, except maybe for the spiked blue hair, nose ring, and tattoos that covered the upper half of his body. "Then what?"

"I landed at a friend's for a couple of nights, bummed around to a few other places, then eventually wound up here. You know the rest."

"The rest …?"

"Yeah, I guess there isn't a *rest*." He took the bottle and finished it off.

"Didn't you say something about someone new?"

"I wish."

"What does that mean?"

"I've met someone, but it's complicated."

"Isn't it always …?" Zambo started to add "… with you?" but didn't. "Chick or dude?"

"Chick. Better than a chick. This one's about something."

"What makes it complicated?"

He grasped the bottle firmly in hopes he could coax a couple more drops from it. He raised it to his lips, then explained Alison's relationship to Adam and Adam's relationship to Yves. Before he could say more, Zambo started laughing hysterically.

"Whatsamattawichu?"

Zambo slipped from the weathered easy chair to the floor, his legs thrashing the air like a kid peddling a runaway tricycle. He slowed down, gasped for air, and managed to get out, "Did you hear yourself, man … the names … Adam and Eve …?"

"I didn't name them."

CHAPTER 10

Same-Sex Spouse Who Sued U.S. Dies at 65,
New York Times, December 24, 2012
Richard Adams, who nearly four decades ago legally married his male partner in Colorado and, in the first lawsuit of its kind, tried unsuccessfully to have their marriage recognized by the federal government, died on Dec. 17 at his home in Los Angeles. He was 65.

Karolos switched on the light to the doorman's office, shed his jeans and jacket, and stripped down to underpants and -shirt. He removed the button-down oxford from the laundry wrapper and his practiced hand unbuttoned it. Posing before the oval mirror, which had acquired a crack down the middle before the dowager in 10-C donated it to the doormen, he observed the split image of himself. Changing from street clothes to uniform transformed Superman to Clark Kent. The street-smart immigrant from the Peloponnese turned before his eyes into a servant to the rich, albeit suave and not without his private opinions. In the immigrant Greek colony of Astoria, Queens, faraway from Park Avenue, he had a sharp retort or a cuff on the neck for anyone who tried to put him down. But here on Park, it was "Good day, Mrs. Donahue," or "How's little Trixie, Miss Cabot?" He even bowed and scraped before the resident Dachsies and Chihuahuas. Had America tamed him beyond recognition?

Before he drew on the shirt, he took a moment to admire his muscular physique in the cracked glass. That strong jawline, curly black hair, and blue eyes, a Greek Adonis—if only the residents of Park could see him as he really was! Not in his undies, but as an Υπεράνθρωπος—a Superman who took orders from no one. Okay, he was well treated on Park. Most residents tipped handsomely, the older ladies made a fuss over him, the young flirted, and some of the gents even doffed their hat to him. Yeah, it was just a courtesy, but maybe not so bad for a guy on his way up from the *patrida*.

But time to man the barricades! He donned his uniform, then saluted his reflection in the mirror. A commotion from the lobby reminded him that James would be impatient to be relieved. Jamie got the day shift—it wouldn't hurt him to wait a bit longer. That pansy had nothing better to do than blow every delivery boy who passed through the lobby.

Emerging from his "dressing room," Karolos almost collided with Mrs. Albert Stover of 9-A.

"Pardon, Madam—"

"Karolos—I'm so glad I've run into you." She put her Bendel's shopping bag down and gave him a broad smile, broad for Mrs. Albert Stover. "I don't mean that *literally*." Her next smile was more deferential.

"I hardly thought you meant that, Madam." Superman and Mrs. 9-A played the game well.

"You know we're expecting quite a crowd tonight?"

A slight nod and a knowing look from the doorman.

"It's Alyssa's doing, of course," she resumed leisurely, as if enjoying a brief flirtation with the handsome doorman. "When they start to arrive— they'll be a younger crowd—please instruct them to take the service elevator to nine, where they'll see the coat racks in the service hall. Signs there will then direct them to the apartment."

"I know just where to send them, *my lady*." He'd recently added the expression to his lexicon and used it only with 9-A. She loved it, he could tell.

◫ ◫ ◫

It was that moment of heightened expectations, the moment they'd antici-pated (and feared) for days, the moment before untold consequences would unfold as in a Greek tragedy (or tragicomedy), if everything went accord-ing to plan, or failed to. They were standing on the threshold of Apartment 9-A. Adam's hand reached out and his finger hovered over the bell.

"Go ahead, what are you waiting for?" dared Yves.

"Nothing, really. Do you want to press it yourself—?"

"I'll ring it if you don't want to."

"I'll ring the damn bell when I'm ready."

"You're not ready now?"

"What's the rush—!?!"

He didn't like the tone of his own voice, harsh and defensive. He stretched his arm across the distance to the bell and let the full weight of his body press upon it.

"I'm proud of you," Yves said, a glint in his eye, as scurrying footsteps resounded from the other side of the door.

Was Yves actually proud of him, or was he being sarcastic? Yves had a sharp tongue, and he didn't hesitate to unleash it. He'd thought he was growing accustomed to Yves' pointed comments, until Yves began to chal-lenge him on a subject he thought they'd put to rest. But just last evening it resurfaced.

He'd risen from his desk after putting the final touches on a sketch for the renovated narthex of an East Village church. He could hear the sonorous strains of a cello—Yves was running through the Passacaille of the Ravel A-minor Trio. The music had insinuated itself into his con-sciousness, and when he recognized the piece, he recalled the time Yves was about to perform the trio with a chamber group in St. Paul's Chapel, shortly after they'd moved in together. He swelled with pride as his lover took his seat with the pianist and violinist to a big round of applause before the noontime crowd that had come over from City Hall and Wall Street to hear the performance.

He joined Yves in the living room, and when the cellist looked up, he asked him,

"All set for the party tomorrow night?"

The barefoot cellist was wearing nothing but his boxers and the fine black hairs curling across his chest.

"Yes, but I can't decide what to wear." Yves sidled up behind him and encircled him in his arms.

"That's funny—I can't decide what to wear either," said Adam.

"Who are you trying to impress, anyway?" Yves' embrace turned into a hearty bear hug as he lifted his architect off the floor.

"It's not as if this goddess my sister calls the most beautiful woman in the world isn't going to be there."

"Sorry, I can't deal with double negatives." Yves dropped him to the floor.

"It's not a double negative."

"The sentence has two *nots* in it."

"Yes, my friend, but that don't make it no double negative."

"You know what I'm trying to say."

"Just what *are* you trying to say?"

Yves reclined on the sofa and it became very still in the room, as if the whole city were listening in.

"Not to put too fine a point to it, but it escapes me why you're so concerned about what this supposedly most beautiful woman in the world will think of you."

"Frankly, it doesn't make a damn bit of difference what she thinks!" His own vehemence surprised him. To tone it down, he offered, "She's a friend of my sister, the one you call the Gorgon. I thought it wouldn't hurt to make an impression."

Yves rose from the sofa and whipped off his boxers. Cupping his hands behind his neck, he challenged, "Want to make an impression on *me* ...?"

Scurrying footsteps had made it to the door of apartment 9-A, and when it swung open, they found themselves face-to-face with Alison and Pietro.

◧   ◧   ◧

It was all there; servers circulated among the preeners and peacocks, while dialogues and trialogues contributed to the pervasive buzz. The affair had jelled; it would be hard for newcomers to worm their way into the banter.

Alyssa, dressed in black velvet and a silver necklace with a large black pearl, was in her element. The party was unfolding exactly as planned. The props were in place, the caterer had made a last-minute check to be sure the edibles had been delivered, and the baristas, male and female, were smartly dressed in mock tuxes. A sullen worker, well built in jeans and muscle shirt, was on duty in the kitchen. He was garnering lascivious looks from the baristas, female and male. Alyssa ran a critical eye over the plates and platters in the pantry heaped with veggies, exotic dips, wafer-thin carpaccio, smoked salmon, whitefish fit for Gentile or Jew, even a bowl of pickled tofu in Mandarin sauce for friends of animals. She wasn't aware of vegetarians among her acquaintances, but Josiah had advised that it was better to cover all bases in case one had slipped in under her radar.

Now the hard part: making sure that all the invited paid proper tribute to the guest of honor. She emerged from the pantry to catch a glimpse of Adam and Yves at the front door, then periscoped to a sofa where Aphrodite was regaling that good-looking fellow from Adam's office, Trent Dunkirk, or whatever his name was. She'd met him at an office party once as Adam's date (he'd forgotten to ask one). Trent could do the honors if Adam failed to tear himself away from that so-and-so of his.

But Trent had left the goddess and was heading toward the foyer to welcome the newcomers. Then she caught sight of Alison's little boy-friend—Chicory, was it? That Ali had a knack for excavating the oddest characters. She crossed the living room to join them but was waylaid by a client-customer she'd hoped to impress by inviting him to the shebang. Had she joined the circle in the foyer, she'd have overheard Adam saying to "Chicory,"

"I remember now, you and Yves met in our apartment, when was it, Ali …?"

Alison had swept her hair up in a French twist and wore a clinging shift of white silk that showed off her figure without appearing to. "It was a rainy afternoon," she replied dreamily, as if her reply hardly mattered. "Someone want to fill in month and day …?"

"It was all too brief an encounter," Pietro offered, his bright eyes dancing around the group but stopping on Yves.

"What's that supposed to mean?" Ali lasered a schoolmarm glance on him as if he were a child. She appeared to be amused as well.

Yves interjected, "It means you never know who'll be on the other side of a door when you open it."

A rich baritone declared, "May I join this charmed circle?"

Trent Duncan stepped into their midst, not from the *patrida* but from a posh Westchester suburb.

"Trent, old man," Adam extended his hand. While still gripping Trent's, he said, "Trent, I'd like you to meet my friend Yves Montjour."

"How do you do?" His office mate replied to the introduction, nodding his approval.

Yves took the proffered hand. "Likewise—and I'll not add 'that any friend of Adam's is a friend of mine' because it goes without saying."

"And my sister Alison," Adam added with renewed enthusiasm, now that he'd finally presented his lover in public.

Alison didn't shake hands but declared, "Allow me to present my friend Pietro." Her comically formal introduction evoked a smile from her brother, while her companion glanced around in mock self-consciousness as if to say, *Who, me?* It was enough to make Yves smile and "loosen up," as Adam put it to him later.

"Perhaps we should join the others in the living room," Adam prompted. "It wouldn't do for Alyssa to accuse me of sequestering you all out here."

"Don't worry," said Alison, "she'll accuse you of something sooner or later."

The little group made for the living room as Alison murmured under her breath, "Time to face the Gorgon."

Pietro looked perplexed. "I thought she was supposed to be a beauty—?"

"I'm talking about my sister."

回   回   回

Alyssa extricated herself from her loquacious client in time to intercept her brother and entourage as they migrated to the grand salon (her term).

"There you are!" She advanced on the quintet, a practiced smile on her face. Thank heaven for Trent Dunstable! She'd make a show over him, the better to downplay the presence of Adam's toy-boy. "I saw you monopolizing my guest of honor just moments ago," she scolded, taking him by both hands and swinging them playfully to belie her implied criticism. "Don't try to deny it—!"

She continued to swing his arms, her version of London Bridge, until Adam cleared his throat.

Alyssa released Trent's hands and leaned in to plant a kiss on Alison's cheek. "Good evening, little sister—"

No sooner had the kiss been implanted than Pietro piped, "My turn." He craned his neck toward her.

Ali explained, "He wants to be kissing cousins."

"That's asking a lot on first acquaintance," said Trent. "*I'm* not even there yet."

To Ali's surprise and relief, Aly bestowed a kiss on Trent, then on Pietro.

Adam maintained the semblance of a smile, hoping his wildly beating heart wasn't showing through his silk dress shirt. Maybe his Liberty of London tie hid it. Why didn't Alyssa notice him? It was the moment he'd dreaded since they'd received her engraved invitation. He was sure he felt the tension rising in Yves. What if Yves took the bull by the horns and introduced himself? Would Yves feel he was forsaking him and take him to task later—if not on the spot?

Next he astounded himself by reaching for Yves' hand as the blood rose to his cheeks. "Aly, I'd like you to meet my friend Yves."

"How do you do," she declared with aplomb.

Yves extended his hand, but she didn't take it.

"Nice crowd you have here," Adam offered, hoping he didn't sound sheepish, hoping he didn't sound conciliatory either.

Alyssa took her brother's hand and pulled him into the living room, leaving the others in the dust. "Come, Ady, I'll introduce you!" A quick glance over his shoulder revealed that both Trent and Treachery had trained their eyes on Yves.

◙　　◙　　◙

He followed her through the collection of guests. It wasn't supposed to unfold this way. He and Yves were a couple—and the world should know it—nothing to hide anymore. He caught a glimpse of his folks standing not far from the sofa chatting with Uncle Max. What would they think when they saw he'd abandoned Yves as soon as he set foot in the door? More to the point, what would Yves think? He could already visualize Yves' pained expression.

But Alyssa had hooked her big catch—him—and he found himself standing in front of the goddess with his prepared line. "Is this the face that launched a thousand ships?"

"That's my friend Helen you're thinking of."

And then, the thrill. It rose from his throat or chest or gonads—he wasn't sure from where. His feet no longer touched the floor. But he descended to sit beside her. And they were babbling all matter of nonsense, he asking her, "Were you really naked when you emerged from the sea?" And she: "Alyssa says you could have designed the Parthenon."

Was she attracted to him? The thought didn't cross his mind till later. It was nearly morning, and he was still tossing and turning in bed, unable to stay asleep. Was Yves having trouble, too? He rolled toward Yves till they touched. Yves "felt" asleep. They hadn't said much to each other at the party. He was busy playing the gracious cohost, so to speak, doing his brotherly duty. And it was hardly an effort. In fact, he couldn't remember when he'd had such a splendid time.

He was surprised he liked Aphrodite. When you hear so much about someone, then fear you're being dragooned into squiring her around, it's enough to turn you off. The thought popped into his mind that he might do both Aphrodite and Alyssa another good turn by inviting the goddess to the country. The Fothergill invitation was still hanging over his head—he hadn't mentioned it to Yves. He was waiting for the right time, still. He'd asked himself frequently what the *right* time would be. Well, he could tell Yves about it now. Tell him he'd decided to ask Aphrodite to the country, to be a good brother. Alyssa would pay him back. Maybe she'd redecorate his, *their*, apartment once he and Yves got married.

Married? He rubbed the nonexistent sleep from his eyes and slid away so that he was no longer touching Yves. At the neutral distance he ruminated, Let's get this straight—you're thinking of marrying Yves but planning a trip to the country with Aphrodite? Okay, people make bargains with the devil all the time. You'll ask Aphrodite to go to the country with you, and when you return, you'll pop the question to Yves. That's a fair deal, isn't it?

CHAPTER 11

Illinois Senate Votes to Back Gay Marriage,
New York Times, February 14, 2013
CHICAGO — With a Valentine's Day vote, the Illinois Senate approved a bill on Thursday that would legalize same-sex marriage, inching the home state of President Obama closer to becoming the 10th in the nation, plus the District of Columbia, to allow gay couples the right to wed.

The legislation passed 34 to 21, a margin many considered almost impossible, even in the Democratic-controlled legislature, just a few years ago. The result was seen not just as a hard-fought victory for gay-rights advocates in Illinois, but also as part of a broader, rapid shift in public opinion on same-sex marriage across the country.

"Did I hear you say I could design another Parthenon …?"

"Why not? You said your designs are all about proportion. And what is the Parthenon if not proportions?"

He went slack for the first time since they were introduced. They'd clicked.

Reaching out to touch his knee, Aphrodite continued, "You'd better return to that drawing board and have something to show me by the end of the week."

"Why wait so long?"

"To make your *drawing*?"

"To get together again."

Her eyelids drooped over darkly violet eyes. "I can't possibly see you before tomorrow morning."

A shadow passed over them, materializing in human form. "Caught you together—!"

Alyssa beamed down, head erect, shoulders back, a Hera of the modern era.

"*Caught* us—did you hear that?" laughed Aphrodite, raising her eyebrows as if scandalized. Adam was about to say something when another shadow crossed over them. Unlike their exuberant hostess, the newcomer stood to the side, with Aphrodite the first to notice. She'd seen him earlier, when he arrived at the same time as Adam. Perhaps they were together? Perhaps one of them should welcome him into the group?

But Alyssa had stiffened to attention, her eyes darting between the couple on the sofa and the interloper. When her brother didn't look up despite the looming presence, she uttered a peremptory "Adam!" He might have been her little boy.

Her sharp tone snapped him out of a haze of awe and admiration. Then he noticed Yves.

"I say, old chap—there you are." He started to rise, but why make a big deal out of an introduction? And why had he called his partner "old chap," a term he'd not used before, as if he were speaking to someone else? "This is Yves, everybody."

Well, it was, wasn't it? No need to make a production out of it. Yves was a meat-and-potatoes kind of guy when it came to social relations; he didn't need grand flourishes when introduced. He, Adam, was the one who deserved a grand flourish now: he'd introduced his partner to the immediate family, including Alyssa, and to some close friends.

Aphrodite extended her hand to the newcomer. Yves clasped it then stood back, as if waiting for someone to run the show.

"Well, we've all met," Alyssa summed up, then wandered off as abruptly as she'd arrived.

Waving his hand to disperse an imaginary cloud of smoke, Adam remarked, "Such a smell of sulfur."

"Sulfur?" queried Aphrodite.

"It's a, you might say, a kind of—"

"Cultural reference," Yves finished the sentence, recalling his *Wizard of Oz*, with the departure of the Wicked Witch of the West in a cloud of smoke.

"You must join us." Aphrodite moved aside to make room on the sofa.

"Thank you, not at the moment." He retreated a step, preparing to leave them. "Pleasure to meet you."

Aphrodite smiled serenely.

"You'll be back?" asked Adam. His face, till now wreathed in smiles, had assumed a serious air, like a boy perplexed.

"When the sulfur dissipates."

◙   ◙   ◙

Pietro's eyes swept the room. Something told him he was not in Pennsylvania anymore, or even Kansas. Sights, sounds, smells blended into the fantasy world before his eyes. Conversation hummed like bees in a hive. He'd never heard such a buzz in Nowhere, Pa.; here, everyone was speaking at the same time, and no raised voices? And that scent, not quite as sweet as perfume, but it reeked of status and privilege, as did the well-heeled guests, everyone wearing Dior or Prada (he didn't know the brands; that would come in time), while he himself had dressed in faded jeans (a hole in one knee) and flannel shirt, his size 8 feet shod in Converse. So this was Park Avenue, and destiny had plunked him down amid the charmed milieu? Actually, Alison was to blame. He'd agreed with some reluctance to accompany her to her sister's bash. It's not that Park Avenue intimidated him; he hardly knew what it was. But she'd been surprisingly insistent that he spend the evening with her; heretofore, she'd seemed indifferent to his presence.

Her insistence was the aphrodisiac that won him over. But before he gave in, he'd commanded: "Describe the scene for me—in one word."

"Swish."

A vision of racy boys and dazzling girls produced his outfit for the soirée. When he stood before the mirror, he decided he looked overdressed in a new pair of jeans (no hole in the knee) and penny loafers, hence the substitution of an old pair with hole and the Converse. When they arrived at the event, his inquisitive eyes began peeling masks off faces to see what lay beneath. He resolved to do vulnerable. That usually got attention in crowds. Yes, after spotting Yves Montjour, he was in a vulnerable mood all right, if vulnerable can be called a mood. What if Yves made a scene? Yves wouldn't, Yves didn't do scenes, Yves was too suave. Cruel as well, if he chose to be. He'd not crossed paths with his beloved cellist since their fate-driven encounter in Adam Stover's apartment, when was it …?

As he and Alison made their way into the living room, Ali's undemanding alto brought him out of his reverie.

"You're acting strange tonight."

"Me, *strange*?"

"Overwrought."

"You've plunked me down among the Park Avenue set and expect me to be a zombie? Do you know all these folks?"

"I should *hope* not!"

"You understand this is not my usual scene—?"

"We're in the same boat, baby. Don't rock it."

A slim young man in white tie and black T-shirt approached with a tray of hors d'oeuvres. "Help yourself," said Alison. "You said you were hungry."

"I didn't say for what." He took a canapé from the tray and popped it into his mouth. As he was swallowing, Ali asked, "Would you be all right if I left you alone for a moment? Gotta say hi to my folks."

"Aren't you going to introduce me?" he hung his head in an attempt to do crestfallen.

"I'm preparing the way."

As soon as she left, his eyes zoomed across the room to Yves. It was now or never. No, it was now. He winnowed his way through the crowd and into the dining room. Yves was standing in a corner near the pantry, schmoozing with a white-tied serving boy. Pietro waited to be noticed. He'd debated standing on his head, climbing onto the dining room table, yelling at the top of his lungs—but why be in character? And while he was deciding, Yves noticed him.

There was only the slightest change in Yves' expression—a tightening of the smile he'd focused on the waiter. Then the server boy scooted off to the scullery while Yves held fast to the spot. Muhammad must go to the Mountain.

When he planted himself in front of Yves, his mind went blank. Then the implacable cellist threw his arms around him and kissed him, holding him so fast it would have been hard to break away.

Till a pointed question uttered by a nearby voice inquired, "What have we here—?"

They disengaged before either noticed that their hostess had posed the question. To which Yves replied,

"Just helping ourselves to an hors d'oeuvre."

"No," corrected Pietro, "dessert."

A frown, then Alyssa swept out of the room in her signature high dudgeon.

Yves trained his gaze on her while demanding, "Tell me what you've been up to, you deplorable little brat—!"

◙   ◙   ◙

"Your son's made quite a hit with our Greek beauty." Max Bombek folded his arms across his chest and caught himself wondering why the young get all the breaks. He conveniently ignored the plus side of his balance sheet—financial affairs in order, and a spacious co-op, cook, and cleaning lady, with the leisure to pick and choose his problems, and his women. All the breaks indeed.

"Or verse-visa," retorted Al. Maybe the world wasn't coming to an end after all, his beloved son making up to a female, of all fantastical creatures. Lenny could stop pouring through brochures of wedding invitations, halt the search for a caterer, stop checking out venues that could hold—how many guests were they planning to invite …?

"I'd say she's got him in her pocket," resumed Max. The Stover lad was a good-looker all right. Takes after his mom, none of the father in him, none of that blather and bluster. "How's business, Al …?"

"Could be better, could be worse …," Al shifted to neutral, his eyes settling on Aphrodite, to whom he was growing more and more beholden for saving his son and heir, a reversal of the Perseus-Andromeda myth. "… as long as Obama doesn't pile more regulations on the market." His eyes avoided Max Bombek, whom he called "Max Bombast" behind his back and, at times, in front of it.

"You know what Clinton said about that," returned Max. "If you want to live like a Republican, vote Democrat."

"Oh, yes," returned Al, "that silly remark that a Republican can't enjoy his dinner unless he sees someone hungry outside his dining room window."

"I wish we had him back," offered Lenora. "Nothing against Obama. Clinton just had a way of getting things done."

"Jennifer Flowers, Paula Jones, Monica Lewinsky—he got 'em done all right," quipped her husband.

"Ah, the Lewd-insky girl," echoed Max. "I was surprised that hulla-baloo didn't arouse a wave of anti-Semitism across the land of the free and the home of the supremacists."

"I didn't realize you were so political, Max," observed Lenora.

"I'm surprised I can still surprise you, my dear." This uttered in a tone of admiration, whether for the lady or himself undetermined.

"Surprises are always welcome." She affected an air of boredom, her best affectation.

Again Max's eye settled on the guest of honor. She'd risen from the sofa and was heading their way, with Adam in tow. Alyssa was bringing up the rear.

Al exchanged glances with his wife as their son drew near. Her look implied the unmistakable message—don't blow it. Watching Alyssa approach, he couldn't help but compare her with his wife. Alyssa was a highly accomplished young lady. But there was something brittle about her that often got in her way and tripped her up. He'd warned her about this over the years, but did she listen? Lenny, on the other hand, was unflap-pable, and still interesting after years of marital servitude. He was a lucky man, and lucky to know it.

"*Maman*, Papá," Alyssa greeted them in franglais, "are you enjoying this fantastic party?"

"We got a full house, I can say that." Addressing Aphrodite, Al asked, "Are you having the time of your life, my dear?"

"How can I not?" came the gracious reply. "Your daughter, she is a super hostess." She squeezed Alyssa's hand. "You must come to Greece and arrange a party for me."

"That's a cool idea." Adam looked immensely pleased, as if the suggestion were his.

"You must accompany Alyssa," said Aphrodite. She took his hand as well. "You can help me put red paint on the town."

"Paint the town red," Alyssa corrected.

"I could go for that," exclaimed Adam. "I'll buy a paintbrush for the occasion."

"I'll buy it for you, and a one-way ticket," Albert offered. "Ouch—!" Lenora's pointed toe had jabbed his ankle.

But Al was pleased with his remark—the jab was worth it. Could it hurt to put ideas in the boy's head? Anything to spirit him away from the Gomorrah of Gotham. Greeks are socially conservative, he recalled from a conversation with one of his daughters. They embrace family values. He was no right-wing zealot, but there was something to be said for boy-meets-girl. And in this, Al Stover was not the first father to embrace conventional wisdom when his children were concerned.

"There's Josiah!" broke in Alyssa, as if they'd all been searching for him. Like the hostess who abandons one set of guests as another captures her attention, she rejoined her beloved and almost collided with a couple edging past them. Treachery and Yves were heading back to the grand salon.

◙　◙　◙

"So you finally showed up," she scolded, as if Josiah had not been in harness all evening, helping out behind the scenes. He gave her a peck on the cheek.

"We're in public, please—!" She turned a sharp eye on him. "And what's your excuse for that tie?"

"I've worn it all evening. Did you just notice?"

Why hadn't she noticed? Did it really matter if Josiah's tie was loud? She'd have to think about that. She couldn't notice everything at once. Her job as hostess was to look after *all* her guests, not just a hapless boyfriend. Though he *had* taken a load off her, despite that tie.

She'd explained to Josiah earlier that she had to keep things moving, the less distinguished guests had to be segregated from the others. He'd asked, "Are there friends here you don't like?" To which she'd replied, "I have lots of friends I don't particularly like." She didn't explain; he'd probably not get it.

"I get it," he'd said. "You're afraid some might look down their noses at others."

"Does anyone worry about noses but you, Josiah? Your tie is loose."

"She reached over to adjust the knot. "Can't have you looking like Sam Spade or something."

"Sounds dashing to me."

"You—dashing?"

"Anyway."

"Do you think he likes her?"

"Who?"

"Aphrodite—Adam."

Josiah cast his gaze toward the sofa where the pair were now locked in conversation.

"He hasn't pulled her hair, and she hasn't slapped him—if that's what you mean."

回　　回　　回

As they passed through the lobby, Karolos sprang to attention. It was always a busy evening when residents entertained on the grand scale. He'd glimpsed the Stovers' guest of honor entering the lobby. *Τι όμορφη κούκλα!* he thought, a living doll.

"Leaving so early, gentlemen?"

"We have to get home to the cats," replied Adam as he and Yves brushed through the lobby. He instantly regretted his offhand remark. Why give the doorman ammo for the gossip mill? Karolos would discover soon enough that he and Yves were a unit and broadcast the news to the building. Besides, nothing was definite. He and Yves hadn't set any kind of date. They hadn't even discussed the subject! Things were fluid.

"I'll hail you a cab, sir." It was the first time Karolos addressed him as "sir." Was this social distancing, or pseudo-respect?

As the line of vehicles passed by, their headlights beaming up and down Park, Karolos ventured, "That friend of your sister—she's some looker."

"We were introduced this evening," came Adam's even reply.

"Yes, we were," echoed Yves.

They rode in silence as the cab wove through traffic down Park, then circumnavigated Grand Central and began its descent on Park Avenue South.

Yves finally broke the silence. "Speaking of cats, have they got your tongue?"

"Mine? No."

He had to tell Yves—he couldn't put it off any longer. Now was as good a time as any, worse things had happened in the backseat of a New York City cab. He'd told himself a thousand times there was nothing to worry about. Yves should understand that he'd merely accepted an invitation for a weekend in the country. All right, he'd invited Aphrodite to the Fothergills' for the weekend.

"I thought you'd understand," he said.

"Understand what?"

"She's from out of town, another country, a friend of Alyssa."

"So—?"

"A way to pay her back, Alyssa."

"Do you always pay your sister back when you've done her a favor?"

"If you have a problem with this, maybe we should discuss it."

"We *are* discussing it. What do you want to say about it?"

"First, are you trying to pick a fight?"

"Why would I do that?"

He gripped the armrest. "Well, you've seemed to be in a touchy mood all evening."

"All evening? You've hardly laid eyes on me all evening."

"You know what I mean."

"No, I don't."

"Okay, so you're pissed I didn't ask you?"

"Ask me what?"

"To go to the country with me."

"I wouldn't say pissed."

"I didn't ask you because—"

The cab swerved onto East Tenth and soon the cabbie pulled over to the curb.

"I've got it," said Adam, reaching for his wallet.

"Maybe we should split … the fare …"

CHAPTER 12

Republicans Sign Brief in Support of Gay Marriage,
New York Times, February 25, 2013
WASHINGTON — Dozens of prominent Republicans — including top advisers
to former President George W. Bush, four former governors and two members of
Congress — have signed a legal brief arguing that gay people have a constitutional
right to marry, a position that amounts to a direct challenge to Speaker John A.
Boehner and reflects the civil war in the party since the November [2012] election.

A curious remark, it stuck in his brain. Neither had said a word about it
after they left the cab and entered the apartment, their "safe spot," they'd
called it since Yves moved in, and were settling down for bed. They didn't
have their late-night snack together. They didn't turn on the radio for a little night music. They didn't exchange a kiss after they turned down the covers and slid beneath the sheets. Or cuddle. Next morning his mind trotted
it out then paraded it around throughout the day. What makes the brain
store up meaningless bits of conversation? And churn them out when least
anticipated? *Maybe we should split …*

Is that what he'd said? It was the cab fare Yves was talking about. They
sometimes split the check at restaurants, too, though usually one or the
other picked up the tab. No one kept track.

Or maybe it wasn't a random remark. Why didn't Yves just hand over
his share of the fare, if he wanted to split it? Why did he have to ask about
it? He dismissed Yves' offer at the time because he had the money in hand.
Time now to forget about it.

But he couldn't. He called Aphrodite later that morning to con-
firm their plans for the weekend. Just before the phone rang, the thought

returned, *maybe we should split*, and he almost dropped the phone into his pocket. But why allow a random remark to shape his behavior?

He put on the best face, uh, voice, when the receiver clicked open at the other end and he had to confront his sister.

"Of course, I'm glad you had a fabulous time!" Alyssa had seldom sounded so pleased with him, or with herself.

He could picture her in triumph. She'd summoned the irresistible Aphrodite from afar to ensnare him. Well, she *was* rather irresistible, but he had no intention of falling in love with her. Besides, wasn't he almost— the word slipped into his mind—*married*?

"Sis, would you put your lovely houseguest on the line …?"

The words were hardly out of his mouth when Alyssa interjected, "She's told me all about it. This trip sounds so exciting, I wish I were going with you."

Though brother and sister seldom saw eye-to-eye, their thoughts converged at that moment to agree that Alyssa's presence would definitely subvert the purpose of the trip, though they would not have agreed on what that purpose was.

Aphrodite spoke into the phone with a simple question: "Are we still on?"

"I've heard many a silly question in my day, but that's the silliest one yet." Could she have doubted the sincerity of his invitation? (Maybe we should split …)

"Could you meet me at my folks' place, Saturday at 9:00 A.M.? My boss will pick us up there. Yes, on Park Avenue."

"A touch of pretentiousness," he'd admitted to Yves the night before he left for the country, feeling the need for complete honesty with the love of his life. He knew it might provoke an argument; he and Yves had sparred more than once about his Park Avenue credentials. Yves would probably throw it up to him that his boss could just as easily have picked them both up at Alyssa's place. But Yves had surprised him; he said absolutely nothing at all, as if he hadn't heard him, or didn't care.

◧   ◧   ◧

"Do you know how many cigarette butts I counted in the hall outside the service elevator ...?"

Lenora kept her attention on the article she was editing, but she managed to reply: "Were you picking them up, or were you just counting them?"

Al, too, was only half paying attention to the conversation, even when he was speaking. "Why would I pick them up? I'm not a collector."

"Excuse me?"

"I said ..." He turned to the next spread of *The Journal*, "I don't collect cigarette butts."

"You don't?"

"Why would I?"

"Search me."

The monotone of their exchange could have passed for chant if overheard in a cloister. The desultory traffic of Sunday morning was light on Park Avenue, until the eruption of several sirens caused Al to glance up for the first time.

"Can you explain why there were so many butts out there?"

"I have no idea. You were always better at numbers than I."

He let the paper fall to his lap as his specs were about to slide off his nose. "I wish you'd be serious!"

She returned the article to the table by her armchair. "How serious would you like me to be about an undetermined number of cigarette butts on a service landing? A least they weren't in the apartment. We probably got off pretty easily, given the size of the crowd."

"I guess it's not such a mess for such a turnout," he admitted. "Alyssa seemed pleased."

"With the mess?"

"The turnout. Did you notice how Ady was taken with her?"

"With Alyssa?"

"With Venus de Milo. That Greek girl was a knockout, I have to give you that." A broad grin crossed his lips. "Ady was tailing her like a puppy."

"I hope it doesn't cause an uproar."

"What's to roar up about? She's a gorgeous girl and he's a gifted guy—a real catch."

"Have you forgotten, he's already caught?"

"Maybe he's not."

◙   ◙   ◙

He'd made the bed with such care it could pass muster in an army barracks, the sheets tightly tucked to the mattress, as if to prevent anyone from entering. A pallid light fell across it, as if mourning the end of day. What had happened to the bright light of a late-summer afternoon? And where had all the traffic gone? Though rush hour had started, the room was unusually quiet.

He slumped onto a chair, stretched his arms, and stared at the ceiling. Motherwell shapes had coalesced there—*Elegy to the Spanish Republic*? His eyes fixed on the shapes. He'd have to summon the will to finish packing.

He surveyed the room once again. Its spare décor pleased him. Adam had a deft touch all right. Less is more. A suitcase and duffle bag waited for him in the doorway. He'd already made arrangements for his cello. Just his satchel left to go. He'd fill it with musical scores and be off.

He flipped through the pile of scores on the desk, relieved to find there weren't that many after all. A quick triage would do the trick.

He discarded the Brahms cello sonatas. They were treasures, but he could replace those scores easily enough. They lacked the sentimental value of Fauré's Piano Quartet in C minor. It was the first piece he'd performed for Adam after he'd moved in, at a concert in St. Paul's Chapel, where the Founding Fathers used to pray, near the site of the former World Trade Center towers. He remembered the evening especially, not for his playing but for the discussion with Adam about those towers. Adam kept insisting that architecturally they were a blight on the skyscape of Lower Manhattan, and he was about to retort, *At the cost of three thousand lives?* But he was burning with love for his partner and for the Fauré quartet, one of his favorite pieces of chamber music. He'd finagled it onto the program, and the performance had come off splendidly. He glanced up frequently to watch Adam in the third row center of the audience. Why mar the effect with an argument? As it turned out, while he held him in his arms later that evening, with the bold strain of Fauré's first movement still in his ears, Adam had whispered, "I wish I could bring the towers back for you."

He was packed now. Glancing around the room for the last time, he slung the satchel over his shoulder and was about to collect his bags, when a small object on his bedside table caught his eye. It was a statuette of an elephant with ivory tusks, a rook that had escaped from an old chess set. They'd seen it in a shop off University Place that specialized in all things chess, vintage and modern. Adam must have returned to the shop later to buy the piece for him.

Knowing that he was an avid chess player, Adam had suggested in the shop, "We should buy a set and you can teach me how to better my game." Adam was especially taken by a set carved in amber based on characters from Proust's *A la Recherche du temps perdu*: the Queen was the Duchess de Guermantes, the Knights were Charles Swann and the Baron de Charlus, the Rooks were M. et Mme Verdurin, and the pawns were eight girls from the little band, Albertine, Andrée, and others.

"I didn't know you played," he'd replied.

"There's probably lots of things you don't know about me…. Say, don't you love that little fellow over there?"

Adam led them to a container of pieces from various chess sets to be sold off individually.

"Flawless," he pronounced the little elephant. "It reminds me of carvings on Hindu temples."

"Have you been to India?"

"No. I'd like to go."

"We'll go on our honeymoon."

It was a first, this reference to a permanent tie between them. And Adam raised the subject once again when they were going to bed that night. He'd taken the elephant from Yves' night table and was turning it this way and that. Then he mused, "Maybe we can bring him to life and he'll guide us to India, once we're married."

He cradled the rook in his hand. The two tiny tusks tickled his palm, as if attempting to send him a message. He was about to drop it in his pocket—he was never without it. But as he was leaving the room, he placed it squarely in the middle of Adam's desk. The desk was bare but for a pad and pencil, and now the rook.

◉   ◉   ◉

Three calls in three days, and still no answer. That was odd—*she* was usually the one to ignore her phone, or switch it off, or forget to take it with her. Had he turned the tables on her? Was Pietro playing hard to get? Had he lost interest in her?

That was hard to believe. His ardor hadn't flagged. At Alyssa's party he was so eager to get her into the sack he nearly dragged her away. She'd even had to inform him, "I'm not a Sabine Woman!" He was a wild man once they got home, all hearth fires and holocausts. But as they got down to business, he kept interrupting himself, as if something besides their lovemaking was tearing at him. He'd launch into diatribes on one subject after another—it was hard to follow him.

So why wasn't he answering her call? She never thought she'd lower herself to drop by his place unannounced, but what else to do? She'd been there once before, when his roommates were out. He'd wanted to show her his "humble dwelling." But soon after he'd opened the door to his disorderly pad—she'd never seen anything like it: a backdoor in the bathroom, a bathtub in the kitchen—he'd tried to put the make on her and she'd fled without completing the tour.

She didn't have a key to his place, and the building had no doorman or on-premise super to let her in, so she'd have to take her chances. She hopped a cab to Alphabet City.

The tenement, a nondescript brick pile, was a reminder that even in a newly fashionable part of town, shabby still flourished. Alternating rows of bricks the color of dried mustard or maroon "decorated" the façade. Here and there along the block, renovated brownstones hinted that the neighborhood was up and coming.

Alison pushed into the vestibule. A panel of mailboxes festooned one wall, most of them lacking nameplates. No matter, she knew the apartment number. On the opposite wall were the intercom buzzers. She buzzed his apartment a couple of times, but no response, so she started pressing buzzers at random. After several moments a response buzzed back and she pushed into the building. There was no lobby, just a stairway paralleling a narrow hallway lined with flats. A whiff of urine hung about the hall.

She climbed the stairs to the third floor and proceeded to his apartment. She rang the bell but no response. She rang again, and again, and was about to give up when the sound of footsteps from the other side raised her hopes. *Creeek*, and the door opened a couple of inches.

Assuming Pietro's face would come in view, or that of a complete stranger should one of his roommates have been home, she was unprepared for the sight—and voice—that met her eyes.

"A pleasure to see you, Alison. Was I expecting you …?"

Yves opened the door a couple more inches. "You're looking for Pietro?"

He opened the door fully and stood before her in a rumpled oxford shirt and jeans. His hair was uncombed, and it occurred to her she might have awakened him from a nap. But what was he doing here?

"Come in and I'll tell you what I'm doing here."

When she hesitated, he coaxed, "I've made a pot of coffee. Will you join me in a cup?" He retreated a pace from the doorway, still clutching the knob, as she took a tentative step across the threshold.

▣ ▣ ▣

An amber sun shone high in the sky as they drove along a country lane winding its way from the city to Upstate New York. "What did I promise you—no traffic!" The voice was cheery but flat, like Muzak.

Elias Fothergill was fond of taking credit when his predictions turned out to be correct, as they occasionally did. He was also fond of providing entire conversations for his unwary guests, with the connivance of his wife. No sooner had he picked up Adam and Aphrodite at the Stovers' apartment than a question-and-answer ensued, with no participation required of the guests. Even as the Mercedes was pulling away from the curb, Fothergill asked, "Where did you two meet?" But before either could answer, his wife leapt in: "Is that really what they call you …?"

"What do you expect them to call her," shushed Elias, "Venus?"

"Let her answer the question, Elias. Where did you two meet?"

"We met at a party," said Adam.

"A party?" echoed Mrs. F.

"It's not what you think, Mrs. Fothergill."

"You must call me Erzsébet."

"Thanks you, Mrs. … Erzsi. The party was at my parents' house."

"A get-acquainted party?" Elias interjected then hit the horn, signaling to pedestrians that he had the right-of-way. "Aphrodite, my dear, did you ever see such a misguided group of pedestrians in your life? I can't imagine they're worse in any other city."

"Perhaps she hasn't been to other cities," suggested the wife.

"That seems unlikely to me. She knows Athens. And I would imagine that such an accomplished young lady would know London and Paris as well, maybe Rome and Barcelona." He half turned for a glimpse at the silent occupants of the backseat.

"Have you entirely forgotten Scandinavia? And, of course, Romania and Bulgaria?" said his wife, the scion of Hungarian royalty. "They're so close to Ellas? Have you had a chance to visit the new Acropolis Museum, my dear?"

"She lives in Athens, forheavenssakes!"

As they neared the city two days later, the sun was sinking, but Adam felt a glow from within. He'd spent a weekend with the most beautiful woman in the world and was about to return to his lover, with a clear conscience! Erzsébat Fothergill had turned over the guest suite upstairs. ("The West Wing, we call it," she'd mentioned, as if their home were a Manderley.) A sitting room was adjoined by two small bedrooms, each with a twin bed and powder room. The common bath was off the hallway leading to another "wing" of the house, as yet unnamed by their hosts.

"This would be ξενοδοχείο in Greece, a hotel." Aphrodite surveyed their quarters, then slipped onto a chaise lounge near the window.

"Do you suppose they offer room service here?" Adam's eyes swept the sitting room then came to rest on her.

"Who needs room service when I have you?" She tossed her straw hat to him.

"What more can I do for m'lady!" he beamed.

"What would please me most now is your company. We'll venture downstairs once we've settled up here, okeydokey?"

"Εντάξει!"

He'd already picked up some Greek lingo. *Εντάξει* was his favorite; it meant "okay," but it could stand for almost anything. They still had the sleeping arrangements to resolve but could cross that mattress when they came to it.

His conscience and his libido wrestled with each other while they spent the rest of the afternoon on a tour of the grounds conducted by Elias. His boss insisted on transporting them on his tractor. This feat required Aphrodite to sandwich herself between him and Elias, who delighted in veering off the path, with slight regard for the bumps and holes in their way.

Several times as they passed a burbling stream, a Victorian gazebo, a stand of birch trees, he'd grasp her around the waist to keep her from sliding off the obstreperous vehicle. Several times, her hand pressed into his thigh to steady herself. Later, after they'd taken turns in the shower and met for iced Chablis in the "downstairs parlor," it was an effort to take his eyes off her, despite the pontifications of his boss and the prattle of the wife, who mentioned that she wanted to introduce her houseguests to a distinguished neighbor. "He's a painter," she explained with unsuppressed pride. When her guests failed to react, she emended somewhat downcast, "Not a *house* painter, *un artiste!*"

Polite conversation nibbled away at dinner and the rest of the evening, till their hostess exclaimed, "You must be ready to retire. Breakfast at nine A.M. tomorrow."

They trailed upstairs and lounged together on the sofa in the sitting room, discussing American films, Greek politics, Balzac and Proust, and indie rock (Aphrodite was well informed), when the first yawns suggested it was time for shuteye. This was the moment he'd awaited. (Should he make a pass? But why? But shouldn't he?) (What would she think if he didn't? Did it matter what she thought? But what if it did?) (What would Yves think? OMG—Yves!) (He didn't have to tell Yves.) (But wasn't that cheating?) (Maybe we should split.) (What was he doing here, anyway? Heaven help us …)

"I'm turning in." Aphrodite hesitated on the edge of the sofa. "Όλα καλά?"

He was good, he told her, then added, "I admire your English—it's so idiomatic."

"You're a boost to my ego, φίλε μου." She rose and retired to her roomette.

Φίλε μου, that settled that. *My friend.*

He undressed for the night in the small room adjoining hers. He'd brought along a pair of gym shorts and a bulky T-shirt for modesty's sake, not knowing whether they'd be sharing a room. He also packed a copy of *Swann's Way*, which he'd been trying to read for some time, catching snatches on the subway to and from work. He was just forming an acquaintance with the Verdurins and beginning to appreciate how the pretentiousness of *la Patronne* was redolent of their hostess, when a knock at the door recalled him from the late nineteenth century.

"Mind if I fuss you?"

"*Bother* me? No bother at all."

She settled on the edge of his bed.

"I'm honored."

"Be my guest—is that right thing to say now?"

"Σωστο," exactly! He admired her sangfroid, the ease with which she'd sailed into his room and entered his bed.

"Are you having trouble falling asleep?"

"I must ask you one more question, παρακαλώ."

"Shoot—it means, Ask."

"Who are you?"

The sun was sinking as they neared the city, casting a scarlet-gold patina over the Harlem River. He'd spent a weekend with the most beautiful woman in the world and was about to return to his lover, his conscience tried but steady. He glanced at Aphrodite with the sun's rays splashing about her and thought he'd remember the beauty of that moment forever. And he did, but not the way he'd expected.

PART III

Treachery

CHAPTER 13

Gay Couples Face a Mixed Geography of Marriage,
New York Times, February 26, 2013
The nation's patchwork geography of same-sex marriage laws was not much of
an issue when just a few states allowed it. But now nine states and the District of
Columbia allow such unions, with Maine, Maryland and Washington voting to
join the list last fall. And the Supreme Court could decide this summer whether
equal marriage protections are a right under the Constitution.

"If you don't mind my saying so, pet ..." A shade of crimson infused Josiah's
cheeks as he sprawled across the bed. It was the first overnight with his
once unrelenting mistress, and the bloom of love incorporated his blush
without betraying his underlying anxiety that an injudicious remark could
send him back to square one. Nonetheless, he declared, "You were a goose
to expect something to come of it."

"I don't know that I'd call myself a *goose*—" Alyssa glanced up
from her magazine. Her silk pajamas might cover a well-kept concubine
or a Chinese peasant, depending on the viewer. The effect she'd hoped to
achieve in such an outfit has not been recorded.

"Of course you wouldn't, pet, but let's face facts."

"Whose facts—?"

"The facts that speak for themselves."

"Please make yourself clear if you want my attention, Josiah."

"It's like this ...," he rolled onto his ample belly and propped his chin
in his hands, peering up at her like a smitten schoolboy. "You say your

brother's taken up with another guy who's actually moved in with him. And you don't think *that's* serious?"

"Not in the least! It's a crazy New York thing. Ady's experimenting, that's all. It wouldn't surprise me if he's made a bet with someone or is trying to prove a point."

"Adam doesn't strike me as a betting man."

She rolled up her magazine as if to swat him, so he tacked on, "I meant to say, he seems to know his own mind."

"Whatever you meant, I'm certain he'll soon grow out of this absurd phase. I'm just giving him a push in the right direction."

"I don't know," said Josiah in a flat tone, as if reading from a teleprompter, "they say two guys will soon be able to marry each other in the Empire State, if they choose to—push or no push."

"That's a choice I'm determined he won't make."

Josiah rolled onto his back and gazed up at the ceiling. Sunlight was dappling it with playful shadows. As the wind cycled through the trees outside the window, the shadows frolicked overhead as if mocking the mortals below.

"What does your friend the goddess have to say about this?"

"Aphro—? She says he's a nice boy."

"We knew that already."

"It doesn't hurt to have it affirmed.

"So she's not interested?"

"I didn't say that."

"I did."

She wasn't sure how to integrate this piece of information into her weltanschauung. She was too proud to ask her brother how he'd got on with Aphrodite, and he'd coughed up nothing when their paths crossed days later at a family dinner. The exchange between the nice boy and his mom revealed little—"How was the country?" "Fine." He'd not fallen head over heels, but he wasn't out of the running either. He was still in harness as far as she was concerned. She'd find out more from Aphrodite herself.

But when she questioned her houseguest about the weekend sortie, she was astonished to learn that the goddess had received an invitation to dinner from an unlikely quarter: a colleague from said nice boy's office. Trent Duncan had thrown his hat into the ring.

◙   ◙   ◙

"How to explain it? We met. I asked her out. End of story."

"Or just the beginning …?"

"Believe me, man, I never intended to encroach on your turf."

Trent took another sip of Dewar's and glanced around the bar to make sure no one from the office was within hearing. This endearing Adam Stover puzzled him. Adam had only recently poured out his heart about the love of his life and seemed to be the happiest man on earth. So why were waves of resistance washing up from his colleague? At least, that's what it felt like as they sat side by side enjoying, or trying to enjoy, a drink after work. His colleague seemed quite shaken by the news of his upcoming date.

Staring into the distance, Adam replied, "It's none of my business, really. I shouldn't have brought it up."

Neither spoke for some time as dusk descended over Midtown. It was a time for hitting the streets, for leaving your job and heading to the clubs, the gym, the theater—the weekend was upon them. Yet neither man appeared to be looking forward to it.

Finally Adam ventured, "Forget about it, my friend. It doesn't matter—it doesn't matter one damn bit."

...

He hardly recognized his own voice. The vision of an empty apartment flashed through his mind, the way it looked when he walked in and discovered Yves had left him. He'd been supremely happy up to that moment. Life was perfect and promised to remain so, at least for the foreseeable future. He'd made a friend of his sister's Athenian and obliged them both by inviting Aphrodite to the country. His boss had taken to her and complimented him twice on his "impeccable taste." His stock at the firm was on the rise. Things were going his way, all right. And then the unthinkable happened.

He'd entered his apartment with a light step, not surprised to find it empty but for Dido and Aeneas, whose utter complacency at his return was no tipoff to the disaster that had befallen. Yves must have been rehearsing or teaching or studying or shopping, he thought, a turn of the latch and he'd soon hear the music of Yves' footsteps. Later he wrote down a mantra—He'll be back—and stuck it on the bathroom mirror.

He had no idea where Yves went. He'd reached for his cell fifteen, fifty times—he'd even learned to do French accent marks, Où es-tu? (Where are you?)—but something always stopped him. He wouldn't hit SEND because he couldn't accept that Yves was gone. He made up stories—urgent family business had called Yves to Montreal; he'd left town for an audition and there was no phone service—all fairy tales. His thoughts had been filled with Yves—Yves' smile, his scent, his cello vibrating in the next room.

Why were the cats staring at him?

The rook had set him straight. He'd spotted it smack in the middle of his desk, as if it had wandered there on its own. He started to pick it up but hesitated. Is this how detectives proceed at a crime scene—don't disturb the evidence? But what was his crime? He'd gone away for the weekend. He'd even explained that he was making the trip to oblige his sister. Yves didn't seem convinced. But surely he'd come to his senses? Could Yves doubt his love, his commitment? He'd asked Yves only recently, "How do you feel when we make love?" The reply: "Consumed." Yves was a man of few words, but he meant them. There could be no doubt about their feelings for each other. They were both consumed, weren't they?

"Would you care for another drink?" Trent asked, noticing his empty glass.

"Why not?"

Trent signaled the waiter. "So you're not sore at me?"

"Why sore?"

"For asking her out."

"Oh, her."

" 'Oh, *her*'?" Trent mimicked. "I thought that was why you clammed up on me."

"No, not sore at all. I don't have the right to expect you not to ask her out, I of all people."

"What's eating you, then, if I may ask?"

"Yves left me."

"Are you certain?"

"Elephants don't lie."

回　　回　　回

"What are you doing here?"

"What are *you* doing here?"

"What are we *all* doing here?" Pietro glanced around the room to assure himself he'd not entered the wrong apartment. Yves and Alison were camped out on his living room floor. "Mind if I butt in on this charmed circle, or ellipse, whatever it is?—I failed geometry." He squatted down between them, his head oscillating from one to the other.

"It's a charmed syzygy, now that *you*'ve arrived," said Alison. "Make yourself at home." She drew her knees up to her chin. "That is, if you still wish to be on speaking terms."

"Speaking terms—?" He swiveled to face her. "Let's get something straight—I never stop speaking to anyone."

"Because you never stop speaking," put in Yves, his smile verging on flirtatious. Or that's what Alison observed. Had Yves changed persona?

Pietro's gaze swerved back to Alison. "Why you here, Ali …?"

"I happened to be in the neighborhood." Technically speaking, it wasn't a lie.

"How'd you know our illustrious Yves was here?"

She and Yves exchanged a complicit glance. "That info will be revealed at a future date."

"Hmm, and they call *me* 'Treachery'." After a moment he said, "While we're sitting around, can I get someone something to drink? We're out of everything—take your pick."

"Pas moi—gotta be going." Yves stood and waved farewell to the pair on the floor. "See you guys later."

"Have your key?" asked Pietro.

Yves nodded and slipped out the door.

The white noise of nearby traffic filtered into the room and filled its neglected corners. It was so still that when Alison spoke, Pietro sat up with a start.

"You're a good Samaritan."

"Case of mistaken identity. Gimme a kiss."

He leaned in to her but she held back.

"What choice did I have? The guy needed a place to crash—I had the place."

"You can say that for a third of New Yorkers on any given day. So why him and why here?"

"Cuz I s'ppose I'm more concerned about his welfare than about that third you wasjusspeakin of."

Her doubting look prompted him to add, "The guy's family, ain't he?"

"They've split. They may never see each other again. I guess you could call that family. But why stretch it?"

Pietro cocked his head left and right. It made her smile in spite of herself. "Let's just say I owe him one."

"You win. I desist. But I don't cease."

He lowered his eyes.

"I won't ask any more about it."

His eyes brightened.

"That's a promise."

"I'll hold you to it."

"I'm as good as my word."

And she was, though her curiosity was only heightened by this mysterious silence of his—he who never held anything back. She was still processing the breakup of her brother and Yves, the first she'd heard of it, and the fact had hardly settled upon her when Pietro walked in on them.

Alison was no dummy; she could maintain two opposing ideas at the same time in her belief system. This allowed her to give a pass to the preposterous. When Yves finished telling her that he'd encountered Pietro at Alyssa's party for Aphrodite and that Pietro had offered his hospitality, she didn't ask whether Yves and Pietro had met before; instead, she was digesting Yves' tale of woe. She'd believed in Adam and Yves from the get-go, despite Alyssa's attempts to break them apart, and Yves' explanation had only skimmed the surface of their split. He'd resolved to move on. "It wasn't meant to be," he'd confessed. She thought his lip trembled when he said that. "It's tragic!" she'd replied, reaching for his hand.

"The tragedy is, we didn't realize it sooner."

◙   ◙   ◙

The sun glinted into the tiny office and did its best to enlarge the claustrophobic setting. N. Nuddelmann was about to speak but instead made an indistinct sound that resembled a *tsk, tsk*. "I would call this a new development."

"Walking out on the love of my life—you bet your sweet ass it is."

"I'm not ordinarily one to place bets," the worthy therapist replied, "but I suspect that's a safe one."

Dr. N *tsk, tsk*-ed again, a sound he'd perfected over thirty years of practice. This particular patient had been a rather difficult nut to crack. The therapist found him so self-contained that he wondered why Montjour Yves Age 29 had even bothered to go into therapy. No matter, Dr. N had recently embarked on a renovation of his chalet in the Catskills and was in no position to sneeze at his income flow. Having *tsk, tsk*-ed this news of his patient as far as he could, he inquired,

"What do you propose to do next …?"

"I hardly know. I guess that's why I'm here now."

"Indeed."

After a pause that threatened to stretch to eternity, Yves asked, "Don't you want to know why I left him?"

"If you care to discuss it."

"I'm not keeping secrets, if that's what you mean."

"Yes, this bears further inquiry." Pause. Pause. Pause. "Was it because of the woman?"

"Aphrodite? Not really. I mean, you could call her the proximate cause, but I think I would have had to bail, sooner or later, whether or not she'd come into the picture."

"Why is that?"

"I'm not the jealous type," he began. "Jealousy is a foolish waste of energy."

"Some of the best novelists of all time have churned out some of the best literature on the theme of jealousy."

"I'm not living in a novel."

"A safe assumption, if you want my professional opinion." (Little did Dr. N know.)

"In fact, if Adam had just had a fling with her, I could have lived with that. I would have chalked it up to something he had to flush out of his system. Maybe ..."

"A passing fling?"

"Yes, a passing thing ... *fling*—I could deal with it, though it wouldn't have made me especially happy. We were supposed to have been in what the poets call that first bloom of love. I'd have hoped my lover had more staying power. But the real issue is, I don't think Adam knows whether he wants to spend the rest of his life with a man."

Norman Nuddelmann took a flying leap. "You don't think it's your job to help him find out ...?"

"No."

"Why not?"

"I'm an interested party. *Too* interested. I'd push him in a particular direction, no matter how much I wanted to keep my hands off. This is something he has to thrash out for himself."

"You're prepared to lose him?"

"I'm prepared for nothing at all—but to love him. I've never loved this way before—it's a new feeling that needs a new word. I think I shall never love again." He broke down and started to cry.

Dr. Nuddelmann nudged his rose-tinted glasses back up from the tip of his nose. It was time to say something to fit the occasion. "I'm afraid our time is up."

◪   ◪   ◪

He wasn't sure how long he'd dozed awake before he sensed something warm beside him. They'd even rubbed together, though he didn't realize at first what he was up against. Then he sensed skin. Why was he lying next to a stranger? A young man with thick hair that all but covered his face occupied the other side of the bed, Yves' side. Adam slipped out of the bed and put on a robe, then turned toward the kitchen to make a pot of coffee.

It was coming back now. A blur of images was melding into a tableau with Trent Duncan in the background. They'd had drinks and parted, a Friday night. He had no plans but he wasn't going home. He took the train downtown and wandered to a questionable destination near the water, to an "establishment" that, at first sighting, might have been an auto repair shop or an abandoned warehouse. He'd passed it in a cab a few times with Yves. One time Yves had glanced from the building and back to him without saying anything; the second time, Yves muttered something he didn't quite catch. A ramshackle entrance—a mere hole in the wall—beckoned.

Inside, a tune of indolent rhythm filled the airwaves as patrons edged around the bar or loitered between tables. At the bar he ordered a vodka and tonic, then waited for something to happen. The faces he encountered ranged from eager expectation to world-weary indifference. Ages ranged just as widely, as bears and daddies brushed shoulders and other parts with twinks and rent boys. And then there was him.

The vodka dulled the emptiness that had filled him all week, if emptiness can fill anything. When the music ramped up, a boy seized him by the belt buckle and pulled him onto the dance floor. The kid—no more than seventeen or eighteen—danced with abandon, as if he were alone. But his firm grip on the belt was a sure sign he had no plans to release his prey. He, Adam, swayed and swerved to the rhythm—he knew how to dance. The amazing thing is that he was keeping up! He'd come alive with the verve of his college days, the one time in his life when he'd let loose on the timber.

In the kitchen his Braun coffeemaker, the Darth Vader of the countertop, was burbling encouragingly. He still had no recollection of how long they'd danced, or managed to land a cab to whisk them back to the apartment, though he did remember fishing in his pocket for the key, with the young man (Hilary? Jeremy?) still clamping on to his belt. Just as the Braun quieted down, producing four cups of java, his "guest" wandered naked into the kitchen. Jeremy/Hilary blinked around the room but showed little surprise at his surroundings, as if it were the most natural thing in the world to awake nude in a strange apartment. Perhaps it was.

"I take mine black," he requested in a gravelly voice out of sync with his slight build.

"Coming right up," replied his host, who was wondering why he was treating the uninvited waif like a dignitary.

The waif yawned and asked,

"What's your beat …?"

"Law—public interest."

"You make much?"

"Depends on what you think is 'much'."

"I see you're a hair-splitter. Let's fuck."

The kitchen floor wasn't the best place for making love, but there wasn't time to find a more suitable venue. The kid was in a hurry.

Afterward he divested himself of the guest by explaining he had an important conference to attend. Then he slipped him a twenty for cab fare to anywhere. Was this how life after Yves was going to be, picking up rough trade in sleazy bars for anonymous sex? Not completely anonymous: Hilary/Jeremy had let out that he'd come to town trying to find work as something or other, maybe theater, maybe banking. He wasn't specific, he'd be in touch. But what did the kid's evanescent plans matter? What did anything matter now? He saw the kid to the door, then returned to the living room, where he collapsed on the sofa and burst into tears.

CHAPTER 14

N.F.L. Is Pressured on Issues of Gay Rights,
New York Times, March 18, 2013
[H]ighly publicized support of same-sex marriage initiatives by some players [as well as a] series of controversial episodes has made the N.F.L. the awkward vessel for grappling with one of sports' most stubborn taboos—that of the gay athlete— and for the country's larger debate about gay rights.

The sheet of paper lay on her desk. What to do with it? She could drop it in a drawer, or she could present it. So why was she delaying? There were consequences: Her star could rise, or it could plummet, or she could lose her job. All because of a thin sheet of paper.

"So whatsa piece'a paper …?" Al asked the night before, when she broached the subject. "It's a sketch, that's all. She can crumple it and toss it if she doesn't like it—straight into the *poubelle*."

"She can toss *me* with it—that's the problem," Lenora sighed. But she couldn't suppress a smile. Where did her husband pick up this habit of dropping French words into their conversations? *Wastebasket*—why would he remember that one?

"You know in business," he continued, "nothing ventured, nothing gained."

"This is fashion, Albert."

"That's *big* business, Lenny. The fashion industry brings in more money to New York than finance or banking." He draped his oxford button-down over his faithful valet stand and sank into the arms of his easy chair in his shorts and T-shirt, neglecting to remove his black socks and the garters that held them up. "Why are you smiling?"

"Those black socks and garters—they make you look like a porn star."

"So you've been watching porn?" He buried his face in his beloved *Journal*. "You get your fashion ideas now from pornography …?"

"Occasionally."

"Probably not a bad place for inspiration—for fashion, that is."

His faithful Lenny watching porn? Maybe fire still blazed in their marriage. Lenny was still a good looker, hardly a wrinkle in that creamy skin, and the figure of a teenage athlete. He had every reason to be proud of his wife. Heads still turned when she entered a room. It's a wonder he wasn't jealous. He had grounds. If that silly Max Bombek wasn't a cousin, he'd be jealous of Sir Max, with his Godiva chocolates ("Sweets for the sweetest"), perfume samples ("the scent brings you to mind"), theater tickets ("for my Sarah Bernhardt")—Max overdid it now and then, mainly now. But Max was a cousin, twice or thrice removed, not removed enough, he'd never gotten the details straight, but then, genealogy wasn't his thing.

"I wanted to present something original," Lenora resumed, "something a bit out of space and time, if you know what I mean …"

He had no idea what she meant, but then again, he understood in a funny kind of way. That's what forty years of marriage does to a man; he could comprehend his wife even when she herself wasn't sure how to express it, whatever "it" was. They often had the same thought at the same time, or if he was looking for something, she found it. When she couldn't explain herself, he supplied the missing *mots*—even in French! They'd developed a seventh sense about each other, elusive but nonetheless real.

"Let me take a look," he offered.

He knew she'd do all the talking. But all that talking with an audience, even one that was only half-listening, would restore her confidence and she'd be better prepared for her confrontation with the boss.

She reached into the folder she'd kept on her night table for the past several days and handed him the sketch.

"You know how she is" was all she said.

"I know."

□   □   □

"I'm always amazed when I peer up these thighs of yours."

Yves lay on his back watching Pietro bat his penis back and forth.

"This stick of yours reminds me of a metronome."

"Isn't that mixing metaphors?"

"It's mixing petronomes."

"What in the hell is a *petronome*?"

"A combination penis + metronome."

Yves smiled and frowned simultaneously. Pietro had never seen such an expression on his friend's ordinarily composed face. "I'll have to take it out next time I perform a challenging piece."

"Maybe you should confine it to practicing."

"On second thought, it doesn't keep the best time."

Pietro was nestled between his legs. He bent down and kissed Yves, brushing his Cupid's bow lips against Yves' symmetrical ones, then ran his hands up and down the inside of Yves' legs. "You know what I call the thighs?"

"I can hardly imagine."

"Highways of Desire."

He planted a kiss on the tip of Yves' penis. Yves was on him in an instant, pinioning him to the mattress. A wave of pleasure engulfed him, but he knew too well what would follow. They'd synch their bodies, find a common rhythm, then go off—to their separate worlds. How strange to be

in command of his thoughts, he thought, during periods of intense pleasure. Ali had told him there was a "disconnect" between his desires and
their fulfillment (but … what about Ali and hers?). That remark hung out
in his brain as Yves grappled him toward climax. Why was he thinking so
clearly when he was supposed to be swept away?

Was it Yves' fault? Was something lacking in the combo Tresceri +
Monjour? Did Italian and French not mix? Is that why he never achieved
complete satisfaction when they made love? Yes, he orgasmed all over the
place. But no matter how close they came—not to mention the bantering
beforehand—Yves was off-limits. Sure, they had great sex, but they always
wound up in separate places. Did Yves feel the same way? He always rolled
away after coupling, dozing off or going to his cello in the next room.

Maybe it was no one's fault. Maybe that's how sex played out with a
guy. What did *he* know? He wasn't experienced with males. Yves was a first
and only.

It was different with Alison. Nothing raw or hasty there, but they
were more intimate, with all kinds of possibilities beckoning when they
took their pleasure. He was still feeling his way with her, giving her time
and space to lure her away from her fears and inhibitions, of which he suspected there might be a few, he being not the least among them.

His budding romance with Alison was in full bloom. Her roommate
was on a world cruise with her parents. Ali's flat was now that most trea-
sured asset in New York City—a place of one's own. And what a cozy place
it was. He felt absolutely domestic—for the first time in his life.

One morning over breakfast, he observed, "You know, sitting here
like this, we could be an old married couple."

"I hope not!" she shuddered.

He was seated across from her at the kitchen table in his briefs and
undershirt. She wore a bright red kimono, her hair piled on top of her head.

"Then will you be my geisha?"

"What does it pay?"

"You modern women—do you have a *single* romantic bone in your body, or have you hopelessly abandoned femininity?"

"It depends entirely on the fee schedule."

"Mammon!" He shrank back in mock horror then took a sip of coffee.

"You look so funny," she said, not without a touch of feeling that she might have preferred to conceal, but he noticed it.

"Who, *moi*?"

"Sitting there so bare in your jockey shorts."

He glanced to his lap and back at her.

"Maybe it's the photographer in me, but you come across as somehow more formal and proper—if I dare apply such a word to the likes of you—than when you've got your clothes on."

"Which way do you like me better?"

"I like you better when you're sleeping."

"Whyizat?"

"Then I can arrange you however I wish. Otherwise, you're always in motion. Has anyone ever told you you're completely protean?"

"Not in so many words. Not even in *one* word, if you're determined to know."

After several moments during which he sipped at his coffee, he said, "It might be premature to ask, but would you like to spend the rest of your life with me?"

"Definitely." She quickly tacked on, "Definitely *premature*—"

"What about the afternoon? You have plans?"

She removed a clip and her hair fell about her shoulders.

The gesture took him by surprise, but never at a loss for words, he exclaimed,

"La mia Botticelli!"

Hadn't Yves called her that when they were first introduced? "I do have plans."

"Could you add me in?"

"Would you like to join me?"

Her hesitation made him fear the offer was already exceeding its shelf life.

"Count me in. Whasup?"

"I'm going to see my brother."

◘   ◘   ◘

The God of Summer had given leave to the denizens of Greenwich Village to wear next to nothing—tanks, camisoles, ripped Tees, sports bras—garments that, fifty years ago, would be worn only as underclothes. In letting it all hang out on such stifling days, New Yorkers had little left to hang.

"It's like watching a pornographic movie," Alyssa fumed as a cab conveyed them through the Village along Seventh Avenue South toward an art gallery in Soho.

"You don't have to look, Pet," suggested Josiah. "If cabs had isinglass curtains like carriages in the olden days, I'd draw them for you."

"Thanks for your help," she replied with ill-concealed exasperation. Her exasperation was due to not knowing whether he was serious or pulling her leg. Her inability to distinguish what Josiah called "fact from fiction" in her relations often led to confusion and then irritation.

Before he could utter more soothing words, she exclaimed, "Isn't that Ali over there … with the little chimp she brought to my party, Chicory, I think it was—?"

Josiah's head bobbed affirmatively amid the jouncing of the cab. "Why do you call him her 'little chimp'?"

"Didn't you see how he was climbing all over the place, into laps, under the table—I'll swear, if my folks had a chandelier he'd have been swinging from it."

"That's not very charitable, Pet. Maybe they can't afford a chandelier."

She glared at her watch by way of reply, but he wasn't ready to let go.

"He seemed like a rather charming fellow to me. Uninhibited, but that kind of added to his charm."

"Did you speak with him?"

"Briefly."

"What on earth did the two of you have to talk about—?"

"He never said. But he was quite amusing; he had a word for everyone. He told your mom he thought Alison was a prodigy, and now that he'd met her mother, he understood why."

"Utterly gratuitous," snapped Alyssa, taking a compact from her Louis Vuitton and dusting the tip of her nose.

"He also announced to Mr. Bombek—that cousin of yours—"

"Of my mom's—don't lay the blame for Uncle Max on *me*—"

"... that if he didn't know him better—just imagine, he'd never even laid eyes on him till that moment!—that he, your uncle—or whoever's uncle—was hopelessly in love with your mother."

Alyssa gripped the door handle. "The kid is certifiably mad."

"Then I overheard him say to your dad that he must be adept—he's quite literate, that chimp, I mean, scamp, frankly, he's an absolutely beguiling scamp—adept at fending off your mom's admirers." Anticipating an outburst from his beloved, Josiah added, "He holds your folks in high esteem."

"What a relief to have his seal of approval." Alyssa glowered as Alison and Pietro disappeared down a tree-lined street west of the avenue. Readers paying close attention to the geography of this tale may recall that they were passing the exact spot where Adam and Yves had rescued their piano, an unwitting syzygy for Stover offspring.

She had a soft spot for her brother. Though he was older by a few years, she felt like his protector. When Ady hoped to play piano but their dad insisted on baseball, she went to bat, *ouch!*, for him, sounding Dad out on the possibility of allowing Adam to do both. He'd brushed her off, claiming that Adam would be busy enough with one activity; his grades might slip with two. She'd replied that busy people get more done than idle ones, and she buttressed her assertion with data from civics class. When Dad refused to budge, she had the last word: "You're making a mistake at Ady's expense."

She'd never before spoken so directly to her father. Dad had only recently broached the subject again. He wasn't his usual direct self; instead, he'd shown a fine degree of subtlety, remarkably more than she'd realized he was capable of.

They'd been talking about the breakup of Adam and Yves, she and her parents. Mom seemed to take it in stride, expressly misquoting Cole Porter: "It was just one of those flings." After Mom left the room, Dad said, "As a parent, you worry that if you thwart your kids at a critical stage, you warp their development." He fingered the tabletop as if he himself were tickling the ivories. "You mustn't blame yourself," she'd replied. Al's self-reflection made her feel generous toward him. "We're pretty hardy—we kids," she told him. "We grow up the way we grow up, and who knows whether anyone has a thing to do with it." She was moved by his concern for Ady; he seemed shaken by the breakup, though he'd not had a kind word to say about the relationship—or Yves—till that moment. "He's a good man," Dad pronounced. When she looked puzzled, he emended, "That Yves of his."

But they were ringing the bell to Adam's apartment. Why was he gawking when he opened the door—had he forgotten their date? Alison blinked several times till he came to life.

"Great to see you guys," he managed to say, leading them into the living room.

How strange the place looked now, she thought, though nothing had changed. It was as if the universe had shifted, and the point of the shift was right where Adam stood when he opened the door to them. The tastefully decorated living room had lost its character. The once beige walls were now a dull gray, and the windows refracted a scrim of colorless light, as if to paint the room in gloomiest tones. Everything was off-kilter.

"I wish I could say 'What a surprise to see you.'" Noticing his sister's downcast expression, he summoned his former graciousness. "Thanks for the heads-up. You gave me time to put my face on."

Pietro looked confused.

"His emotions, not his makeup," she explained sotto voce. Then she and Pietro took seats on the sofa, where Aeneas & Dido were lounging, their heads stuffed with thoughts of damnation as they retreated to make way for the oversize interlopers.

"I'll get us something to drink," Adam smiled bravely. "Then we'll get to the dope."

Again Pietro was confused. As her brother left for the kitchen, Ali translated, "The lowdown."

Pietro still looked muddled.

"He's going to let down his hair—got that?"

Pietro's bronze curls shook in sudden recognition. "You gotta forgive my density," he explained. "I ain't no vocabularist."

Adam returned with a crystal pitcher filled with a deep plum liquid. On the tray beside it was a bottle of rum, a silver ice bucket, silver tongs, and three goblets.

"Would you like to do the honors, Ali?"

"Whatzisss we're about to imbibe—?" Pietro fixed his eyes on the brew.

"Spécialité de la maison," she replied. It was not the first time Adam had asked her to serve what he called his "elisir d'amore." But his gaze wandered off somewhere, leaving a wan smile in its wake. Then he said, though no one had asked, "No, I don't know where he is."

Ali held her tongue. She didn't blurt out that she and Pietro knew exactly where Yves was. It was a curious arrangement, and she was still perplexed that her boyfriend was putting up a guy with whom he had but a nodding acquaintance. And why had Yves squatted in what was little more than a glorified pigsty? She recalled their earlier conversation on the subject. Pietro had coughed up an explanation of sorts: "He seemed like a nice guy when we chatted at your sister's party, and when he mentioned he might be looking for a place to stay, well, you know never-think-twice me—if I think at all. I told him he could crash at my pad till he got settled, if he could put up with scattered obstructions here and there. I mean, he seemed respectable enough, like everyone else at that shindig. I mean, a Park Avenue happening—? I bet your sis doesn't know a soul who's not ultra-respectable—except moi, but that goes without saying."

Pietro's explanation was plausible. But why was Yves thinking of splitting while he was at the party for Aphrodite of Athens? Adam hadn't mentioned or even hinted at any problems. They seemed like the perfect couple; she'd never seen her brother so happy before.

"… and I guess I should leave it to him to seek me out, if he has anything he wants to say to me," Adam resumed, again with that vacant stare.

Finally, she asked, "Why did Yves leave you?"

"I'm still trying to figure that out …"

"You don't *know*?" Pietro exclaimed, his incredulity unvarnished.

Adam looked as if he'd been slapped in the face. "Frankly, no."

Ali started to speak but Adam cut in. "I guess that makes me a pretty big dummy."

"Don't be hard on yourself," Pietro chimed sympathetically. "You have a broken heart, not a broken brain, that's what needs fixing, your heart."

It was a neat little package, tied with a gold lamé ribbon with no tape, over high-gloss white stock. Tape as an adhesive was verboten at Tiffany & Co. But the question was, how did it get to her desk? She'd quizzed her secretary, but Marna shook her Shirley Temple curls with convincing vigor. Marna loved conspiracy and intrigue more than anyone since Sherlock Holmes. She was in the right profession all right at *Fashionista*.

Lenora was tempted to unwrap the package and take a peek, but she knew as soon as she removed the ribbon an inquisitive head would materialize at her door and want to know what was up. It was not worth the risk. Besides, she was expecting a visitor, and she had to collect herself.

It had come as a surprise, his request for "an audience," as he'd somewhat formally put it. He'd called her at the office several days ago, saying that they could get it over with in a few words. Alison had expressed the opinion that Adam and Yves would find a way back together; even her husband gave out that if they became a number again, he for one wouldn't stand in their way. Her views were not often aligned with those of her older daughter, but like Alyssa, she had little faith that they'd reunite. And now Yves was waiting in the anteroom outside her office.

She ran an eye over the face in her compact. It stared back, betraying no emotion, her stock-in-trade. Her makeup was in order and every hair in place. She'd been called into the boss's office this morning and was given the go-ahead for a new line of dresses she'd proposed with her recent sketch. It was her moment of triumph. If her hair was good enough for the boss lady, it was good enough for Yves Montjour!

"You may show him in, Marna," she instructed her secretary, her voice unwavering; she was surprised she sounded so cool under the circumstances. "And please close the door after you've delivered him."

Marna flashed her an inappropriate wink. Her underling's attempts at familiarity grated, but she tolerated her in the expectation that soon enough there'd be a reason to fire her. When she reappeared with her visitor, she declared, "It's Yves, Ms. Stover."

Forcing a smile, Lenora returned, "Always introduce callers by their first *and* last names, as we've agreed, my dear."

"I didn't give my last name." Yves nodded across the room as she signaled for him to take a seat by her desk.

"That's right, Ms. Stover—I couldn't force it out of the gentleman."

"I also told her I was not a gentleman," Yves put in.

"Definitely not," agreed Marna. "That is, he definitely did *not* tell me." She turned to leave but failed to close the door behind her.

"Let me," said Yves. He closed the door then moved his chair closer to her desk.

"Now, where were we?" she asked.

"I'll come straight to the point." The light had fallen over his eyes, and she noticed for the first time the violet hue that distinguished them from other blue eyes. They resembled a woman's eyes, Elizabeth Taylor's— they were too beautiful for a man's face.

"I haven't seen your son since I left, and I don't know what he may have told you, but I owe you an explanation."

"You owe me nothing. But that's very considerate of you," she allowed.

"I loved Adam—" He paused. "I *love* Adam—with all my heart, with everything I've got."

"But that's not why you left?"

"I began to fear that, as time went by, I couldn't make him happy."

"Does one ever make another happy?"

"A fair question."

Her phone rang but she made no move to answer it. The office was softly lit and shadows lingered here and there, as if awaiting her instructions.

"It may be presumptuous of me to say this—"

"Please speak freely."

"Your son doesn't know his own mind enough—not yet, at any rate—to commit to me ... or probably to anyone else."

"You're very wise."

"I'm practical."

"I mean what I said." She leaned back in her chair to view him from a different angle. "You're younger than Adam, if I recall. Yet you seem older. More sure of yourself."

He smiled for the first time since entering her office. "He has a bit of growing up to do, our Adam."

"Our Adam," she repeated, without Yves' wistfulness.

"I won't take any more of your time, Mrs. Stover ... Lenora." He stood to depart. "Thank you for seeing me."

"I'm grateful you came."

"Don't get up—I'll see myself out."

She sat quietly for several moments. A thought crossed her mind—she couldn't recall where she'd read it—*There's no afterlife for love.*

CHAPTER 15

British House of Commons Approves Gay Marriage,
New York Times, February 5, 2013
The House of Commons voted overwhelmingly on Tuesday to approve a bill legalizing same-sex marriage in Britain.... After a six-hour debate, the Commons vote was 400 to 175 for the bill. The legislation, which applies to England and Wales, would permit civil marriage between same-sex couples, but specifically exempt the Church of England and other faiths from an obligation to perform such ceremonies. Some faith groups, including the Quakers, have said they want the legal right to perform same-sex marriages.

After Ali left, he remained on the sofa, while Dido and Aeneas maneuvered over him to resolve which would settle on his belly, their Mamayev Kurgan. His sister's visit, however well motivated, had drained his emotional reserves. And that boyfriend of hers? They'd met a couple of times before, once even at his apartment, when he pulled off that disappearing act. Peculiar, to say the least.

The cats were unrelenting in their attentions, rather, in their demand for food. He was of a mind to tell them to fix their own supper. But their mewling reached his heart, and he scratched Plan B.

He opened a can of tuna and divided the contents, content to set his mind on a simple task and a break from worrying. He sprinkled gourmet Kat-Treets over both bowls and set them on the floor for his finicky felines. He was about to change their water when a phone rang. It wasn't his cell but the landline.

"Mom ...?"

Unlike the helicopter moms of today, Lenora Stover seldom called her son. She claimed she was not a "phone personality" and still had trouble using her cell, which no one seemed to call but Uncle Max. She hardly needed to tell them; they knew because she'd leave her phone at home and others intercepted her calls.

Her invitation was to the point. "Lunch?"

He'd seen her only once since the breakup with Yves, and they'd not been alone together. When he asked whether there was an occasion, she replied, "Do we need one?"

He took the day off and met her in Midtown at a new bistro as yet undiscovered by hoi polloi. She awaited him in front wearing a black-and-white sheath that stopped mid-calf and a necklace of red coral, he in sport jacket, tie, and black Converses.

Her kiss just brushed his cheek. "How are you, dear?"

"I wish I felt as good as you look."

"Is there an ulterior motive in that observation?"

"I refuse to say." He smiled ruefully. "Shall we get a table?"

The maître d' seated them at a window facing the street through which splashes of sunlight bounced around the room.

"How's your appetite?" she asked after the waiter rattled off the specials.

"It's gone, I'm afraid."

"That's not good."

"Everything's gone—and nothing's good."

She reached across the table and her fingertips grazed his hand.

She was a remarkably undemonstrative mother. He couldn't remember the last time she'd touched him. And he was puzzled by her request to lunch. "There has to be a reason for this invitation."

"No there doesn't. But I do have something to tell you."

"Good or bad."

"You decide."

"I'm all ears, as they say."

Their imperious waiter interrupted before she could proceed. "Frightfully sorry, Madam, but we're out of the Oysters Rockefeller. Would you care to make a substitution?"

"If she didn't," said Adam querulously, "she'd have nothing to eat, would she?"

"Why not Coquilles St.-Jacques?" she replied coolly. When the waiter left them, she said, "I saw Yves."

The bistro became terribly quiet: Voices ceased, traffic stilled outside, and the entire wait staff froze in place, all waiting for his response. Or that's how he remembered the stillness after she spoke. The waiter tried to horn in again, but he shooshed him away. "How is he?"

"He seems well."

"And …?"

"Yes, dear …?"

"C'mon, Mom—you must have more to report than that?"

"He's resigned to the breakup."

"Is that supposed to make me happy?"

"I think he thinks it's for the best—for both of you."

"Oh, then it's to make us *both* happy—?"

He brushed away a tear about to trickle down his cheek. "Damn that Alyssa!"

Lenora drew back as if from a physical assault.

"It was the date with Aphrodite that did it. I'm sure of it. It was all Alyssa's doing." He crumpled his napkin and made ready to leave but she sensed his intention and raised her hand.

"Your sister can be hard-driving at times, but you mustn't blame her for wanting to give you the chance to—"

"—chance to what, ruin my life forever?"

"Don't be dramatic, dear."

How could a mom treat this gut-wrenching discussion as if it were a talk about the weather? He was tempted to toss his napkin at her. "So I'm supposed to take this lying down, and everyone's happy again because now I can pursue a woman and you can breathe a collective sigh of relief because everyone will think your son is normal, is that what this is about?"

"You know that's not how we feel, Adam. We just want you to be happy. Your father and I have done nothing to stand in the way of your happiness. But if it's not meant to be with Yves, then perhaps it's time to think of moving on."

"So you're saying, that was the message from Yves?"

She left him to draw the conclusion.

The waiter brought their meal and they ate in silence, till she declared, "I don't pretend to understand men, dear—one kind or the other."

▣   ▣   ▣

A persistent buzzing filled his mind when he left the restaurant—*one kind or the other*. Was he now but a category? Had it not been for a chance encounter on his way back to the subway, his mom's remark might have rankled indefinitely.

What did he notice first—the sun glinting through her hair, the mauve dress that stood out from the other dresses on the street, all of them NYC Black. A bare shoulder, the other crossed by a spaghetti strap, the skirt angled across the front so that it rose toward the hip on one side. There was a radiance about her that set her apart, as if she'd just emerged from the sea. Yet it was the way she moved, as if completely unaware of her looks, that made several men passing by stop and stare.

"Just the man I want to see," Aphrodite declared as they drew abreast of each other. She extended her cheek to receive his peck of a kiss.

He was tempted to seize her and cover her with kisses, if only to break out of his despondency over Yves, but her tone was too playful. He glanced to right and left, as if she might have meant someone else, then said, "Εγώ …?"

"Yes, *you.* Your Greek has advanced considerably since we last met," she teased. She took his hand and they proceeded down Fifth Avenue.

"Where are we off to?"

"Bergdorf Goodman," she said, drawing him to her side. "I must select gift for your sister, and I could use advice—though I'm not sure you'll be much help if you're like most men."

Like most men—the phrase caught in his brain, just as his mom's casual remark stuck there. Or was it so casual? The buzzing was starting up again, offering thought-bites such as "if you were a man" and "real man." But he was determined to squelch it this time around. He didn't intend to spend the afternoon fretting over innuendoes and hidden meanings, not when he could enjoy the company of a beautiful woman strolling up Fifth Avenue, the Main Street of the World, past Bendel's, Rizzoli, the brownstone Presbyterian Church to the emporium of Bergdorf Goodman. Life could be worse.

An aura of expensive well-being enveloped them inside the storied department store, which began as a tailor's shop near Union Square in 1899. Its windows faced onto Fifth Avenue, Grand Army Plaza, and Central Park beyond. The smell was feminine and discreet—fine-grained leather mingled with eau de cologne and bath salts. It brought to mind the visits he'd made here with his mom after trips to the allergist when he was a child. He'd linger in plush surroundings while she disappeared inside countless dressing rooms, only to reappear in all manner of garb while prune-faced matrons clucked and tutted at each item she tried on. Sometimes the dressing room doors opened to expose ladies in slips or petticoats or pulling skirts over their heads. They'd smile or make a moue, as if the presence of a well-behaved boy was acceptable, if rather irregular.

"I was thinking of something in leather," mused Aphrodite as they came to the handbag department, "something in good taste, not too expensive-looking."

"I don't know why you think you need me along," he returned. "You've hit the nail on the head when it comes to my sister."

A complacent smile graced her lips as she reinserted her arm through his. For several moments he enjoyed the sensation of being part of a couple. The fleeting sensation didn't square with the image of himself as a little boy. So was he a man, or was he simply playing the part here amid the feminine backdrop? He suddenly felt self-conscious then lost then over-whelmed with longing—for Yves.

Aphrodite didn't notice. Her eye had led her to a smart little clutch of black calf with a rhinestone-studded silver clasp.

"I think it's just the thing," he declared, forgetting the wave of desire and desperation that had threatened to consume him moments before. "Alyssa will love it."

"I knew your presence was all I needed. You're that rare πρίγκιπας among men—a prince."

◙   ◙   ◙

He passed one more night alone, not without tossing and turning; Morpheus was determined to elude him. Was it the messages on his machine after he got home? All from the same person, Hilary or Jeremy? He still hadn't sorted out the name, hadn't decided what to do about it, or him. The kid wanted to see him again. "Hook up tonight, man?" "Hey, you, I've called twice already." The question was, did he want to spend another night with another Jeremy or Hilary? The answer was no, but then why was he still awake?

Next day was Saturday. He'd earmarked it for an expedition to Macy's. Trips to Macy's were always expeditions. With its interminable corridors and countless boutiques thronged by bargain hunters of the middle brow, it made no sense to shop there for just a single item. He needed to crisp up his fall wardrobe: dress shirts, lightweight jacket, T-shirts & boxers. Despite the size of this Pentagon of a department store, it was next to impossible to locate a salesperson—no tutting and clucking salesladies anywhere.

As he rode the escalator to the fifth floor, he was still traveling light, with just a single package in hand. There was a soothing quality to those moving stairs. They'd exerted a fascination for him since boyhood, when Alyssa first described them to him. Mom had taken her on a shopping spree, and when she returned, she explained that you stood still while the stairs transported you a flight at a time and you didn't have to lift a foot. He'd asked her where the stairs went after you got off. She explained that they disappeared under the floor. When he inquired how the passengers themselves kept from disappearing, all she said was "Dummy."

While pondering that long-unanswered question and wondering how it would feel to disappear beneath the floorboards now, he snapped out of his reverie: he'd just caught sight of Yves descending in the opposite direction.

It happened so quickly the apparition hardly registered. Was he mistaken? Impossible—he'd recognize Yves anywhere. The escalator deposited him one flight up while Yves descended in the opposite direction. He froze in place, immobilized by a jumble of feelings. After several seconds, he raced to the descending escalator to follow Yves down, taking the stairs two at a time. But no sign of Yves. Had Yves retraced his steps in hopes of encountering him on the upper floor? Or were they heading in opposite directions? He'd never before wished to be in two places at once. Why did they have to meet (or *not* meet) this way? Why hadn't he tried to contact Yves a single time since Yves walked out on him? Why hadn't he made that call?

He reached the ground floor and slid off the moving stairs into menswear. Signs heralding GEOFFREY BEENE, PERRY ELLIS, YVES SAINT-Whoever led nowhere (where was Yves?). His head swiveled left to right. No Yves in sight. How would he find the needle of Yves in the haystack of the world's largest store when he didn't even know which direction Yves took? Overwhelmed by defeat, he slunk out onto the street and descended into the subway. When he arrived on the platform, a train was pulling out of the station. Its doors had clammed shut and it had just begun to move. As the first, then the second car glided past him gathering speed, he came face-to-face with Yves again, on the other side of the doors. Then the bitter realization—twice that day, a mechanical device had kept him apart from the man he loved.

回　回　回

When he emerged from the subway the sun's golden glow was painting a Millet canvas of peace and harmony over the neighborhood, minus the Gleaners. How could couples he passed on the sidewalk look so contented when he faced another night alone?

But what was this—?

He almost stumbled over a figure perched on the steps in front of his building.

"You're here, finally!" exclaimed the voice before he saw who it was. Then he recognized the bronze curls of the fellow he'd heard referred to as "Treachery." This beau of his baby sister, so intimate and familiar, so oddly ingratiating, yet somehow mysterious—Churchill's riddle. What the hell was he doing on his doorstep?

"Something for *you.*" Pietro held up a package wrapped in brown paper. Were those bright eyes twinkling on their own, or was it the light from a streetlamp falling across them? His tone was conspiratorial, as if he were reporting on a secret mission.

The unwitting host held the door as his visitor slipped into the lobby ahead of him. As they pressed together in the narrow cage of the elevator, he asked, "Are you going to hand over this 'something'?"

"Oh, that? Glad you mentioned it—I almost forgot. Once we're inside."

"You're inviting yourself in?"

"I ain't inviting myself out."

Adam mentally shook his head as they entered the apartment. The guy was over the top, amusing in a way that kept you coming back—maybe not for more, but for something indefinable. An actor not quite right for the part whose performance improves before he leaves the stage, then returns.

"Great place you got here—did I ever tell you?" Pietro slid onto the sofa and reclined with his hands behind his head. His slight frame took up little space. Aeneas and Dido nestled against his legs as Pietro glanced down at them. "Brazen hussies, you two—!"

"Have you had the tour?" Adam sat across from him in a roomy wing-back. "As I recall, the first time you were here you vanished almost as soon as you set foot inside the door. You must have seen a ghost or something?"

"Or something," said Pietro, brushing off the remark. "Here's your book."

Adam opened the bag. He took a pair of reading glasses from his pocket and slid them onto his nose.

"You look cool in those specs," prompted his guest, now sprawling on the sofa.

"I wear them to look intellectual."

"You look plenty intellectual enough."

"I do?"

"You look plenty *everything* enough."

"Hmm ..." said Adam.

He opened the book. *DOS for Lovers*. Did anyone care about DOS anymore, or even remember what it was?

"You see," lectured the guest, as if addressing an obedient child, "love, like computers, has its own operating system."

Adam flipped through several pages, then read aloud: "A relationship that's crashed can be rebooted." He tried to suppress a smile. "So you're presuming to help me figure out my nonexistent love life?"

"Someone's gotta do it. I'll take that tour now."

He hopped off the sofa and cast a glance at his host that suggested *What the hell are you waiting for?*

Pietro repeated *Nice, Nice* at whatever caught his fancy: a picture of Lenora Stover (the same one Yves once admired), the view from the bedroom window over the leafy treetops (Yves liked that, too), the flat-screen TV (he and Yves used to watch every night). He summed up as they returned to the living room, "You gotta great setup here. Now, back to the Missing Persons Bureau."

"Is that one of the lessons in this book?" Adam turned the pages again till he came upon another quote that he read aloud: " 'Leave a door open if you exit for good.' What's that supposed to mean—?"

Pietro bolted upright. "Are you as naïve as you act …?"

Adam crossed the room and sat beside his guest. He placed his hands on Pietro's shoulders and declared, "This isn't an act, my friend—this is the real me."

"Who *is* this real *me*, then?"

"That's what I'm figuring out."

The pianist-model-stripper had never met anyone like this ex lover of his present lover (not to mention his girlfriend's bro). This hopelessly attractive Adam Stover, living by his lonesome? What was wrong with this picture, DOS?

Beneath the pressure of Adam's palms on his shoulders, he felt an electric current passing through him. His free-floating amorosity was transferring feelings he'd heretofore reserved for Alison and Yves to this individual who united all three in his person, whose musky scent of a discreet cologne mingled with aromatic male sweat. Adam the Architect, who'd fashioned all sorts of constructions, was now fashioning an eroticized object out of him.

If Adam had realized his gesture was arousing this lover of his sister, he'd have scooted to the other end of the couch, or maybe the earth. But he was charmed by the disarming figure beside him. Treachery (what was his real name again?) seemed to have time on his hands and little to do with it. Maybe he should invite him to stay for supper, if only one of the frozen dinners he kept in the fridge for such occasions. (Though what might this particular occasion be?)

He removed his hands from those sloping shoulders and asked, "Would you like to stay for a bite?"

"Will it hurt?"

"Not if you hold still."

His cell started to ring.

"I might be persuaded."

"What inducement might I offer?"

"Inducement—?"

Adam cocked his head to the side for a different view of his intruder-guest. "Do you stay, or do I answer the phone?"

"If I accept your dinner invite, are you going to turn around and ask me to spend the night?"

The cell commenced its third ring.

"I have no plans to turn around."

"I have no plans to leave."

CHAPTER 16

Delaware, Continuing a Trend, Becomes the 11th State to
Allow Same-Sex Unions, *New York Times*, May 7, 2013
Delaware on Tuesday became the 11th state to permit same-sex marriage, the latest in a string of victories for those working to extend marital rights to gay and
lesbian couples.

...

Delaware adopted same-sex marriage just five days after a similar decision in Rhode
Island and after ballot-box victories last fall in Maine, Maryland and Washington.

It was a perfumed evening when strange particles invade the minds of
young men of more dash and daring than discretion. The frozen dinners
turned out to be unpalatable, so the host ordered in pizza, the National
Dish. Then they watched a rerun of *Casablanca*, cheered at the same parts,
and teared up when "La Marseillaise" was sung. Now night was upon them
as Rick and Louis ambled off the screen to start their beautiful friendship.
That was when Adam asked,

"What now—?"

"I guess I'm spending the night."

Adam hit the remote. "Making yourself at home then?"

"Any objection?"

"Fine with me."

"I have an objection—I have nothing to wear."

"Let's see what my closet has to offer."

It was a peculiar state of affairs, spending the night with his sister's presumptuous, forgivably overbearing Pietro (he remembered the name). He opened the closet door and pointed to a couple of silk robes.

"I mean, they're elegant, but not my style—"

"Not to worry." Adam opened a chest of drawers to display a collection of T-shirts and gym shorts. "By the way, what *is* your style?"

The guest slid his hand over them. "I sleep nude."

"Suit yourself,

"You mean *unsuit*?"

He was the first to hit the sack, as Pietro stripped down to nothing then clambered in beside him. He flicked off the lamp and pulled the sheet over his chest. Ali's young man intrigued him. He fancied him a kind of Cupid, alighting wherever he saw applecarts to upset. As for himself, he'd had enough one-nighters of late and didn't need another, certainly not with an "in-law." On top of all this, he wanted Yves. If he'd ever doubted that, he was sure of it now. The image of his former lover on that escalator gliding into, then out of his life left its mark more than any Cupid's arrow. If he hadn't missed Yves so much, he'd probably not have let his in-law sleep over.

A perky voice drew him out of his reverie.

"Here we are."

"I think that's safe to say."

"Playing it safe, eh?"

He ran a hand through his bedmate's locks. The tight curls rippled through his fingers like sheep's hair. "Sonny boy …," he began, then thought better of it.

"I'm waiting."

"Do you know what you want?"

"Does it matter to you?"

"Yes, if I'm the one lying next to you."

"Good question, man. Never thought about it."

After some delay, Pietro added, "I can honestly say there's only one thing I've ever wanted."

"Which is …?"

"All I can get."

"Sometimes, 'less is more,' if I may quote from architectural lore."

"I'm not trying to build anything."

"Then be careful you don't tear something down while you're at it."

"May I ask you something, since you're so free with the questions?"

"Shoot."

"What do *you* want?"

"Me? All I want is something impossible."

"Then we're back to the Missing Persons Bureau."

Adam nodded in the darkness.

Pietro rolled onto his side. "I could use some beauty rest now, if you'll excuse me." His tone suggested Adam had been keeping him awake.

"Sweet dreams," murmured Adam, "no charge for them in this house."

◙　　◙　　◙

Al stepped into his club in late afternoon and joined the boys at the bar. Bernie McGregor was holding forth like the potentate he wasn't, regaling his captive audience with accounts of the big deals he hoped to bring off. Bernie gave a wave and he waved back, remembering the noises Bernie had made about sending business Adam's way. Then—bizarrely—Bernie's inquiry into Adam's marriage plans. He'd brushed that one aside; it was none of the SOB's business about his boy's business. Besides, there wasn't going to be any "business," certainly no tying the knot. Time was when he'd have flipped handsprings to learn that Adam was no longer "involved" with a rinky-dink musician. But his feet remained planted on the ground, for his boy had never looked so glum.

He first noticed this change when he invited Adam to lunch. They met at the historic Fraunces Tavern in the Financial District, where the Founding Fathers often supped. When he arrived, Adam was propped against the back of his chair. He was holding a menu but staring into space, the color drained from his face. He could have passed for forty or so.

Adam usually stood and hugged him when they met. Today he just glanced up.

Al sank onto the seat across from him and, instead of launching into the litany of father-son questions, asked, "How have you been, son?"

Had he been too short with his boy over the years? Had he failed to take time to know him? His own father never had a heart-to-heart with him, except when he told him once, "Always carry rubbers on you and don't try it with nice girls."

"Oh, I'm okay." Adam barely breathed out the words.

"What's up?"

"Oh, nothing much ..."

He started to make light of the situation but instead repeated, "No, really, how've you been—tell me."

"Well, not so hot, ... if you want to know ..."

Of course he wanted to know, he wanted to know more than anything else he could think of. But how do you draw out a lovelorn son whose partner is, *was* another guy? Maybe start with something funny.

"Do you remember that time Ali was quizzing you about the Milky Way?"

"It was Alyssa, quizzing me about the solar system."

"And you remembered all the planets' names but the last one out?"

"It's not a planet, technically speaking."

"And when she hinted that planet number ten—"

"Nine—"

"... is named for a Disney character—"

"Walt Disney wasn't born when the planets were named—"

"You blurted out Goofy? Pretty funny, right?"

He reached across the table and gave Adam a punch in the shoulder. He wished he could have held him close and said *Everything will work out.*

"Those were the days," Adam sighed, in a half-hearted roll with the punch.

"Were they, son?"

"They were simpler than nowadays, I think we'd have to admit."

"You still alone—?"

Adam barely nodded. "Please don't say it's for the best, Dad."

"I wasn't going to." He glanced at the menu. "Nothing's for the best if you're not happy. So what do you think's going to happen?"

"Do you mean, will he come back? I don't think so."

"Any plans to go after him?"

It was the first time anyone had put it to him directly, his dad of all people.

"It's hopeless."

"How do you know?"

"I just know."

"That's no answer."

The waiter took their order and they ate in silence, Al having decided there wasn't more to be said on the subject for now. He'd revisit it another time if Adam seemed amenable.

When he asked for the check, a stranger appeared to be waving to him from across the room. He suppressed the impulse to wave back.

Maybe the guy was trying to get someone else's attention—he'd look a fool if he waved without knowing who it was. But suddenly he knew. And with unintended urgency he exclaimed,

"Lunch is on me—no need to wait for the check, Ady. I'm sure you've got plenty to do at the office."

Adam nodded, slid off his chair, then bent down to kiss his cheek. "Thanks, Dad," he said, but Al's eyes were following the man coming toward him as Adam departed. The gentleman in question had evidently been watching the two of them, for he paused to give Adam time to step out of the room. Then he came forward with an assured step.

The waving man reached his table. He was Al's age, same height and weight, same ruddy coloring with gray streaking his hair; they might have been brothers, this stranger he recalled with the force of sudden recognition.

"Goober—?"

"How you doin', Al? You recognized me."

How could he *not* recognize him? The man who'd lived by his side for two years, the only man with whom he'd shared an emotional tie till he had a son. Did the tremble in his hand and knee show?

Helmut Bryce aka Goober. His army buddy at Fort Benning (the army post's name may change as the nation's conscience adjusts to the murder of George Floyd). They'd endured basic training together and wound up in the same barracks. They had little in common outwardly, the brash New Yorker and the good ol' Southern boy from the Georgia Piedmont. They surely weren't "meant" to be thick as thieves, the one with his singsong Southern drawl, the other with the Brooklyn bouillabaisse of an accent. How had it all begun?

Perhaps it was the night he'd been confined to his bunk for mouthing off to a sergeant. As he tossed and turned after the lights went down, his stomach growling with hunger, a hand descended from the upper bunk. It delivered a brown paper lunch bag filled with a peach, a hotdog, and a

Milky Way. When he thanked the donor on the parade ground next morning, Helmut explained the choice of grub. "All soft stuff, boy [Helmut pronounced it à la Southern: BO-ah], so no one couldn't hear you crunchin.'"

"And I was jus' wishin' someone'd hand me a bag o' grub," he replied, pleased that he'd started picking up the local lingo that pervaded the camp.

Their paths hardly crossed the following week. Then one night …

It was outside an off-limits shack not far from camp. He'd consumed enough beer to float him to that primitive dwelling, where he used his last condom. As he staggered out to wait for the ride that would spirit him back to camp, the sound of a scuffle behind the house drew his attention. There a couple of locals were beating up on a guy in uniform, who turned out to be his upper-bunk mate. He plunged into the fray, throwing punches as much to the wind as to the tangle of bodies, hollering every curse known to New Yorkese. He was bruised and bloodied in the end, but the assailants of his buddy—for that's how he thought of Helmut now—vanished from the scene.

"You okay, Goober …?" The name came without forethought as he was speaking, and it stuck.

By way of thanks, Helmut replied, "You sorry sonvabitch, jus' look at that face 'a yourn—!"

The incident led to an unspoken pact to watch each other's back. Soon they were palling around every chance they got, and their friendship grew like a hardy weed. That friendship failed to escape notice at the camp, and they soon came to be thought of as a pair. One prankster even posted a "sign-in" sheet on their bunk, headed by Al's name along with times for checking in and out, as if Helmut monitored his every move.

Before he and Helmut, reunited now in a plush New York restaurant, could exchange another word, the memory of that sheet flashed back and the ribbing that came of it. And then the evasive recollection of a night near the end of their service, when they found themselves in a cheap hotel at a resort on the Georgia coast, drunk, of course, and exhausted from a weekend of carousing. The only available room had a double bed that they fell into without undressing. At some point, Helmut's arm flopped over his chest. The weight of that arm as he lay beneath it produced a strange but not unpleasant sensation. After several minutes—time wasn't registering—he fell asleep. When he awoke next morning, the arm still lay athwart him.

He tried to put the incident, if that's what it was, out of his mind. Nothing was ever said about it. Then a short time later they were discharged and went their separate ways. Years passed, and now Helmut was standing before him.

◎　　◎　　◎

It was the oddest feeling, gliding down that escalator and coming face-to-face with an apparition that quickly assumed corporeal form before disappearing to the floor above. His stomach churned, and the ground smacked under his feet as the escalator delivered him to the floor below. He nearly tripped stepping off the moving stairs but forged ahead, dodging the string of makeup artists handing out scented coupons and samples as he fled through the store. What if Adam came after him? He had to get away, to avoid an encounter the thought of which filled him with a queasy kind of dread, he wasn't sure why.

He pushed through the revolving door onto the teeming corner of Thirty-fourth and Seventh, then skittered down the stairs to the subway and made his way through the crowd to the downtown side of the station. Waiting on the platform for the next train, amid sweaty bodies and garlic-laced breath, he wondered what he'd do if Adam followed him. When the No. 1 creaked into the station, he stepped into a car and felt the train revving up to resume its course. As the doors closed and it picked up speed, Adam appeared on the other side of the doors.

He left the train at the next stop, raced out of the station onto Fashion Avenue, and hailed a cab, his heart pushing up toward his throat. He felt like a cornered animal. While the cab sped toward his, Pietro's, apartment, his wide-eyed stare took in the familiar blocks as if he'd never seen them before. When the cabbie turned onto his street, he caught sight of Pietro on the sidewalk. He told the cabbie to stop and signaled for Pietro to climb in.

His "landlord" slid onto the seat beside him, as unconcerned about this change of pace and place as if he'd merely turned a page in a book he wasn't reading.

"Want to get drunk?"

"Why not?"

"How'd you know about this joint?" Pietro took a sip of Budweiser. Yves had led them to a bar below street level you might overlook on the narrow alley in this quiet quarter of the Village.

Yves tongued his Bombay Gin, savoring the burn of lemon on the rim of the glass. He'd downed most of it in the several minutes since they'd taken a booth. The dark, cool air enfolded them, and for the first time since fleeing Macy's he felt undiscoverable. Pietro was clearly intrigued. But did he want to tell him what had happened? The waiter was already setting their second round of drinks on the table before them. His companion had chosen the seat beside, not across from, him.

Before he could reply, Pietro lobbed the next question: "Why did you drag me here kicking and screaming?" He sidled closer, nestling his leg against Yves'. "That ain't like the cool, cruel cellist I know."

Despite the gin circulating through his system, a self-protective force checked him. He was fond of the rapscallion, but to trust him might be madness.

"We haven't talked in a couple of days. It's a quiet spot here to catch up."

"You've never wanted to catch up before."

"I think it's time."

"I don't believe a word you're saying."

"That makes it easier, doesn't it?"

Another gin and another beer, and Pietro's mood slipped from suspicious to mellow to aroused. He was anticipating a wild ride in the sack with his "tenant" once they got home. But when they finished their last round, Yves paid the check, then slid out from the booth.

"You off to the john or somewhere—?" asked his startled companion.

"Somewhere."

"Somewhere *where*, man—?"

"To the wider world. Take care of yourself, mon brave."

Did he notice that Pietro followed him?

CHAPTER 17

Minnesota: Governor Signs Same-Sex Marriage
Into Law, *New York Times, May 14, 2013*
Gov. Mark Dayton signed a measure Tuesday giving gay couples the right to
marry, making Minnesota the 12th state in the nation to permit same-sex marriage. During a signing ceremony outside the State Capitol in St. Paul, where thousands of Minnesotans gathered and cheered in 90-degree weather, Mr. Dayton, a
Democrat, praised the choices of state lawmakers as changing the course of history.

The State Legislature, controlled by Democrats, approved the measure in recent
days, marking the first state in the Midwest to allow same-sex marriage through
legislative action, rather than a court action.

Two strands of conversation wove through his mind that afternoon. At
times they coalesced and the words of his son intermingled with those of
his army buddy Goober. While trying to sort out who actually said what, he
decided to take the subway home instead of the usual cab. He pushed onto
the perpetually overcrowded Lexington line, the sole underground train
on the East Side of Manhattan while the much-delayed Second Avenue
subway languished among the sewers beneath the avenue.

"Kalimera, Kyrie Stover," Karolos greeted him in his native Greek.
Before he could reply, the doorman tacked on, "Your missus just went
upstairs ...," he glanced at his watch, good Cerberus that he was, "... I'd say,
... no more than ten minutes ago."

He barely nodded, his thoughts still entangled in the events of the
afternoon. Yet he did notice that the doorman was eyeing him intently, as
if he had something more to say but wasn't sure how to express it. Then as

he was about to step into the elevator Karolos asked, "The missus expecting you, sir …?"

An odd question, was his wife awaiting him in his own apartment? Before he could reply, Karolos tacked on, as if anticipating his reaction, "You're home somewhat early, sir, I notice."

"It's me all right" was all he had time to sputter when the door slid shut and he began his ascent to the ninth floor.

That Karolos was a funny chap—friendly to a fault, but wily too; he knew his way around. The Greek certainly had an eye for the ladies. He first noticed it when Karolos started paying what he thought was undue atten- tion to his daughters as they grew into "teen queens," as the dashing door- man dubbed them. Karolos excelled at peppering his speech with slang and idioms he'd picked up from English, though he could be off the mark. He once called Alyssa a "one-woman power station." The co-op board rated him highly—efficient and dependable. Even Lenny had succumbed to his charms, Lenny the Cool and Aloof. He hadn't missed her beaming smiles at the doorman, their whispered asides.

When he turned the knob to the door of his apartment, it seemed to jam, then he realized the door was locked. What was this? Lenny always left it open for him, a ritual she never failed to observe.

He fished for his key in the recesses of his pocket, his fingers encoun- tering a gum wrapper, a shiny penny he'd picked up off the street, and Goober's phone number, scribbled on a scrap of paper. When he opened the door, the apartment seemed unnaturally quiet. Of course, it was always quiet when he got home, unless one of the kids was there with friends or talking with their mother. Why did today strike him as different? His mind wavered back to Helmut and their meeting in the restaurant, then Lenny appeared from out of nowhere, or that's how it seemed to him. He decided not to mention Helmut, not right now.

Her kiss barely grazed his five-o'clock stubble. She sank into an arm- chair and asked, "How was your day, Albert?"

Again he was thrown. She'd never asked him such a question. She was usually involved in a project, making sketches, reading through her magazines. The formality struck him.

"Fine, fine." He started for the stairs but paused then asked, "Anything special happen in *your* day …?

"Yes, as a matter of fact."

He took a seat across from her and propped his feet on an ottoman squatting in attendance.

"I had a visitor at the office."

"Someone I know?"

"Hmm."

"Want to say who …?"

His impatience was rising faster than his curiosity; it seemed she was pointlessly drawing out her news, if it even *was* news.

"Yes," she replied after hesitation, "a certain Yves Montjour."

The name didn't register at first. He continued to stare, expecting an explanation. After a moment she said, "Ady's musician."

"*That* Yves—yes, I know who he is."

When she ventured nothing further he urged,

"Well …?"

She eyed him for some time, as if to be sure she had his attention. She may have also wished to buy time. She hadn't thought much about Yves' visit, though it had come as a surprise. She wasn't certain what to tell her husband about it. He had a way of jumping to conclusions and getting wrong ideas from mere tidbits of information. For that matter, she wasn't sure herself what to make of Yves' confession.

"You know," she began, "whatever else you might think about him—"

"I don't think about him—"

"He seems older than Adam."

"He *is* older."

"No, he's just more mature."

"What makes you think that?"

She drew her legs up beneath her, reminding him of a cat. "I can't imagine—if the situation were reversed—that Adam would do what Yves did, coming to me."

"You think Adam's not honest—?"

"It has nothing to do with honesty. He's just not that forthcoming."

"Maybe it's just as well. What did the boyfriend tell you?"

"It sounds odd when you put it that way."

"That's how I put things. He is—*was*—the boyfriend. Or did I misconceive the situation?"

She trained her eyes on him, then glanced off at an angle. "It wasn't meant to work out."

"No?" He took this in. "And what brought him—or you—to that conclusion?"

"They're too different."

"Why should *that* matter? You and I are different—"

"Maybe we weren't always so different."

He wondered why she was suddenly disparaging Adam's relationship. She'd voiced no objections when he was with Yves. In fact, he couldn't recall her uttering a single opinion on the subject. He had no idea what she made of their son's attachment to another man. Was she relieved—happy—that the relationship had ended? Or was she unfeeling about her son's feelings? He felt a flash of irritation at what he'd always admired about her—her cool. Was she so cool as to be frozen? He found himself unexpectedly in the position of wanting to make a case for the relationship, though the parties to it had declared it null and void.

◱   ◱   ◱

The sun had not yet hit the horizon. Only a feeble light streamed into the bedroom from adjacent apartments; neighbors were rising early, or perhaps some had not yet gone to bed, this being New York. He would remember that the call awakened him before dawn.

"Yes, … who is it—?"

He was blinking the sleep from his eyes, wondering whether he was dreaming. The voice at the other end sounded unfamiliar at first. A wrong number, but so urgent?

"Can you meet me there in half an hour—?"

"What hospital—?

"Emergency room—be quick—"

Pietro hung up before he could ask another question.

He rolled out of bed, splashed cold water on his face, and slipped into wingtips, khakis, and an oxford button-down—office casual. He could return to work later without going home to change. But why was he thinking about office wear when Yves was lying somewhere in a hospital bed—? He'd remember that too, long afterward.

He dashed into the street and hailed a cab to Bellevue, that receptacle for the city's down-and-out or accident-prone or mental cases nobody wanted, the oldest public hospital in the USA. It was early enough to beat the worst traffic, and he arrived within ten minutes at the collection of red brick buildings hulking near the East River. Pietro was pacing outside the ER amid the surrounding scramble and sounds of distress. When he caught sight of Adam rushing toward him, he signaled for him to follow with a toss of his head.

They passed the admitting desk—Pietro had already settled the preliminaries—and headed down an interminable corridor. The scent of disinfectant lined his nostrils as he sprang aside to avoid tripping over a body lying on a mattress against the wall. Nurses and orderlies scurried past them in spasms of efficiency as they passed through a set of double doors and entered a large room.

A clerk looked up and Pietro supplied the name. The clerk glanced at a sheet on his clipboard, ran a finger down it, then glanced up again.

"Are you family?" he inquired.

"*He* is," said Pietro with exaggerated authority.

The clerk gave Adam a once-over then nodded tentatively, as if unwilling to grant permission for entry but not withholding it either.

Pietro's hand pressed into the small of Adam's back, propelling him along the corridor.

Beds with curtains partly pulled around them lined the passageway. Pietro's hand continued pressing into his back, until they came to a bed nearly hidden behind a curtain. Two nurses stood on either side, one taking the patient's pulse, the other monitoring a machine that clicked and ticked at his side.

He and Pietro froze in place till the nurses departed, one of them glancing back at them, no expression on her face. Pietro held the curtain aside as Adam approached the bed.

Yves was covered to the chin in sheet and blanket. Bandages swathed his face without completely concealing the bluish-purple bruises. His lower lip was fissured, and a stream of saliva ran down from the corner of his mouth across his chin to the sheet.

◙　　◙　　◙

The Stover dining room was a hexagon whose proportions would have pleased the ancient Egyptians. The windows, as holds true for most Manhattan dining rooms, faced an inner court with little light—your eyes are supposed to be on your meal, not the view outside. The dining room was the first that Lenora redecorated when she became mistress of the domain. "Too gloomy," she explained to her husband, who was content to leave the decorating details to her. Till cost estimates poured in. Then he assumed a more active role. "Do we really need flocked wallpaper?" he'd grilled her one morning. She compromised, "You pick it out, then." He was defeated. "Think of all the meals we'll be eating in here," she reasoned. "Then why'd you enlarge the kitchen so we could eat in there?" Her retort ended the discussion: "So we might dine in separate rooms."

"Pass the potato salad, please, Josiah—and let's not sniff it when you do."

Alyssa and beau were spending their first evening alone with her folks, and Alyssa was making sure her paramour committed no gaucheries. She was quite practiced now at directing his behavior, and he'd become expert at taking orders without complaint, though what yoked beast is not without its private opinions? Lenora had just called them to the dining table, where she served from the buffet but with certain dishes strategically placed around the table, including the potato salad, that had to be passed from diner to diner. It was an activity to keep the conversation from flagging, though she suspected that between Al and Aly there'd be no lull.

Al had trained his vision on Josiah since the pair's arrival, on the high forehead, dark brown hair streaked with youthful gray, the prominent nose, and wide mouth that looked perpetually as if it were breaking into a grin. It was starting to dawn on him that his elder daughter had a serious interest in the young man—and better yet, he in her. So Theo Witherspoon was out the window? He'd met Josiah socially a couple of times and decided to check him out before it was too late, he wasn't sure for what.

"How's that business of yours?" he inquired, sending up a trial balloon.

"It's a *store*, Dad," Alyssa corrected. "Josiah's making money. I can vouch for that."

"I'd like to hear it from the horse's mouth," said Dad.

"The horse will tell you the same thing."

"Then let the horse tell me." Al removed his reading glasses and, like a judge in chambers, awaited the equine testimony.

Josiah was uncertain how much to repeat of what he'd already told his host. The subject had come up a couple of times, but always amid gatherings with lots of chatter. He wasn't sure whether Al had listened, even if he'd heard.

"Well, sir, I guess you could say I'm in the book and bedding business."

"A curious combination," returned Al.

"You see," put in Alyssa, "he's named his store—"

"Let *him* tell me, Aly. I'm sure your book-and-bed man can speak for himself." Al replaced his glasses over his nose, as if to embellish his next observation, almost an aside. "If he can't, he'll be in for a heap of trouble in this family."

Her dad's allusion to "family" gave their guest's ego a needed boost. He'd made headway on the romance front, but his beloved seemed determined to keep him in his place when her family was concerned, though she'd not made clear where that place might be. She'd relented ever so slowly in her initial determination to keep him at arms' length, and she was becoming a willing, even active bedmate. Yet he'd not had the temerity to suggest, let alone propose, that they might form a more perfect union.

"Well," Josiah hesitated, to make sure his one-and-only wouldn't interrupt, "when I first opened the place, customers wondering in off the street asked for sheets and pillowslips as often as books, perhaps because of the store's name—"

"What's that name again?" queried Al.

"Between the Covers."

"Very clever," Al brimmed while glancing around the table, as if he himself had named the establishment.

"Thank you, sir," beamed Josiah. "So I decided to capitalize on the double entendre and offer a line of bed linens as well as books."

"I like that," said Lenora, who'd been a quiet observer.

"The sheets or the books?" asked Alyssa.

"The 'double entendre,'" she returned. "Three cheers for literacy."

Alyssa damned with faint praise: "Josiah's vocabulary is perfectly adequate, you can take my word—though I'm not sure he could complete the *Times* crossword."

"Thank you, pet," came the guest's polite rejoinder. "Your potato salad is *scrumptious*, Mrs. Stover."

"Call her Lenny," piped Al.

"*Lenora*, Dad," corrected Alyssa.

"Aly, let your mama speak for herself. We're all grownups here."

Alyssa's pout suggested she might not be in total accord. "On another subject," she asked, "How's Ady? Anyone seen him lately?"

Mom & Dad exchanged glances before she replied, "Not lately. He spends his free time at the hospital."

"Has he been sick?" asked Josiah.

"His friend."

"That Everett?" asked Alyssa.

"That Yves," retorted Al.

"I thought that business was over with and done."

"It is. *Was*."

"Then what's he doing at the hospital? And what's wrong with that guy, anyway?"

"Injury," said Al.

Dad & Mom exchanged another glance.

"Let's just hope he doesn't get mixed up with him again—for everyone's sake," said Alyssa. "Now, may we change the subject? We're embarrassing Josiah."

◙   ◙   ◙

The mask of death, the mask of immobility—it was coming to life. The face—it was coming back now, the beloved features. It had taken on a touch of color in the cheeks, at the temples. There was even motion, if you could call it that, a fluttering of the eyelids. And a trembling of the right hand, the hand that holds the bow. (Was he trying to play his cello?) The doctors said "It means nothing." The nurses said "It could mean anything." The nurses left room for hope. He vowed to listen to them and ignore the doctors. What did doctors know about sick people?

In three days they'd come some way together, the watchful at the bedside, the moribund in the narrow metal bed. Only three days ago—it seemed a lifetime—the patient had resembled a corpse. One of the order-lies had taken his visitor aside to murmur, "I know this ain't easy for you." He'd steeled himself after Pietro's call, ready for anything, to be near Yves once more, to watch over him—and that's almost all he'd done for the past three days.

The staff had been kind. They knew what he was going through, or acted as if they did. Some assumed he was next of kin, otherwise why did they allow him to haunt that hospital room, coming and going whenever he pleased? "No, I'm not family," he'd confessed to the nurse on duty a cou-ple of days after Yves was admitted. Then drawing himself up in a fit of indignation, he'd declared, "I'm *more* than family." The nurse understood—this was New York. She told him he could visit as much as he pleased, that the patient "came to life" when he was there, the vital signs steadier. He'd hardly noticed any changes himself. Was he watching too closely?

Then on the fourth day, Yves' eyes popped open and stared at him, eyes etched by dark circles like bull's-eyes. He moved his chair closer to the bed and clasped Yves' hand. They sat that way for the next hour, without speaking, Yves now and then peering into his eyes.

Then Yves drifted off, his eyelids drooping then closing altogether as he slipped back into oblivion. Twice, thrice as Yves drifted away, he called his name—Yves, Yves … *Yves.* He hoped Yves heard him, how he hoped.

Next day when he returned to the bedside, Yves awoke and asked, "How long have you been here?" The question was frank and to the point—vintage Yves.

"Forever, I guess." It felt like eternity.

Yves smiled, his first since awakening from the ordeal. "I might have known."

"You okay?" asked Adam. The question was idiotic, but what else to say?

"Fabulous—can't you see …?"

"You look fabulous to me." They clasped hands more firmly and sat for a while in silence, then he noticed a tear from Yves' eye. The harsh fluorescent light lit a silvery trail down his cheek. He was tempted to wipe it away, but Yves was drifting back to sleep. He didn't want to disturb him. He continued holding his hand.

"You spendin' the rest of your sorry life here …?" A head poked in at the doorway, its roguish expression that of a precocious child actor who'd just said his first line.

Adam glanced at his watch. "I'm here as long as he needs me."

"Behold the noble husband," Pietro mocked, not without a broad grin.

"Shut up, asshole." Yves frowned then winked at the newcomer.

Their offhand exchange took Adam by surprise. He felt a pang of jealousy. Jealousy had never been his thing; it wasn't worth the energy. But this familiarity between Yves and Pietro? He'd not thought of them as friends. They just had an arrangement—Yves had taken temporary refuge in Pietro's apartment when he left him. But how would Yves have known to go there? Why would he have *wanted* to go there? Was it Alison who'd explained that Pietro had made friends with Yves at Alyssa's party and offered him shelter after the breakup? There was some connection between Yves and Pietro, else why was Pietro the one to let him know about Yves' horrendous injury? Injury? He still didn't know all the details. Something about a fight somewhere—Pietro called it an "ambush"—outside a gay bar near a rough stretch by the Hudson. They'd not discussed the matter, faute de time or inclination. And then there was that odd occurrence when Pietro had beat a hasty exit from the apartment when he, Adam, was living with Yves, right after they were introduced. He still wondered what *that* was about.

But a nurse had entered the room to check the patient's blood pressure.

PART IV

The Piano

CHAPTER 18

With New Legal Challenge, Gay Marriage Debate in New
Mexico Heats Up, *New York Times, June 6, 2013*
The definition of marriage in the New Mexico Constitution—"a civil contract,
for which the consent of contracting parties, capable in law of contracting, is
essential"—makes no mention of gender, and that is the central argument of
both lawsuits.

...

It is exactly this ambiguity in the "statutory framework," ... said [state Attorney
General Gary King], that has made the state's marriage statute the subject of conflicting interpretations, fueling battles in court and in the court of public opinion.
According to recent polls, more voters support making same-sex marriage illegal
than legalizing it, though by small margins. Among young voters, though, there is
solid support for same-sex marriage, mirroring national surveys.

When will it stop, the infernal circling round ... around—? It starts up each
time he drifts into the bliss of forgetting, but then the circling, spiraling
downward, down ...he's hitting bottom—*crash*! But something breaks his
fall. The voice—far away, yet in his ear ... Someone faraway, yet near—He
tries to ask, sit up, but his head falls back onto the pillow, then the circling—

It was just a moment ago, months, when the voice was speaking ...
He was fleeing, putting as much distance between them as he could—mental images kaleidoscoping, escalators veering off to nowhere, subway doors
slamming shut—Pietro inside ...? But Pietro was drinking beer ... pressing against him while he ... ran off to the river—? To get away from—?
... after the train brought him to that place by the river, a haunt of leather
fetishists, sweaty homos pressed together—couldn't breathe, had to get out,

stumbling onto the sidewalk. The taste of blood on his teeth, blows to the head …

He remembered the place, he'd paid a call years back, when he burst onto the New York scene, feeling his way after a cosseted upbringing in … Miami … *Montreal*. It was a reason he came to the city, to Sodom … yes, darling Cello, you too, but a man is flesh, he has to live.… He remembered those dingy walls, sweaty, leather-clad bodies—back then. But—wasn't he just there … staggering out the door, falling against some goons, fists flying, a knee to the groin—the pavement hitting him smack in the face?

Adam's voice, that's whose it was, Adam beside him. It was hard to see, eyes swollen shut, but he recognized the silhouette against the light from the window, he'd know it anywhere, even without the voice. The chiseled nose in perfect proportion to the face, small ears sticking out like a teddy bear's, squared chin with dimple, between firm jaws—Adonis or Apollo sitting next to him …? He got it. That was when the tear trickled down his cheek. Adam … his little boy.

He hadn't taken very good care of his little boy, leaving without a word. Adam had no chance to tell his side of the story. He'd sailed out of his, *their* life without looking back. And the crime—? A date with his sister's girlfriend …?

He'd given the matter little thought since the breakup. Why dwell on the past?—his lifelong refrain. But happiness without Adam? He was a vagabond now, an exile in Pietro's overpopulated digs. Maybe it was time to dwell … for once in his life. He'd shut the door on the past and it was past, though Faulkner wouldn't agree. Adam … sitting by him now? sitting there for how long …? Holding his hand, his soothing words, the moments stretching back and forth in time.

But if Adam loved him, why did he leave him for a weekend with a woman he barely knew, when he could have invited him instead? Aphrodite, gorgeous beyond compare—but would he have to be wary of every attractive woman who'd cross their path? Was Adam fickle …? Adam the golden boy of his architectural firm—is *that* why he chose Aphrodite over him, to protect his rep at the firm, if word got out that he, Adam ...?

These questions had slalomed through his brain many times, but this hospital stay made him reconsider the past in a new light. After they brought him to Bellevue a bloody mass, the hospital had not contacted his mom in Canada; they relied on Adam as "next of kin," once Pietro put them in touch. He'd heard that Adam even weighed in on medical advice (allergic to codeine), dietary preferences (loved cauliflower, detested Brussels sprouts) and restrictions (gets asthma from red onions), underwear size (waist 34, T-shirts medium).

The nursing staff—they all made a fuss over Adam. He'd become a favorite in no time, his easy charm, modest manner. "You're the best friend a guy could have," quipped the head nurse. "You never leave his side." A pert Irish orderly declared to Yves, "This bloke knows all about you there be to know. Make a copy of him—in case you lose the original." Another quipped, "If you're making copies, make one for me!"

No, Adam was no immature kid who didn't know his own mind. He was suave, sophisticated, judicious. So why had he showed him the door (actually, showed himself the door) when Adam did something that displeased—or disappointed—him? Was he, the patient laid out in a forlorn hospital bed, that insecure? If he was so mature, why would he feel displaced by a beautiful woman? Was it the end of everything if his partner wasn't ready to come out to that rarefied world he was immured in? He tried to imagine Adam's private life—his home and family, the profession in which he was distinguishing himself, his many posh friends. Adam wasn't a driven musician from distant Canada; maybe it was just harder for him to turn his back on Park Avenue and set off onto uncharted waters.

◎　　◎　　◎

"Aren't you looking bright and shiny—almost like new?"

Alison was standing by his bedside, a bouquet of snapdragons in one hand, a book in the other, Shakespeare's sonnets. She had that balanced appearance, he thought, a goddess of wisdom and youth, if two such deities ever merge into a single being.

He flashed her a smile. Not a big one, not the kind you bestow on close friends and loved ones, a smile more of recognition.

"Why do they call such pretty things *snapdragons*?" he asked.

She held one to his face and pinched the flower's tiny pouch. It made the "mouth" above it open and close. "Because they snap, like dragons."

She started to say, *I brought these for you.* But he'd know that—why tell him? Especially when there was much more to discuss, and she hadn't come to exchange platitudes.

"Have a seat," he managed, his eyes indicating a chair near the door. When she'd pulled it to bedside, placing the book on his bed while still holding on to the flowers, she cast about for a receptacle and, finding none, stuck the snapdragons in the plastic water pitcher on his bed tray. "It's not Steuben glass," she offered, "but maybe the nurses can bring you another?"

"A Steuben glass vase—? I'll put in a request." He hesitated. "Or maybe I should leave that to your brother."

"Adam?"

"The nurses would do anything for him."

"Glad to hear that. So how are you?"

He tried to sit up. She tucked an extra pillow beneath his head to help him prop.

"I'm coming along. They might even release me one of these days, if I'm able to walk and hold a cup to beg with."

A look of concern crossed her face. "You haven't hurt your hands—?"

He flexed them, winced, then bounced each finger against the thumb to demonstrate their dexterity. One finger-thumb combo he couldn't quite manage.

"You act proud of them, as if they were your children."

"I often think they're the only thing about me worth saving."

"Do I detect a note of self-pity?"

He looked her in the eye. "I deserve what I got."

"Deserve it or not—and I highly doubt that you did—how's our Adam?"

"Our Adam?" He noticed she was leaning forward in the chair. "I'd say he's a regular Florence Nightingale."

"We kind of lost track of him, then found out he was spending all his time here with you." She wavered for an instant. "I can't imagine why."

"He's been a real Father Theresa."

"You love him, don't you?"

"The question is superfluous, is it not?"

"No one knows better than you."

"I don't deserve him."

"Does anyone ever deserve anyone else? Besides, we're not talking about deserving here. Do you want him back?"

"A more apt question might be, does he want *me* back."

"While we're quizzing each other, what do *you* want, anyway—?"

"A loaded question."

"Speaking of loaded questions, I know about you and Pietro."

"How did you know—?"

"Let's just say I figured it out."

◙　　◙　　◙

It hadn't come to her immediately; such things seldom do. It was the most peculiar configuration—she and Pietro, Pietro and Adam, Pietro and Yves. Was every man in the world turning gay on her? Was gay so in fashion, gay boyfriends, gay lovers, gay partners? What next—gay husbands?

She felt like a guileless fool, a dupe of those she'd loved and trusted, her own boyfriend sleeping with her brother's boyfriend?

But now that she knew, what to do about it? On the one hand, she wanted to ditch the bastards and move on with her life. But they weren't cornhusks to be shucked—she couldn't very well abandon her brother, who was innocent in this mix-up. If anything, Adam needed *her* protection. As for Yves, Adam had to sort that out for himself. She couldn't imagine Adam abandoning a lover, even a former one, who was prostrate in the hospital, his career in jeopardy. But Pietro …?

She understood his nickname now. She should have been suspicious from the start. Treachery—effervescent, over the top, loving and sly at the same time, showering compliments on her, the "Empress of my Heart." The sad thing was, she was just starting to believe him, to be comfortable with the idea of "them," and, worst of all, to trust him.

He'd dogged her for a week with phone calls and text messages, imploring then insisting she give him his day in court. She'd agreed to meet him for "a final talk"—that was her term and condition to see him one more time. She'd committed to this last meeting, in a café near University Place. Surrounded by the clank and clatter of flatware and crockery in the bustling establishment, she sat across from him at the table where he awaited her. Only after a waitress took their order did she speak.

"So your dirty secret's out now."

"So it's *dirty* because I've had sex with a man—is that it, Miss Holier Than Thou? I thought you billed yourself as a modern woman—!"

"You mean, 'modern' as in women who let men run roughshod over them?" she shot back. "This has nothing to do with modern—it's about honesty, and you should know it—!"

"I can't see why you go ballistic cuz I made it with a guy. I thought people stopped raising eyebrows over that since the Renaissance or the Twenties, whenever it was."

"I could care less who has a prick. You were doing it behind my back, while pretending I was, well, someone special. And now you'd be a complete fool if you didn't think I was one for believing you."

For an awful moment she hated the way she sounded, a giant cliché in a ticky-tacky café. No wonder he seemed unsympathetic!

He tried to snatch her hand, but she yanked it back as their waiter delivered two steaming cappuccinos.

"So why do you think you're any less special because I've stuck my dick in some guy or other?"

"Guy or *other*—? He happens to be my brother's partner!"

"*Ex*-partner."

"Spare me the correctives. You know what I mean."

"No, I don't quite … know … what … you … m-e-a-n," he spelled the last word.

"Then you're morally obtuse, to say the least."

"Did it ever occur to you that Yves and I might have had a life together before you and Adam ever came on the scene?" He seized her hand and managed to hold it.

She wondered whether she'd lost her common sense. She understood that men without pasts were mythical beasts or mama's boys, a fact easily overlooked by someone in love. We like to believe that our lovers come to us freshly minted, Pygmalion presenting them just for us, the way Pietro stepped down as naked as Galatea from his pedestal that day in sketch class.

But what was this about an earlier life with Yves? Was he slithering off the hook—or telling the truth? The question provoked a memory from the not too distant past, when Pietro left—*fled*—right after being "introduced" to Yves that first time she took him to Adam's apartment. So perhaps he *did* know Yves before she met him, and was embarrassed to meet him again for some reason. His excuse was seeming a bit more plausible.

"Whether you knew him or not," she conceded, "I can't grasp why you were interested in me if you were making it with him all that time."

"It wasn't 'all that time," he objected. "It was *before* I ever had the good fortune to lay eyes on you. If it would interest you to know, in fact, it was before he and I ever met you and your brother—we each had a life of our own even then, as hard to believe as that might be."

She blew the steam off her cappuccino, then gazed out the window before settling her eyes on him again. "If I grant that I might believe you knew Yves before you met Adam and me, what I'm having trouble wrapping my head around is that you like guys."

"I'm completely heterosexual—I like both."

A ray of sunlight brightened his smiling face. It was the smile of a precocious child who'd just reported some great accomplishment.

"I'd say you're bisexual."

"We're *all* bisexual." He released her hand and raised both of his, framing his next comment in giant quotations marks. "Everyone has the capacity to love and have sex with anyone else, the same or opposite—ask any anthropologist worth his sperm."

He was taking her in, ascertaining whether he had her with him in this. "In my book, if you make it with dudes and dolls both, then you're hetero. That's referring to the *choice* rather than the person who makes it, which is much more accurate and more fair. I might add, we wouldn't have any Matthew Shepards if the world adopted my weltanschauung, despite what your Republican friends might make of it."

"I don't have any Republican friends," she retorted. "At least, none I know of."

"I'm glad we got *that* out of the way," he heaved a big sigh, as if they'd finally resolved the issue at hand.

But she wasn't ready to let him off the hook.

"There's still some things about you I don't get, Treachery."

He winced at the name, the first time she'd called him by it. It was okay if everyone else did, but Ali?

"Shoot!" he fired back, "But aim gently."

"How can you be so fired up over me, as you claim to be, when you're just as capable of hitting the sack with any guy who comes along?"

"So now, *promiscuity* is the charge—?"

It wasn't a fair charge and she knew it. But he'd hurt her with this latest round of revelations. It was the first time she'd made herself vulnerable to a man, and now to find out he liked guys as well? What chance did she have? How did feminine wiles (not that she employed them) count for anything if she was competing with every cute male who'd flit between his crosshairs? She had no objection to homosexuality or bisexuality per se, only to his. A feeling of hopelessness engulfed her as she sipped her cappuccino. It tasted bitter. She was of a mind to get up and walk out on him. But something was holding her back, and it wasn't just the frayed thread of hope that she might salvage the situation. She'd made a huge, maybe reckless investment in this intriguing, seductive creature clutching her hand. She was feeling her way, still uncertain what she wanted. But there was someone else to consider in this mass of confusion.

"Tell me about Yves."

He left the hospital that dusky afternoon—he'd noticed the days were growing shorter, as if a heavenly utility company were rationing the light. Only recently was he living the Golden Age of eternal sunshine, he reflected, at least it had felt like that as he stepped from the antiseptic hospital ward into the cinnamon scent of an early fall evening. There was a time when life promised endless happiness, at least it made broad hints in that direction. But now he had more feelings than he could sort through as he tried to make sense of his life and where he was heading, or where he was stuck. As he walked south on First Avenue, he found himself wondering whether the good New Yorkers he passed on the street had any idea of his confusion. Could onlookers and passersby glimpse the sadness that filled his heart?

They'd moved Yves to a semiprivate room, and he'd spent every free hour at his bedside, propping pillows, filling water pitchers, feeding him—each minute spent with Yves a reprieve, a path forward though into terra incognita. Yet Yves would soon be released; he'd be going home. But where was "home"? He'd continue to look after him, there was hardly a question of that. He'd see that Yves had everything he needed. But would Yves agree to move back in with him again, and their piano? Or would he return to Pietro's pad? Yves had even mentioned something about going home to Canada until his hand healed and he could resume work. Yves said he had no idea how long that might be.

New York without Yves—inconc-Yves-able! That's when he tripped on the curb and fell in the street. Plenty of onlookers were watching him now with their own thoughts about his confusion as he picked himself up and dusted off his trousers. Heaven knew what they were thinking. He himself was thinking he couldn't let Yves go. But would Yves be willing to stay in New York?

CHAPTER 19

Supreme Court Allows Same-Sex Marriages to Proceed in
South Carolina, *New York Times, November 20, 2014*
WASHINGTON — Over the dissents of two justices, the Supreme Court on
Thursday allowed same-sex marriages to proceed in South Carolina, rejecting an
emergency application seeking a stay of a judge's order striking down the state's
ban on such unions.
In urging the Supreme Court to intercede, state officials had stressed federalism
concerns, saying that South Carolina's voters rather than the federal government
should be allowed to decide questions of "domestic relations," including marriage.

Hell's Kitchen. A floor-to-ceiling mirror covers a wall of the foyer. It opens
into a sunny living room whose windows face south over endless rooftops,
with slices of the Hudson River between the buildings lining Tenth Avenue
to the west. From the living room is a view of a NYC kitchen—in which
one person can barely turn around. Beyond the kitchen, a hallway leads to
the bath and bedroom.

Overnight guests could park on a sofa bed in the living room, Jenn
explained when Alison agreed to rent the apartment. Jenn, a trust fund
baby, had interviewed prospective roommates for weeks before Ali turned
up and expressed interest. Ali added that she didn't expect to have anyone "crashing" there, thus no need for the sofa bed. This was before she
met Pietro.

When she returned to the apartment from the hospital later that
afternoon, she felt as if she were entering a box that tipped back or forth
when she moved. In the foyer, she stared at herself in the large mirror that
Adam had installed. "I told you the trompe l'oeil effect would make this

room twice as big," her architect brother had proclaimed about his housewarming gift, as he and Yves drove the last nail into the wall.

Adam and Yves. How fitting she'd be thinking of them now as she gazed into that mirror. Would they ever get back together? Yves had seemed the perfect companion for her brother—cultured, warmhearted and witty, talented. And that music he made with his beloved cello, his demanding "mistress," he called "her."

The first time she heard him play was by accident. She'd let herself into Adam's apartment, forgetting that her brother had a roommate now. Yves was practicing in the living room and didn't stop, despite her unexpected intrusion; he barely looked up. He was barefoot and had wrapped his body around his beloved, while clad only in boxers, oblivious to the world around him. He was at one with his instrument. She'd heard that expression before, but never witnessed it firsthand. That day, as the strains of the Brahms E-minor Sonata soared out to the world, Yves revealed his "inner soul." That's how she'd described him and her private "concert" to her parents the following evening. Any doubts she might have had as to his suitability for her brother vanished like morning mist in a hot sun.

But what had become of Yves and his beloved? Was the cellist in shining armor still the right match for her brother? Recent history had a way of refashioning the past, which had become quite unpredictable. Yves was not only her brother's ex but was tangled up with her own boyfriend, or maybe *former* boyfriend, the way things were going.

Adam and Yves. The box tilted again and she reached for the wall to steady herself as she walked down the hallway to the bedroom, from which she heard the *click-clacking* of Jenn's Royal as she typed out words, phrases, anagrams for all she knew.

The sight of her roommate reclining on the bed in harem pants, the typewriter balanced on her knees, punctured her reverie, and she exclaimed, "Just the man I want to see!"—Jenn's gender notwithstanding.

She sank onto her bed across from Jenn's. "Mind if we talk …?"

"Be my guest," Jenn sat straight as the Royal slid down her calves toward her feet. "But mind if we order in? I'm famished after an afternoon on the keys."

They kept a menu from a Chinese takeout—that lifesaving institution for Manhattanites—on the nightstand between their beds, their Gideon Bible. With menu in hand, Jenn called in their order. It was always the same.

After the call, Jenn said, "Now, what's on that mind of yours? I can tell when your hard drive's been whirring."

A jumble of words poured forth for her patient roommate from Topeka, who was as serene as a Kansas cornfield. She startled herself at times by her revelations to this roommate, who was a complete stranger only months ago. When she finally wound down, she'd bequeathed an X-ray of her heart to her listener.

But the intercom bell was ringing. She sprang up to answer it; Jenn had paid for their last two meals from their "kitchen away from home," as Jenn dubbed it. After she paid the delivery man, she carried their dinner back to the bedroom—hot-and-sour chicken, moo shu pork, and egg rolls.

Jenn digested her rambling account along with her dinner and was ready with a verdict.

"I think you've been too easy on him. I can think of worse things to call him than 'little bastard.'"

"My sister calls him 'Chicory.'"

"Clearly, he's all things to all people. But what about *you*?"

Alison's chopsticks nudged the remaining pieces around the orange hot-and-sour sauce. This was the first time she'd shared her feelings with anyone on the grand scale, her "big messy mess of a mess," as she pondered it.

"I mean," Jenn resumed, biting into a packet of Chinese mustard, "who does this little twerp think he is?"

"Good question," Alison replied, spearing a pineapple nugget. "The problem is, there's been no indication to date that even *he* knows who he is." To Jenn's inquiring glance she elaborated, "He's such a schizzy guy. Do you think he can be held accountable—in fairness—for his behavior? I don't mean to excuse him." She was stretching to the limit, and she knew it.

"Don't let him off the hook. The guy claims to love you, expects you to put out for him—"

"He keeps saying he wants to spend the rest of his life with me—"

"Next thing, you find out he's been making it not just with guys but with some of your significant others—some life he must have in mind."

"You're not thinking he and Adam—"?

"I refuse to think about it." Jenn shifted position amid the pile of cushions, "and I don't profess to be a fortune-teller."

"You could be, in your odalisque outfit," Alison couldn't help remarking, her photographer's eye following the sinuous curves of Jenn's Ingresque body as she propped on her collection of pillows. "I've been thinking about acquiring a pair of harem pants myself."

"Maybe you should be thinking about acquiring a new boyfriend."

She couldn't quibble, but was she prepared to leave Pietro? Her feelings for him aside, if she let him loose, would he go back to Yves? Then what would become of Adam? But was it her job to reconcile her brother to his ex, if his ex was in danger of being ensnared by her … ex? And was Pietro actually an "ex" yet, an echt ex? She was rescued from the dilemma by the ringing of her cellphone.

"Drop whatever you're doing and come uptown immediately!" the peremptory command rang through the receiver.

"Is there a fire or something …?"

"We've got to talk—now!"

She put the carton of takeout on the nightstand and cast a rueful glance at her roommate, still chewing, as Ali formulated her next statement: "My sister never beats around the bush."

Jenn's puzzled look questioned, *Everything all right?*

"Family emergency. At least, that's what my sister calls it."

"I hope it's not too serious?"

"It could be a hangnail, for all I know."

◙   ◙   ◙

She'd passed the coffee shop on Lexington Avenue countless times without going in. The place was too close to her folks' apartment, a block over on Park, for her to need to stop there. But this time, in she went.

A convivial din filled the space, and she could see how the homey atmosphere might attract a loyal clientele. Most of the diners and coffee sippers looked like regulars. They could be wallpaper.

She proceeded down the aisle toward the back, where she spotted Alyssa. A curious little cap perched atop her head and a pair of black reading glasses crowned her nose. She reminded Ali of an ancient scribe. Alyssa was locked in conversation with a man concealed behind the diners seated in front of them. As she approached the table, she saw it was Josiah sitting beside her.

"Greetings, sister," called his cheery voice over the blur of conversations. He stood to kiss her cheek. She found him a reassuring presence.

"Now do you understand why we couldn't meet at the folk's apartment?" asked Alyssa, the steam from her coffee cup fogging her reading glasses.

"You haven't told her the reason we've met yet, Pet," rhymed Josiah.

The steam rising from the coffee appeared to be rising from Alyssa's head. Alison slipped into the booth across from them.

"It's about mom."

"What about mom?"

"That's just it," exclaimed Aly, as if she'd imparted a detailed explanation. "Thank heaven I found out in time."

"Found out *what*—?"

"About her and that wretched Uncle Maximilian." She grimaced. "It's time to stop calling him uncle, by the way."

"What should we call him?"

"I'm too much of a lady to say," she harrumphed.

"So what did mom *do*—?"

She's involved with that man!"

"How did you find out?"

"Her cell."

"She's always careless about leaving it around," mused Ali. "I don't think she takes her phone seriously."

"You don't seem very concerned, Alison."

"Would it advance the case if I were?"

"At least I'd have the satisfaction of knowing that what I just revealed had registered with you."

"It registered. Does Ady know about this?"

"Adam—?" Alyssa removed her specs. "What would *he* know? He's a baby."

"He's probably more experienced at this kind of thing than we are."

But then she remembered her latest round of worries with her man. *Her* man? Hadn't she brushed him out of her life—almost? Wasn't she the "experienced" one now? She wasn't into schadenfreude, but it was a relief to find out there was trouble elsewhere in paradise, even if her own mother was among that select group, if Alyssa was to be believed.

"At any rate," her sister resumed, "the cellphone tells the sorry tale."

"This is the first time I've heard of someone's cell betraying them," said Ali.

"It's not as if it called me and tattled," corrected Alyssa, "but that's the gist of it—mom's having an affair."

"Is that what the phone told you?"

"Not in so many words, but it left little room for doubt. And now—" She drew in her breath to punctuate her next statement. "What I've called you here for is to devise a plan of action."

Ali exchanged glances with Josiah. "What kind of action?"

"First, of course, we have to confront her, put a stop to it, and then—"

"Hold on," interrupted Alison. Why are we doing *anything*?"

"I had the same question," put in Josiah.

"Are you serious, Ali? And let matters run their course—?"

"That's what matters generally do," ventured her younger sister.

"I agree," said Josiah.

"Your opinions aren't helpful, Josiah, s'il vous plaît, this is a family matter," ordered Alyssa. "I think if we both confront her—"

"Count me out," exclaimed Alison. "I have no intention of getting involved in this."

"Don't you care about mom—and dad …?"

"Of course I do. That's why I won't get mixed up in any hare-brained scheme."

"I agree," put in Josiah.

"Please stop being so agreeable, Josiah!" snapped Alyssa. "Ali and I can resolve this without outside interference."

"But *we* are the ones interfering," objected Alison, "if we get involved the way you're demanding. Do you want to break dad's heart? What is he supposed to think if he found out? And to betray your own mother—"

"She's betraying dad—"

"That's *her* business. And none of ours. I have no intention of getting mixed up in this, and I hope you'll stay out of it too."

She slid out of the booth and left the café. Visions of Pietro, Adam, Yves, her folks tumbled through her head as she made her way to the Park Avenue apartment. She found her parents in the living room. She couldn't tell whether they were having a conversation or just settling in. As she entered the room, dad asked,

"What's up with you …?"

"Nothing—nothing at all. And I fervently hope you can say the same."

◙   ◙   ◙

She materialized out of nowhere at the foot of his bed, as if she'd descended in Glinda's magic bubble. Removing several items from her handbag, she placed them on his bedside tray: a box of chocolates, a miniature bottle of Cognac, a notepad-and-pen set, and, curiously, a compass.

Yves rubbed his eyes. "What in the world is *that* for—?"

Aphrodite handed him the compass. "You'll soon be recovered and out on your own again, if doctors and gods are to be believed. This little gadget—you say *gadget* in English?—it's to help you find your way, once you reenter the wide world."

"Thank you, I suppose." His taut mien gave way to a smile. "Aren't you supposed to be in Greece these days …?"

"Can't a girl be in two places at once?"

"I've never heard of such a thing."

"Neither have I, but here I am—so it must be possible."

Aphrodite slid onto a chair and trained her gaze on him. "I thought while I was here, I'd pay you a visit."

His head bobbed; he was touched by her concern and wondered how she knew he was hospitalized. On top of this, her beauty mesmerized him. They'd met once before, but he wasn't paying attention. He'd only recently started going with Adam, and when he encountered Pietro unexpectedly, at the home of Adam's parents of all places, he hardly noticed anything else.

He waited for her to speak, or maybe the ball was now in his court. The thought crossed his mind that if he were straight, he'd make a play for her. (As Adam had done?)

"Speaking of Adam," he began, still confused by her presence and unmindful that Adam's name had not been mentioned, "have you seen him lately?"

"Adam …?"

Her tone suggested that Adam had been far from her thoughts, if he'd been in them at all, "I haven't seen him since the last time I was here. You are friends, are you not? How is he?"

"Well," he hesitated, not sure what to respond, "he's well, as well as well ever is, I guess you could say."

"If you shall run into him, remember him to me—is that how you say in English?"

"Yes," he replied with uncustomary tact, "that's just how I'd say it. Will you be here for a while?"

"In New York, or in this chair?"

"Either."

"It depends."

"Do you care to say what it depends on?"

"I haven't decided."

He was deciding she had an expansive sense of humor, or maybe she was just charmingly whimsical. "So these lovely gifts that you've brought me...," his eyes swept over them on the tray.

She held up each in turn as she explained. "I predict that you are going to take trip. This chocolate here fortifies you at start of journey. The compass helps you find your way. The pad and paper are for chronicling what you will learn. And the Cognac, a reward for learning it." She added,

"But do not rush the voyage in the least."

His eyes lit up in sudden recognition. "Better it last for many years," he replied.[1]

"I think your trip has begun."

◙   ◙   ◙

When Adam arrived at the hospital later that day, Yves debated whether to tell him about Aphrodite's visit. Of course, her gifts would require an explanation, but they were no longer on the bedside tray. Perhaps an orderly had tucked them in a drawer for safe keeping? Thefts were not unknown in the hospital, especially from the sick.

But was he "sick"? The doctors' prognosis warned that his hospital days were numbered. The nurses were even more encouraging. "Frankly speaking," the head nurse announced just the day before, "I'm in worse shape than you, honey. Frankly speaking, *I'm* the one who should be in that bed of yours." He flashed her a devilish grin: "You're welcome to join me." To which she replied, "You've just proven my point."

Adam slid onto a chair by the bed. Had Yves' eyes been closed, he'd have recognized his cologne, woodsy with hint of lemon. His response—a fire in his loins.

[1] From C.P. Cavafy, "Ιθάκη" [Ithaca], in *C.P. Cavafy, The Collected Poems*, ed. by Anthony Hirst, trans. by Evangelos Sachperoglou (New York: Oxford University Press, 2008), p. 39.

"They say you'll soon be out of here." Adam gave a nod of satisfaction, as if he'd had a hand in the matter. "Have you thought of your next move."

"You make it sound like a game of chess."

"That's life, isn't it—a chess game? Speaking of chess, I've brought you something." He reached into his jacket pocket and withdrew a small package wrapped in tissue paper. He hesitated before handing it to Yves.

Yves removed the paper to reveal a small figurine.

"My rook ...?"

"*Our* rook."

Neither spoke for some time.

He swept through the hospital lobby after taking an elevator for the Orthodox, tears streaming down his cheeks. Once he was outside on gritty First Avenue, to the accompaniment of rumbling buses and screeching tires, his sobs broke forth. Blinded by tears, he stumbled homeward, stopping to lean against a parked car, where the sobs redoubled. A passing couple offered their assistance. He was too overcome to speak, but he reached out and the woman took his hand. When they offered their help again, he choked, "Thank you—it's hopeless." The man patted his back, then the couple moved on.

Why was he crying his eyes out in the middle of a busy New York City avenue? He'd always been self-contained, a combination of upbringing and temperament. He'd not had such a cry in years.

Was it the rook? The rook symbolized the months he'd spent with Yves, their Golden Past. He couldn't decide whether it would have been worse to hold on to it or to surrender the little piece to Yves. Yves' reaction—perhaps that was it? He recalled the silence that filled the room when Yves unwrapped it. He was expecting some kind of declaration from Yves, perhaps a confession of how much he'd missed him, how he regretted their being apart.

But Yves showed no reaction at all. He held the piece for several moments, and instead of pocketing it, placed it on the bedside tray between them. There it stood, as if it'd taken on a life of its own but had no idea where to go. When he left, the rook stood alone on the tray. For all he knew, Yves would drift off to sleep and a passing orderly would abscond with it.

He managed to stop crying by the time he reached home. When he picked up his mail, he sifted slowly through the bills and circulars if only to delay entering the apartment. He dreaded the emptiness he'd find there. Once inside, he left the mail on his desk and flopped on the bed, overcome by a feeling of opportunities lost. Why hadn't he pinned Yves down, made him reveal his plans, or even persuaded him to give them—*them!*—another chance? Why did he listen passively, as if he had no stake in the conversation, when Yves brought up the subject of returning to Canada, perhaps to recuperate from his injuries? Why hadn't he declared, *Don't be foolish—Come home to me—I'll watch over you till you're back on your feet—I'll watch over you for all time?*

And their piano—what about it?

CHAPTER 20

Supreme Court Ruling Makes Same-Sex Marriage a
Right Nationwide, *New York Times*, June 26, 2015
In a long-sought victory for the gay rights movement, the Supreme Court ruled
by a 5-to-4 vote on Friday that the Constitution guarantees a right to same-sex
marriage.... "No longer may this liberty be denied," Justice Anthony M. Kennedy
wrote for the majority in the historic decision [*Obergefell vs. Hodges*].

A soft light suffused the library at the Stover residence on Park Avenue.
Late afternoon traffic began its surge as nearby offices let out amid the
clamor of honking and police whistles. Without looking up from his
WSJ, Albert Stover remarked to his wife, "Those honky cars remind me of
quacking ducks."

"When was the last time you heard a duck quack?"

Instead of a direct reply, he said,

"How was your day ...?" His eyes remained on his paper.

"Nothing exciting to report."

This time he did look up. "It was exciting but you don't want to
report it?"

"To tell the truth," she returned, "your implied accusation is the most
exciting thing that's happened to me today."

"What about yesterday?"

"How far back are we going to go?"

"What time are you expecting the kids?"

"We're both expecting the kids. In fact, they should be arriving within the hour. We should get dressed and I'll see about dinner."

"What are you serving?"

"Takeout."

Adam arrived later than his sisters. As was his custom since he had his own apartment, he rang the bell rather than letting himself in. Aly and Ali opened the door together.

"I didn't expect a welcoming committee," he declared.

"Are you okay?" they asked in unison.

A sad little smile broke out as he replied, "Why wouldn't I be?"

Alyssa led the way into the living room as he explained, "I got held up by a phone call."

"Indeed?" said Alyssa, her tone suggesting he should be more responsible.

"Nothing important—it took more time than I'd anticipated."

"There you are," exclaimed Lenora, joining them from the kitchen. She was still wearing an apron as she gave her son a kiss.

"I don't think I've seen you in an apron in years, Mom."

"It's just for show." She held up an edge of the black voile with a big red rose appliqué.

"For *show*?" queried Alyssa.

"Yes, darling—don't you sometimes do things for show?"

"I'll admit appearances are important, sometimes *very* important. Especially if you have something to cover up."

"And what might that be?" returned Lenora.

"Don't ask me—I'm not needing to keep up appearances, if that's what you mean."

"I don't mean anything."

"Where's Dad?" resumed Alyssa. "We have things to talk about."

"What things?"

"Just general kinds of things," said Alison with assurance.

Lenora was heading for the kitchen again when she turned and asked, "Is anything the matter?"

"What could be the matter?" returned Alison, determined to downplay any drama her sister might inject into the proceedings. "We haven't been together as a family in a while."

Al had just come downstairs to join the gathering, ready to plunge into the melee, as he called family get-togethers.

"What have we here—die ganze mischpoke—?"

"How have you been, Dad?" Ali brushed his cheek with a kiss. As his arm encircled her waist, Alyssa said, "Let's all take a seat. We have things to talk about."

"What things?" asked Alison.

"The usual general things, I'd bet," put in Adam. He'd taken a seat on a settee near the fireplace.

Lenora returned with a platter of hors d'oeuvres as Al scooted next to his son on the sofa.

"Speaking of 'things,' how are they, my boy?"

"Oh, you know—same old things."

"You seem downbeat, more than usual."

"Do I?" A text message earlier in the day followed by a phone call was still distracting him: "Call me."

For once, Pietro was short on words. He hesitated to return the call, wondering whether he should put it off till later in the day. He'd not yet had his morning coffee and wasn't up to facing the topsy-turvy world of Pietro Tresceri. But the message had a sharp tone, and he called back. "He's out of the hospital." "Where is he—?" "With me." "Why with you—?" "His things." "What about his things—" "They're here, at my place." "So he's at your place—?" "Last time I checked." "Why did he leave the hospital—?" "They kicked him out." "What do you mean, *kicked* him out—?" "Time to go. Said so themselves. He was well." "*Well*—?" "Well enough to go. They needed his bed."

Al resumed, "I worry about you, son."

"You shouldn't."

"What do you mean, I shouldn't? Who *should* if not me …?"

Adam stood abruptly and scuttled to the dining room. His dad had not seen him cry since he was a boy.

Noticing that his daughters were ogling the platter that Lenny had set on the coffee table, he trailed Adam to the kitchen.

There he said as gruffly as he could, "It's not a crime to cry in this house, you know. Now what's eating you—?"

Feeling as if he'd morphed into a boy of five, his shoulders shaking from his sobs, Adam coughed out, "It's about Yves …, unfortunately, … you know …"

"Oh course I know! What's going on?"

"He's left the hospital. He didn't tell me himself. I found out from a friend. Why didn't he tell *me*? Why did I have to hear it secondhand …?"

"Quit crying and go after him."

"He won't come back."

"You don't have a crystal ball, Ady. But if you have any balls at all, you'll be on his tail before you do anything else, except maybe dry those tears first."

He handed Adam his hankie. Adam dabbed his eyes with it. "Dad, do you think I'm throwing my life out the window?"

"No, but you'd better start chasing after it, before it gets away from you."

"There've been women, you know ..."

"What do women have to do with it?"

"And Aphrodite, we spent a weekend together ..."

"What does Aphrodite have to do with it?"

"Well, I *do* like women."

"Everyone likes women. What does that have to do with it?"

"It's just that—" He drew in his breath. "It's so hard to explain, about the confusion and all ..."

"What confusion, son?"

"Between, well, liking women or liking men, Dad. What should I do?"

"You're asking *me*?" Al pondered a moment. A vision of Helmut Bryce flashed through his mind and he knew this was it. "There's one sure way to find out, Ady. Follow your dick. Now move your ass!"

The soirée wound down but Adam paid little attention, and was twice called out by Alyssa for drifting off to another world. He'd paid almost no heed to the conversation. His mom and sisters might have been speaking Gujarati, their assorted remarks hardly registering—"Watch your step," "So much at stake"—followed by evasions and non sequiturs—"Think about the future," "One false step." In spite of the gibberish, he formed a plan and decided to carry it out first thing next morning. He'd call Pietro to forewarn him.

回　　回　　回

It was misting lightly when Alyssa left her folks accompanied by Josiah, who'd joined the family gathering later. A soothing rain mixed with gentle breezes promised hope and wellbeing if you were paying attention to the weather and not to the report. As they peered into the evening from the doorway amid the murmurings of leisurely traffic, Josiah said, "I didn't bring an umbrella."

"Karolos will have a spare, won't you?" Alyssa said to the doorman. It was more an assertion than a question.

"At your service," replied the obliging Greek, who disappeared into a small room off the lobby and returned with a large umbrella. As the couple meandered onto Park Avenue, the doorman wondered what kind of patience a man must have to deal with such a number as Miss Stover (she'd asked him not to call her by her first name; "Lady Stover now," he'd informed the staff).

"Shall we walk or cab it?" asked Josiah, extending his hand to gauge the intensity of the rain.

"It's not far," she replied. "I could use some fresh air." She put her arm through his and led him off to her apartment.

They walked in silence toward the corner. Then Josiah commented, "I must say, that was some confabulation with your folks."

"I just hope we got through to her."

"It's hard to tell with your mom. She plays her cards pretty close to the vest."

"I wish she wouldn't hold them so close," returned Alyssa, as if Lenora went around with a deck of cards in her hands. "I wish I could be direct with her."

"You're direct with everyone, darling."

"What's that supposed to mean—?"

They'd stepped too soon off the curb and the honking of an angry motorist obscured Josiah's soft-spoken reply. Our couple ambled down the gently sloping side street, and as they approached Lex, she said, "I just hope she got the point and acts on it. Do you think I was too subtle …?"

"You? Never."

"I'd hate to have to go to dad."

"Surely even *you* wouldn't do such a thing—?"

"What if she doesn't break off the affair?"

"We'll have to live with the consequences."

"But think how bad it will look, if people find out! They always do, you know."

"Ah, people."

Once inside her apartment, they made for the bedroom and started to undress. Midevening sex had become a part of their routine. It gave a boost to their evolving relationship by cutting down on the talking, which could lead to controversy. It also helped matters that Josiah had changed his style of underwear, to smartly fitted boxers and undershirts with sleeves. When he made the transition, she'd adjudged, "You no longer present as a janitor."

As they slipped into bed, an event of momentous consequence occurred. Josiah accidentally knocked a framed photograph from the bed-side table to the floor. As he leaned over to retrieve it, the back fell off the frame and the photo slipped out onto the carpet.

"Don't!" cried Alyssa as he reached down to pick it up. But the command came too late. He turned the photo over to discover that it was a picture clipped from a magazine. It was the same "photograph" that he'd noticed in her workroom.

"So this is Theophilus Witherspoon IV …?"

Debonair Theo had haunted the hopeful suitor since he began his pursuit. Theo this, Theo that—his name seldom failed to worm its way into their conversations. And the oddest thing, she refused to reveal almost any details about this one-time lover, but that he was a prince among men, peerless in every conceivable way, and had left her to go to Africa or South America. He might come back one day.

"Now you know," she confessed with trademark candor.

"But—why, pet?"

She leaned back on the pillow and sighed. "I was already a woman of a certain age when you met me. How do you think it would have looked, when we met, if I'd not had a distinguished beau or two in my past … when you met me?"

"If you'd had a thousand lovers and wild sex with them every night, it would hardly have changed my opinion of you."

"It wouldn't—have??"

He reflected. "Give me time to emend that statement, darling. I might want to alter it ever so slightly."

"How much time do you think you'll need?"

"Alyssa," he began, his turn to sigh, "It's time for you to make it up with Adam."

"Make up *what* with Adam—?"

"To accept him."

"I *do* accept him. He's my brother."

"To accept him the way he is, and everything about him, and all his endeavors, and especially—Yves."

"What about this Yves? He's out of the picture, you know."

"He's going to get him back. He won't give up till he does. And you mustn't be an obstacle to his happiness."

"I've never thought of myself as an obstacle."

"Take it as a compliment. But embrace him—*them*. Take them into your heart and love them, do you hear me?"

She sat up abruptly. "You're impossible, Josiah! You ask too much of me, while you prance around on your merry way, accepting everybody just the way they are. My little sister is mixed up with a clown who'd hang from the chandelier if given a chance, my brother's involved with a Canuck who might as well be from outer space, and my mother—well, enough said about her. How do you think all this looks—?"

"It's called family, darling." He took her hand. "Consider it this way: your mom's having an affair, your brother's a faggot, you're shacked up with a Yid—and you're still worried about appearances …?"

◉　　◉　　◉

He was a good driver and knew the complex pattern of Manhattan traffic. Though most visitors to the city quail at the thought of driving in New York, most of the streets and avenues extend in only one direction, except when they suddenly change at an intersection and reverse, or become two-lane, or dead-end. He found an empty space near the address he was seeking and parked the U-Haul. Then with a rapidly beating heart, he advanced on his destination and rang the bell of the dilapidated tenement.

No response. Wasn't Pietro expecting him? He rang again with the same result. In a fit of impatience, he turned the doorknob as if it would bow to his will, and it did. (It was either a faulty lock or the door had been left unlocked. So much for security.) He pushed into the makeshift lobby and mounted the stairs, the only sound the tread of his shoes, evidently a building of late risers or ghosts. Several cardboard boxes lined the hallway outside Pietro's apartment, neatly stacked in two piles.

When no one answered the bell, he repeated his performance of downstairs, turned the knob—it gave—and pushed into the apartment. The blinds were partly drawn and the small living room was only dimly lit. The room was neater than he'd expected—furniture in place, no beer cans on the orange-crate coffee table, no clothes strewn about the floor, contrary to reports from Alison. While he was getting his bearings and wondering what to do next, a figure emerged in a terrycloth robe.

"You're not dressed?"

"I wasn't expecting you."

"But the fact is, I'm here. So if you'll throw some clothes on, we can get started."

"What's going on, anyway—?"

"Moving day. No one told you? Sorry for the oversight. Shall we get going? I'm paying by the hour for a U-Haul. We can grab a coffee later."

Yves stood in place and blinked once, twice. Then he left the room.

Pietro had done a thorough job. Adam's call of the evening before alerted him to pack up Yves' belongings on the sly. The resourceful landlord/pianist/stripper had raided the local liquor store for empty boxes, then managed to fill them with Yves' things after his lodger went to bed. When Adam appeared next morning, Pietro had moved all Yves' affairs into the public hallway except for a small suitcase and his cello.

Shortly Yves returned, dressed in Bermuda shorts and a polo shirt. After pacing around the room a couple of times, he asked, "What's the meaning of this—barging in here and taking over?"

"It's called a fait accompli. Now, if you can get yourself downstairs and wait by the U-Haul, Pietro and I will tote the boxes and the cello."

"*I'll* take the cello," piped Pietro. "I'm the musician of this moving company." He'd been on an errand and joined them in the living room. In faded jeans and tank top, he could pass for a teenager.

"Watch your step with that cello," Yves commanded, as if he'd been on board with the moving plan all along.

"Don't worry, man," said Pietro, "I've been watching my step my entire life."

Shaking his head but without another word, Yves proceeded down the stairs.

Adam followed carrying the first box, while Pietro brought up the rear with the cello, thinking *Thank god he's not a pianist.*

After they loaded all the boxes in the U-Haul, Yves climbed onto the front seat with the cello, and Pietro hopped into the back with the boxes, while Adam drove.

When he pulled up in front of his apartment, he took a key from his pocket and handed it to Yves. "Let yourself in while we unpack."

"I have a key."

Adam leaned in and kissed him.

During the following week, Adam and Yves set up a routine to which, of course, neither had given a thought till they'd settled Yves in the apartment. Yves said he preferred to sleep on the living room sofa—recovering from his injuries and all that. Adam was sorely tempted to respond that he could recover just as quickly lying beside him in a bed, but he held his tongue.

As soon as they'd unpacked that first day, Yves brought up the subject of money. "I won't be performing for a while, until this hand heals, so I won't be bringing in much cash, if any."

"Alison tells me there's an opening or two for string tutors at NYU, one at Juilliard as well—she's checked it out."

"I'm not sure how much that would pay."

"The good news is, your credit's perfectly good here. I wouldn't worry about money."

"But I *do* worry—"

"Well, don't—I've had a raise."

"I'm not going to sponge off you, Ad."

A great sadness welled up in Adam's breast. It frightened him at first. It recalled the time in his teens when a giant wave almost carried him out to sea. This time he didn't try to fight it; he rode with it, and in no time it exalted him, empowering him to pour out his heart as he'd never done before. "I love you, Yves ... I love you." He said it again and again, not like a man convincing himself or someone else, but as a song of praise. The sadness tried to well up once more, but something pushed it down and allowed him to ride forward. "You left me once, Yves," he resumed, "but I won't let you this time—I won't stand for it." He hesitated. "I love you, Yves, do you hear me, Yves …? I love you."

Yves brushed a tear away as he left the room.

◙　　◙　　◙

Several days later, and the bell from the lobby was ringing insistently.

"That must be Alyssa."

"What in the hell is she doing here?" asked Yves.

"She was unusually vague for Alyssa, so I didn't mention it to you," Adam faltered. "She wanted to deliver something …"

When Adam opened the door, his sister exclaimed, "I'm glad I found you both here." She was wearing a simple black shift and a tailored jacket with embroidered edges.

Adam and Yves exchanged glances, Adam's one of relief, Yves' more perplexed.

"I've brought you something," she announced, advancing into the room.

"It must be awfully tiny if it could fit into that little purse you're carrying." He'd not overlooked its ornate silver clasp.

"It's not in my purse, actually," she explained, laying the clutch bag on a table, "and I'm sorry I couldn't wrap it."

Yves and Adam exchanged glances again, this time identical.

Alyssa surveyed the room then declared, "This must be that famous piano of yours…" She walked over to the instrument and raised the lid. Then she noticed something on the piano.

"What's this here …?"

"Oh, that," said Adam "It's a chess piece—a rook."

She picked it up and turned it this way and that. Then as if it were an afterthought, "Would you mind if I played something?"

"Go ahead," Adam nodded, too startled by the request to say anything more.

She returned the rook to its resting place on the piano and sat down on the piano bench.

As soon as her fingers touched the keys, a cascade of sound filled the room. Her right hand raced up and down the keyboard in unending arpeggios, while the left accompanied with emphatic octaves.

Adam moved closer to the piano. He'd never heard her play this way before. The playing wasn't as polished or precise as when she was younger—he was sure he was hearing some wrong notes—but there was fire and passion in her performance. And her face—it was contorted with the effort; she'd surely not practiced in years, but she was getting through it.

The music penetrated his body, and he was shaking with emotion as the piece resolved to its end. When she removed her hands from the keyboard, he couldn't speak.

"Magnificent," was all Yves managed.

"Well, I've said what I came to say," she declared. And without further ado, she kissed each on the cheek, collected her purse, and left.

When the door clicked shut, Yves wrapped his arms around Adam, who went slack in his embrace, as if he needed Yves' support to continue standing.

"Did you recognize the piece?" Yves murmured.

"Of course," whispered Adam, "It's the Chopin étude, the National Anthem of you and me."

They continued to hold each other as a breeze blew through the room and the cats brushed against their legs, to be sure the bipeds realized life's more important matters were about to resume, no matter how long they wished to stay locked in each other's arms. It was time to be fed.

At length, Adam asked, under his breath, "What now…?"

"It's time to find a piano." Yves took his hand and led him to the Baldwin. "And here it is."

Weddings

The New York Times, May 31, 20—
Yves Montjour
Adam Stover

A Match Made by an Abandoned Piano and a Chopin Étude

When Yves Montjour spotted an abandoned piano on a Greenwich Village sidewalk, he never imagined it would change his life. A freelance classical musician from Montreal, he couldn't resist trying out the weathered instrument. He was soon startled when Adam Stover, a passerby, stopped to listen and correctly identified the piece as Chopin's Étude in C Major from opus 10. The pair struck up a conversation, and Mr. Stover, an architect, offered to help Mr. Montjour transport the piano back to his apartment. Mr. Montjour agreed, impressed with Mr. Stover's knowledge of classical music. "The piece is not that well known," he said. "I knew then that the guy was a safe bet. I mean, how many ax murderers would recognize that étude?"

Mr. Stover, it turns out, was familiar with Chopin's fiendishly difficult étude from listening to his sister Alyssa Stover practice it for hours on end when they were younger. But the two men soon discovered that they had much more in common than Chopin. Their wedding took place at the Park Avenue residence of Mr. Stover's parents, Lenora and Albert Stover. Mr. Stover is a broker at the Wall Street firm of Barley, Bane & Bunn. Mrs. Stover is an editor at *Fashionista* magazine. Among the out-of-town guests was Helmut Bryce, a wholesale liquor dealer at Glazer's Distributors of Arkansas, Little Rock branch.

At the reception following the ceremony, the newlyweds toasted Ms. Stover and her diligence in mastering the music that brought them together. They also congratulated her on performing the piece to unanimous acclaim at a recent private concert.

Mr. Stover is a partner in the architectural firm Appleby, Bartleby & Drumm. Trent Duncan, a colleague of Mr. Stover, and his wife Aphrodite served as his best couple. Pietro Tresceri, a freelance pianist and jazz composer, was Mr. Montjour's best man. At the reception, Mr. Tresceri played the world premiere of his "Jazzy Variations on Here Come the Grooms." He continued to entertain the gathering by successfully essaying a backflip, a somersault, and a handspring, landing on both feet all three times.

An Episcopal priest and a rabbi officiated at the ceremony; all five Stovers are half-Jewish. Ms. Stover provided the floral arrangements for the event, assisted by her fiancé, Josiah Grynszpan, owner of the Lexington Avenue book and bedding store Between the Covers. Alison Stover, younger sister of the groom and Ms. Stover, served as photographer. She was assisted by Mr. Tresceri, called a colleague and collaborator, when he was not at the keyboard or tossing off flips.

After the reception, Mr. Stover and Mr. Montjour set sail on their honeymoon. They will be spending it at their apartment in Greenwich Village, and they expect it to last indefinitely. Those who have observed the happy couple have no reason to doubt them.

QUESTIONS FOR BOOK CLUBS

1. What is the attitude of Adam's parents to his relationship with Yves? Is one more accepting than the other? Why do you think so?

2. Who is your favorite character in *Adam & Yves*? Why is that?

3. Aphrodite of Athens is the namesake of the Greek Goddess of Love. Is she a real character in the novel? Explain.

4. What is your take on the sexuality of Pietro Tresceri?

5. If any character represents a moral force in the novel, who might that character be, and why?

6. Alison Stover expresses apprehensions about her relationship with Pietro. To what extent do you think she is justified?

7. Is the nickname "Treachery" appropriate for Pietro? Why or why not?

8. For all her concern with appearances, why does Alyssa Stover become involved with Josiah Grynszpan?

9. Lenora Stover is considered the "cool head" of the family. Do you think she's too cool? Give examples.

10. Why did Yves leave Adam? Do you think he was justified? Explain.

11. How well does Adam understand why Yves left him? Explain.

12. Helmut Bryce aka Goober appears late in the novel. What is the function of this man who was close to Al Stover when they were army buddies?

13. Do you perceive a similarity in the sexuality of the three Stover siblings? Elaborate.

14. When Yves was in the hospital, what did he make of Adam's many visits?

15. Why did Alyssa play the Chopin étude at Adam and Yves' apartment?

16. Adam and Yves have different reactions when they encounter each other on the escalator in Macy's. Describe them.

17. Why did Yves react the way he did when he saw Adam on the escalator in Macy's?

WHY I WROTE *ADAM & YVES*

When I ask myself what are the most significant moments in modern history, say, since the Renaissance, two events come to mind. The first is the French Revolution, which abolished the notion of the divine right of kings and queens to rule over us. Along with the Declaration of the Rights of Man (unfortunately not of Woman), men and, much later, women became the center of our world, not to be governed by unelected representatives, at least this became the rule in many venues. The second event came much later: the development and availability of the birth control pill, which for the first time gave women control over their bodies. Such control offered opportunities for women to pursue whatever life's work they chose by allowing them to delay having children, or not have them at all. Now some seventy-five years later comes another "most significant moment": the U.S. Supreme Court's decision in *Obergefell vs. Hodges*, legitimizing same-sex unions. Until that time, you might be scorned and shunned for openly loving someone of the same sex. You might even lose your job and become an outcast from society. But *Obergefell* has changed that. It is to celebrate the historic decision that I wrote *Adam & Yves*.

ACKNOWLEDGMENTS

Several individuals made significant contributions to this novel and it is a great pleasure to thank them here. Terry Trucco's journalistic expertise helped me craft what I hope is a convincing end of the tale. From the beginning, Shira Nayman offered something more valuable than praise or cash—enthusiasm. And her astute editorial suggestions helped remove the scaffolding that first held the whole thing up then threatened to bring it down. Barbara Hoffert's highly perceptive, slash-and-burn editing ironed out illogicalities, confused time sequences, and hazy characterizations, and helped give the novel its final shape. My gratitude to you all. Any errors are mine.

ABOUT THE AUTHOR

ED CONE is a father, writer, editor, book reviewer, former tap dancer, aspiring pianist, and licensed New York City tour guide. He originated in the South but moved to New York to study at Columbia University's School of International Affairs, and decided to stay. He lives with his wife and children in Manhattan. *Adam & Yves* is the second of his fourteen novels to be published, after *The Counterfeiter*.